The Last
Dragonslayer

'He must have been wanting to spare my feelings, for when I got back there was nothing left of him but his suit, hat and silver-topped cane...'

THE LAST
DRAGONSLAYER

JASPER FFORDE

HODDER

First published in Great Britain in 2010 by Hodder & Stoughton
An Hachette UK company

This paperback edition published 2016

2

Copyright © Jasper Fforde 2010

The right of Jasper Fforde to be identified as the Author
of the Work has been asserted by him in accordance with the
Copyright, Designs and Patents Act 1988.

A CIP catalogue record for this title is available from the British Library

ISBN 978 1 473 65128 9

Typeset in Bembo 13/15.5pt by Palimpsest Book Production Limited,
Falkirk, Stirlingshire

Printed and bound by Clays Ltd, St Ives plc

Hodder & Stoughton policy is to use papers that are natural, renewable
and recyclable products and made from wood grown in sustainable
forests. The logging and manufacturing processes are expected to
conform to the environmental regulations of the country of origin.

Hodder & Stoughton Ltd
Carmelite House
50 Victoria Embankment
London EC4Y 0DZ

www.hodder.co.uk

For Stella Morel
1897-1933
2010-
The grandmother I never knew
The daughter I will

The Last Dragonslayer

JASPER FFORDE

Once, I was famous. My face appeared on T-shirts, badges, commemorative mugs and posters. I made front-page news, appeared on TV and was even a special guest on *The Yogi Baird Show*. *The Daily Clam* called me 'The year's most influential teenager' and I was the *Mollusc on Sunday*'s woman of the year. Two people tried to kill me, I was threatened with jail, had sixteen offers of marriage and was outlawed by King Snodd. All that and more besides, and in less than a week.

My name is Jennifer Strange.

Practical Magic

It looked set to become even hotter by the afternoon, just when the job was becoming more fiddly and needed extra concentration. But the fair weather brought at least one advantage: dry air makes magic work better and fly farther. Moisture has a moderating effect on the Mystical Arts. No sorcerer worth their sparkle ever did productive work in the rain – which probably accounts for why getting showers to *start* was once considered easy, but getting them to *stop* was nigh-on impossible.

We hadn't been able to afford a towncar for years, so the three sorcerers, myself and the beast were packed into my rust-and-orange-but-mostly-rust Volkswagen for the short journey from Hereford to Dinmore. Lady Mawgon had insisted on sitting in the passenger seat because 'that's how it will be', which meant that Wizard Moobin and the well-proportioned 'Full' Price were in the back seat, with the Quarkbeast sitting between the two of them and panting in the heat. I was driving, which might have been unusual anywhere but here in the Kingdom of Snodd, which was unique in the Ununited Kingdoms for having driving tests based on maturity, not age. Which explained why I'd had a licence since I was thirteen, while some blokes were still failing to make the grade at forty. It was lucky I could. Sorcerers are easily distracted, and letting them drive is about as safe as waving around a chainsaw at full throttle in a crowded disco.

We had lots to talk about – the job we were driving to, the weather, experimental spells or failing that, King Snodd's sometimes eccentric ways. But we didn't. Price, Moobin and Mawgon, despite being our best sorcerers, didn't really get along. It wasn't anything personal; sorcerers are just like that – temperamental, and apt to break out into petulant posturing that takes time and energy to smooth over. Running Kazam was less about spells and enchantments, diplomacy and bureaucracy, and more about child-minding. Working with those versed in the Mystical Arts was sometimes like trying to knit with wet spaghetti: just when you thought you'd got somewhere it all came to pieces in your hands. But truth to tell, I didn't really mind: were they frustrating? Frequently. Were they boring? Never.

'I do wish you wouldn't do that,' said Lady Mawgon in an aggrieved tone as she shot a disapproving glance at Full Price. He was changing from a human to a walrus and then back again in slow, measured transformations. The Quarkbeast was staring at him strangely, and with each transformation there wafted an unpleasant smell of fish around the small car. It was a good job the windows were open. To Lady Mawgon, who in better days had once been sorceress to royalty, transforming within potential view of the public was the mark of the hopelessly ill-bred.

'Groof, groof,' said Full Price, trying to speak while a walrus, which is never satisfactory. 'I'm just tuning up,' he added in an indignant fashion once de-walrussed or re-humanned, depending on which way you looked at it, 'don't tell me you don't need to.'

Both I and Wizard Moobin looked at Lady Mawgon, eager to know how she *was* tuning up. Moobin had prepared for the job by tinkering with the print of the *Hereford Daily Eyestrain*. Since leaving the office twenty minutes before he had filled in the crossword. Not unusual in itself since the *Eyestrain*'s crossword is seldom hard, except that he had used printed letters from elsewhere on the page and *dragged* them across using his mind alone. The crossword was now complete and more or less correct – but it left an article on Queen Mimosa's patronage of the Troll War Widows Fund looking a trifle disjointed.

'I am not required to answer your question,' replied Lady Mawgon in a haughty tone, 'and what's more, I detest the term "tuning up". It's *Quazafucating*, and always has been.'

'Using the old language makes us sound archaic and out of touch,' replied Price.

'It makes us sound as we are meant to be,' replied Lady Mawgon, 'of a noble calling.'

Of a *once* noble calling, thought Moobin, inadvertently broadcasting his subconscious on an alpha so low even I could sense it. Lady Mawgon swivelled in her chair to glare at him.

'Keep your thoughts to yourself, young man.'

Moobin thought something to her but in high-alpha, so only she could hear it. I don't know what he thought, but Lady Mawgon said 'Well!' in a haughty manner and stared out of the side window in an aggrieved fashion.

I sighed. This was my life.

Of the forty-five sorcerers, movers, soothsayers, shifters, weathermongers, carpeteers and other assorted Mystical Artisans at Kazam, most were off the active list either through infirmity, insanity or loss or damage to the vitally important index fingers, either through accident or rheumatoid arthritis. Of these forty-five, thirteen were potentially capable of working, but only nine had current licences – two carpeteers, a pair of pre-cogs and, most importantly, five sorcerers legally empowered to carry out Acts of Enchantment. Like everyone else Lady Mawgon's powers had faded dramatically over the past three decades or so, but unlike everyone else, she'd not really come to terms with it. In her defence, she had fallen farther than the rest of them, but this wasn't really an excuse: the Sisters

Karamazov could also claim once-royal patronage, and they were nice as apricot pie. Mad as a knapsack of onions the pair of them, but pleasant nonetheless.

I might have felt more sorry for Mawgon if she wasn't so difficult all the time. She had an intimidating manner that made me feel small and ill at ease, and she rarely if ever missed an opportunity to put me in my place. Since Mr Zambini's disappearance, she'd got worse, not better.

'Quark,' said the Quarkbeast.

'Did we have to bring the beast?' asked Full Price, who had never really got along with it.

'It jumped in the car when I opened the door.'

The Quarkbeast yawned, revealing several rows of razor-sharp fangs. Despite his placid nature, the beast's ferocious appearance almost guaranteed that no one ever completely shrugged off the possibility that it might try to take a chunk out of them when they weren't looking.

'I would be failing in my duty as acting manager of Kazam,' I said in an attempt to direct the sorcerers away from grumpiness and more in the direction of teamwork, 'if I didn't mention how important this job is. Mr Zambini always said that we needed to adapt to survive, and if we get this right we could possibly tap a lucrative market that we badly need.'

'Humph!' said Lady Mawgon.

'We all need to be in *tune* and ready to hit the

ground running,' I added. 'I told Mr Digby we'd all be done by six this evening.'

They didn't argue. I think they knew the score well enough. In silent answer, Lady Mawgon snapped her fingers and the Volkswagen's gearbox, which up until that moment had been making an expensive-sounding rumbling noise, suddenly fell silent. If Mawgon could replace gearbox bushings while the engine was running, she was tuned enough for all of them.

I knocked on the door of a red-brick house at the edge of the village, and a middle-aged man with a ruddy face answered.

'Mr Digby? My name is Jennifer Strange of Kazam, acting manager for Mr Zambini. We spoke on the phone.'

He looked me up and down.

'You seem a bit young to be running an agency.'

'I'm sixteen,' I said in a friendly manner.

'Sixteen?'

'In two weeks I'll be sixteen, yes.'

'Then you're actually fifteen?'

I thought for a moment.

'I'm in my sixteenth *year*.'

Mr Digby narrowed his eyes. 'Then shouldn't you be in school or something?'

'Indentured servitude,' I answered as brightly as I could, trying to sidestep the contempt that most free citizens had for people like me. I had been brought up by the Sisterhood who'd sold me to Kazam four years before. I still had two years of unpaid work before I could even *think* of applying for the first form that would one day lead me, fourteen tiers of paper-work and bureaucracy later, to freedom.

'Indentured or not,' replied Mr Digby, who wasn't so easily put off, 'where's Mr Zambini?'

'He's indisposed at present,' I replied, attempting to sound as mature as I could. 'I have temporarily assumed his responsibilities.'

'Temporarily assumed his responsibilities?' he repeated, 'Why her and not one of you?' He was addressing the three sorcerers who stood waiting at the car.

'Bureaucracy is for little people,' retorted Lady Mawgon in an imperious tone.

'I am too busy, and paperwork exacerbates my receding-hair issues,' said Full Price.

'We have complete confidence in Jennifer,' added Wizard Moobin, who appreciated what I did perhaps more than most. 'Foundlings mature quicker than most. May we get started?'

'Very well,' replied Mr Digby, and after a long pause in which he looked at us all in turn several times with a 'shall I cancel?' sort of look. But he didn't, and even-tually went and fetched his hat and coat.

'But we agreed you'd be done by six, yes?'

I said that this was so, and he handed me his house keys and left. He took a wide berth to avoid the

Quarkbeast, climbed into his car and drove away. It was not a good idea to have civilians about when sorcery was afoot. Even the stoutest incantations carried redundant strands of spell that could cause havoc if allowed to settle on the general public. Nothing serious ever happened; it was mostly rapid nose hair growth, oinking like a pig, blue wee, that sort of stuff. It soon wore off, but it was bad PR – and the threat of litigation or worse was never far from our thoughts.

'Right,' I said to the three of them, 'over to you.'

The three mages looked at each other.

'I used to conjure up storms,' said Lady Mawgon with a sigh.

'So could we all,' replied the Wizard Moobin.

'Quark,' said the Quarkbeast.

I moved away from where the three sorcerers were discussing the best place to start. None of them had rewired a house by spell before, but by reconfiguring the root directory on the core spell language of ARAMAIC, it was found that such a project could be done, and with relative ease – so long as the three of them pooled their resources. It was Mr Zambini's idea to move into the home improvement market. Charming moles from gardens, resizing stuff for the self-storage industry and finding lost things was easy work, but it didn't pay well. Rewiring, however, was quite different. Unlike conventional electricians, we didn't need to touch the house in order to do it. No mess, no problems, and all done in under a day.

I sat in my Volkswagen to be near the car radiophone. Any calls to the office would be directed through to here. I wasn't just Kazam's manager, I was also the receptionist, bookings clerk and accountant. I had to look after the forty-five sorcerers in my charge, deal with the shabby building that housed them all, and fill out the numerous forms that the Magical Powers (amended 1966) Act required when even the *tiniest* spell was undertaken. The reasons why I was doing all this were threefold: firstly, the Great Zambini couldn't because he was missing, secondly, because I'd been part of Kazam since I was twelve and knew the Mystical Arts Management business inside out. Thirdly, no one else wanted to.

The radiophone bleeped.

'The Kazam Agency,' I said in my jolliest tone, 'can I help you?'

'I hope so,' said a timid teenager's voice on the other end. 'Do you have something to make Patty Simcox fall in love with me?'

'How about flowers?' I asked.

'Flowers?'

'Sure. Cinema, a few jokes. Dinner, dance, Bodmin aftershave?'

'Bodmin aftershave?'

'Sure. You do shave?'

'Once a week now,' replied the teenager. 'It's

becoming something of a drag. But listen, I was thinking it would be easier—'

'We *could* do something, but it wouldn't be Patty Simcox. Just a bit of her, the most pliable part. It would be like having a date with a tailor's dummy. Love is something that it's really better not to mess with. If you want my advice, you'd do better to try the more traditional approach.'

The phone seemed to go dead but he was just digesting my thoughts.

'What sort of flowers?'

I gave him some tips and the addresses of a few good restaurants. He thanked me and hung up. I looked across to where Wizard Moobin, Lady Mawgon and Full Price were sizing up the house. Sorcery wasn't about mumbling a spell and letting fly – it was more a case of appraising the problem, planning the various incantations to greatest effect, *then* mumbling a spell and letting fly. The three of them were still in the 'appraising' stage, which generally meant a good deal of staring, tea, discussion, argument, more discussion, tea, then more staring.

The radiophone beeped again.

'Jenny? It's Perkins.'

The Youthful Perkins was the youngest sorcerer at Kazam. He'd been inducted during a rare moment of financial stability and was serving a loose apprenticeship. His particular field of interest was Remote Suggestion, although he wasn't very good at it. He'd once attempted to get us to like him more by sending out a broad 'Am I cool or what?!' suggestion on the wide sub-alpha, but mixed it up with the suggestion that he often cheated at Scrabble, and then wondered why everyone stared at him and shook their heads sadly. It had been very amusing until it wore off, but not to him. Because we were of a similar age, we got on fairly well and I actually quite liked him. But since this might have been a *suggestion* generated by him, I had no way of knowing if I truly liked him or not. So despite his frequent invitations for us to see a movie, or take tea, or simply watch the gas flare at the refinery during sundown, we had not progressed beyond a friendly 'Hey!' when meeting.

'Hey, Perkins,' I said, 'did you get Patrick off to work in time?'

'Just about. But I think he's back on the marzipan again.'

This was worrying. Patrick of Ludlow was a Mover. Although not possessed of the sharpest mind, he was kind and gentle and exceptionally gifted at levitation, and earned a regular wage for Kazam by removing illegally parked cars for the city's clamping unit. It took a lot of effort – he would sleep fourteen hours in twenty-four – and the marzipan echoed back to a darker time in his life that he didn't care to speak of.

'So what's up?'

'The Sisterhood sent round your replacement. What do you want me to do with him?'

I'd been wondering when this would happen. The Sisterhood traditionally supplied Kazam with a foundling every four years as it took a long time to train someone up for the somewhat unique set of skills and mildly elastic regard to reality required for Mystical Arts Management, and the drop-out rate was high. Sharon Zoiks had been the fourth, I had been the sixth, and this new one would be the seventh. We didn't talk about the fifth.

'Pop him in a taxi and send him up. No, cancel that. It'll be too expensive. Ask Nasil to carpet him up. Usual precautions. Cardboard box, yes?'

'Absolutely. By the way, I've got two tickets to see Sir Matt Grifflon live in concert. Do you want to go?'

'Who with?'

'With? Why *me*, of course.'

'I'll think about it.'

'Right,' he said, then mumbled something about how he knew at least twelve people who would literally kill to see singing sensation Sir Matt, and hung up.

In truth, I would very much like to see Grifflon in concert. Aside from being one of King Snodd's favourites, he was a recording star of some note and quite handsome in a lantern-jaw-and-flowing-mane kind of way. After a moment's reflection I considered that I would pass, despite my curiosity on finding out what going on a date was like. Even if Perkins *was* using some beguiling spell, it was a bad idea to get involved with anyone in the Mystical Arts. There was a very good reason why they were all single. Love and magic were like oil and water – they just didn't mix.

I stood there and watched the three sorcerers stare at the house from every direction, apparently doing nothing. I knew better than to ask them what was going on or how they were doing. A moment's distraction could unravel a spell in a twinkling. Moobin and Price were dressed casually and without any metal for fear of burns, but Lady Mawgon was in traditional garb. She wore long black crinolines that rustled like leaves when she walked, and sparkled like distant fireworks in the darkness. During the Kingdom's frequent power cuts, I could always tell when it was she gliding down one of Zambini Tower's endless corridors. Once, in a daring moment, someone had pinned some stars and a moon cut from silver foil to her black dress, something that sent her incandescent with rage. She ranted on at Mr Zambini for almost twenty minutes about how 'no one was taking their calling seriously' and how could she 'be expected to work with such infantile nincompoops'. Zambini spoke to everyone in turn, but he probably found it as funny as the rest of us. We never discovered who did it, but I reckoned it was Full Price's smaller twin, Half. He once turned the local cats green for a joke, which backfired badly when someone complained and the cops got involved. 'Vexatious, troublesome or malicious enchantments or beguilings' were strictly prohibited even *with* the necessary paperwork, and natural prejudice against wizards had been high ever since the whole 'Quake in terror puny minions and obey Blix the Barbarous' episode in the eighteenth century. To deflect any trouble over Half Price's prank, the Great Zambini had to turn six hundred random cats green around the Ununited Kingdoms. We could thus argue convincingly that the feline colouring issue might not have been an illegal enchantment at all but 'a dodgy batch of Moggilicious cat food'.

With little else to do except keep an eye on the three sorcerers, I sat down in the car and read Wizard Moobin's newspaper. The text that he had moved around the paper was still fixed, and I frowned. Tuning spells like these were usually temporary and I would have expected the text to drift back to its original position. It takes almost twice as much energy to fix something as it does to change it, so most wizards saved their energy and the spell would unravel in time, like an unsecured plait. Sorcery was like running a marathon – you needed to pace yourself. Sprint too early and you could find yourself in trouble near the finishing line. Moobin must have been feeling confident to tie off the end of the spell. I looked under the car and noted that the gearbox was shiny like new, and didn't have a leak. It looked like Lady Mawgon was having a good day too.

'Quark.'

'Where?'

The Quarkbeast pointed one of his razor-sharp claws towards the east as Prince Nasil streaked past a good deal faster than he should have. He banked steeply, circled the house twice and came in for a perfect landing just next to me. He like to carpet standing up, a little like a surfer, much to the disdain of our only other carpeteer, Owen of Rhayder, who sat in the more traditional cross-legged position at the rear. Nasil wore baggy shorts and a Hawaiian shirt, too, which didn't go down with Lady Mawgon.

'Hi, Jenny,' said Nasil with a grin as he handed me a flight log to sign, 'delivery for you.'

On the front of the carpet was a large Yummy-Flakes cardboard box, and it opened to reveal an eleven-year-old boy who seemed tall and gangly for his age. He had close-curled sandy-coloured hair and freckles that danced around a snub nose. He was wearing what were very obviously hand-me-down clothes and stared at me with the air of someone recently displaced, and still confused over how they should feel about it.

Tiger Prawns

'Hello,' I said, holding out a hand, 'I'm Jennifer Strange.'

'They speak well of you back at the orphanage,' he replied cautiously, shaking my hand as he climbed from the box, 'I'm pleased to meet you. My name's Horton Prawns. Most people call me Tiger.'

'Can I call you Tiger?'

'I'd like that.'

He gave me a shy smile, but I could see he was uncertain with his new surroundings. He would have been twelve, as that was the age I had joined Kazam. Like me, he would be a foundling brought up by the Lobsterhood, or to give them their official title, The Blessed Ladies of the Lobster. Their convent was in what was once Clifford Castle, not far from the Dragonlands.

Tiger held up an envelope.

'Mother Zenobia told me to give this to the Great Zambini.'

'I'm the acting manager,' I told him, 'you'd better give it to me.'

'A foundling is the acting manager of a House of Enchantment?'

'You're not the first to be surprised – and I'll wager not the last. The envelope?'

But Tiger wasn't so easily swung.

'Mother Zenobia told me to hand it *only* to the Great Zambini.'

'He disappeared,' I replied, 'and I don't know when he's coming back.'

'Then I'll wait.'

'You'll give the envelope to me.'

'No, I'm—'

We tussled over the envelope for a while until I plucked it from his fingers, tore it open and looked at the contents. It was his declaration of servitude, which was essentially little more than a receipt. I didn't read it, didn't need to. Tiger belonged to Kazam until he was eighteen years old, same as me.

'Welcome to Kazam,' I said, stuffing the envelope into my bag, 'where unimaginable horrors share the day with moments of confusing perplexity and utter randomness. To call it a madhouse would insult even the maddest of madhouses.'

'Double weird with added weird?'

'Pretty much. You'll be fine. Compared to the Sisterhood it's almost normal. How is Mother Zenobia these days?'

Mother Zenobia was the principal – a craggy old ex-enchantress who was as wrinkled as a walnut, and about as resilient.

'I'm sorry to report that she's stark staring bonkers,' replied Tiger.

'No change, then.'

'Listen,' said the Prince, 'if you don't need me, I've got a kidney to deliver to Aberystwyth.'

'Yours?' asked Tiger.

I thanked Nasil for bringing Tiger over, and he gave us a cheery wave, lifted into the hover and then sped off to the west. I had yet to break the news to both our carpeteers that the live organ delivery contract would be shortly coming to an end.

'I was also brought up by the Sisterhood,' I said, eager to help Tiger settle in. My first few weeks at Kazam had been smoothed over by the fifth foundling – the one we didn't talk about – and I hoped to show the same kindness she had shown me, although to be honest, being brought up by the Sisterhood made you pretty tough. They weren't cruel, but they were strict. I didn't know that you could talk without first being talked to until I was eight.

'Mother Zenobia speaks very highly of you,' said Tiger.

'And I of her.'

'Miss Strange?'

'Call me Jenny.'

'Miss Jenny, why did I have to stay hidden in a cardboard box for the trip?'

'Carpets aren't permitted to take passengers. Nasil

18

and Owen transport organs for transplant these days – and deliver takeaways.'

'I hope they don't get them mixed up.'

I smiled.

'Not usually. How did you get allocated to Kazam?'

'I took a test with five other boys,' replied Tiger.

'How did you do?'

'I failed.'

This wasn't unusual. A half-century ago Mystical Arts Management was considered a sound career choice and citizens fought for a place. These days, it was servitude only, as with agricultural labour, hotels and fast-food joints. Of the twenty or so Houses of Enchantment that had existed fifty years ago, only Kazam in the Kingdom of Hereford and Industrial Magic over in Stroud were still going. It was an industry in terminal decline. The power of magic had been ebbing for centuries and, with it, the relevance of sorcerers. Once a wizard would have the ear of a king; today we rewire houses and unblock drains.

'The sorcery business grows on you.'

'Like mould?'

'Pretty much, but don't talk like that to the others. They were once mighty. You have to respect what they *were* rather than what they *are* if you're going to fit in, and you need to. Six years can be an eternity with people you don't like. Don't start off on the wrong foot. The enchanters are a quirky bunch and they can be so annoying you want to beat them with sticks, but you'll get to love them like family – as I do.'

'Six years?'

'Six years. But time passes quickly here. It's the variety.'

The radiophone bleeped again.

'It's Kevin.'

He had told me he would call me at this time several days ago, but as is normal with those able to see a hazy version of the future, was uncertain of precisely *why*. He seemed to know now.

'Can you get back to the Towers?'

I glanced up at the three sorcerers, who were concentrating hard on doing nothing.

'Not really. Why?'

'I've had a premonition.'

I was about to say it was about time too, as a sooth-sayer who can't see the future is about as useless as a Buzonji with only four legs, but I didn't.

'What kind of premonition?'

'A biggie. Full colour, stereo *and* 3D. I've not had one of those for years. I need to tell you about it.'

And the radiophone went dead.

'So, listen—'

I stopped because Tiger had a look of abject fear and horror on his face. Eyes wide and staring, left leg shaking uncontrollably and a strange strangled noise in his throat. I'd seen this before.

'That's the Quarkbeast', I told him. 'He may look like an open knife drawer on legs and just one step away from tearing you to shreds, but he's actually a sweetie and rarely, if ever, eats cats. Isn't that so, Quarkbeast?'

'Quark,' said the Quarkbeast.

'He'll not harm a hair on your head,' I said, and the Quarkbeast, to show friendly intent, elected to perform his second-best trick: he picked up a concrete garden gnome in his teeth and ground it with his powerful jaws until it was powder. He then blew it into the air as a dust-ring which he then jumped through. Tiger gave a half-smile and the Quarkbeast wagged his weighted tail, which was sadly a little too close to the Volkswagen, and added one more dent to the already badly damaged front wing.

Tiger wiped his eyes with my handkerchief and patted the Quarkbeast, who kept his mouth closed in order not to frighten him further.

'I hate it here already,' said Tiger, 'so I already like it twice as much as the Sisterhood. Did Sister Assumpta beat you when you were there?'

'No.'

'Me neither. But I was always frightened that she would.'

And he gave a nervous laugh. There was a pause,

and he thought for a moment. I could see there were hundreds of questions going around in his head, and he really didn't know where to start.

'What happened to the Great Zambini?'

'*Officially* it's plain "Mr Zambini" these days,' I told him, 'he hasn't carried the accolade "Great" for over ten years.'

'You don't have it for life?'

'It's based on power. See the one dressed in black over there?'

'The grumpy-looking one?'

'The *dignified*-looking one. Sixty years ago she was Master Sorceress the Lady Mawgon, She-Who-the-Winds-Obey. Now she's just plain Lady Mawgon. If the background wizidrical power falls any farther, she'll be plain Daphne Mawgon and no different to you or me. Watch and learn.'

We stood there for a moment.

'The fat one looks as though he's playing a harp,' said Tiger, with a lot less respect than he should have shown.

'He's the once-venerable Dennis Price,' I told him testily, 'and you should learn to hold your tongue. Price's nickname is "Full". He has a brother called David, but we all call him "Half".'

'Whatever his name, he *still* looks like he's playing an invisible harp.'

'We call it *harping* because the hand movements

that precede the firing of a spell look like someone trying to play an invisible harp.'

'I'd never have guessed. Don't they use wands or something?'

'Wands, broomsticks and pointy hats are for the storybooks.' I held up my index fingers. 'These are what they use. We used to insure their fingers in the old days, but we can't afford the premiums now. Can you feel that?'

The faint buzz of a spell was in the air. A mild tingling sensation, not unlike static electricity. As we watched, Price let fly. There was a crackle like scrunched Cellophane, and with a tremor, the entire internal wiring of Mr Digby's house, complete with all light switches, sockets, fuse boxes and light fittings, swung out of the house as a single entity – a three-dimensional framework of worn wiring, cracked Bakelite and blackened cables. It hung there in midair over the lawn, rocking gently. After a moment, Full Price nodded to Lady Mawgon and then relaxed. The network of wires – which closely resembled the shape of the house – simply hovered a couple of feet above the ground. Price had managed to do something in an hour that trained electricians would have taken a week to do – and he hadn't even touched the wallpaper or plasterwork.

'Well held, Daphne,' said Price.

'I'm not holding it,' said Lady Mawgon, 'I wasn't ready. Moobin?'

'Not I,' he replied, and they looked around to see who else might be involved. And that's when they saw Tiger.

'Who's this little twerp?' asked Lady Mawgon as she strode up.

'The seventh foundling,' I explained, 'Tiger Prawns. Tiger, this is Full Price, Wizard Moobin and Lady Mawgon.'

Price and Moobin gave him a cheery 'hello' but Lady Mawgon was less welcoming.

'I shall call you F7 until you prove yourself worthy,' she remarked imperiously. 'Show me your tongue, boy.'

Tiger, who to my relief was quite able to be polite if required, bowed politely and stuck out his tongue. Lady Mawgon touched the tip of his tongue with her little finger, and frowned.

'It's not him. Mr Price, I think you've just *surged*.'

'You do?'

And they then fell into one of those very long and complex conversations that enchanters have when they want to discuss the arts. And since it was in Aramaic, Latin, Greek and English, I could understand only one word in four – to be honest, they probably did too.

'Tongue in, Tiger' I said.

When they had decided that it might indeed have been a surge of wizidrical power, such as happens from time to time, they drank some tea out of a thermos, nibbled a doughnut and talked some more, then began the delicate work of replicating the worn-out wiring with an identical model hanging in the air next to it, only from new wires, switches and fuse boxes. They would then reinsert the new wiring into the old house, separate out the copper from the waste for recycling – and then do it all again for the plumbing, both domestic water and central heating.

'I have to go back to Zambini Towers,' I said. 'Will you be okay here on your own?'

They said they would, and after nodding to the Quarkbeast, who jumped in the back of my Volkswagen, Tiger and I left them to get on with it.

Zambini Towers

'So what are my duties?' asked Tiger as soon as we were on our way.

'Did you do any laundry at the Sisterhood?'

He groaned audibly.

'There's that, and answering phones and general running around. I'm glad you're here, to be honest. Since we lost the fifth foundling two years ago and Zambini last year, I've been doing everything on my own.'

'Everything?'

'Except the cooking. We have Unstable Mabel to do that for us, and you'll be glad to hear that the washing up is handled by spell. Stay out of her kitchen, by the way. Mabel has a nasty temper and is a demon shot with a soup ladle.'

'Can't the sorcerers do their own laundry?'

'They could, but they won't. Their power has to be conserved to be useful.'

'Can't we use the washing-up spell to do the laundry?'

'It was written in the ancient RUNIX spell-language,' I explained, 'and is Read-Only and can't be modified.'

'Oh. Do I have to be called F7 by the grumpy one?'

'You'll get used to it. It's better than "Oi, you". She called me F6 until only a month ago.'

'I'm not you. And besides, you still haven't told me what happened to Mr Zambini.'

'Ooh,' I said, turning up the radio to listen to the *Yogi Baird Radio Show*. I liked the show but didn't really need to listen to it. I just didn't want to talk about Mr Zambini's disappearance. At least, not yet.

Twenty minutes later we pulled up outside Zambini Towers, a large property that had once been the luxurious Majestic hotel. It was the second-highest building in Hereford after King Snodd's Parliament, but was not so well maintained. The guttering hung loose, the windows were grimy and cracked, and small tufts of grass were poking out from the gaps between the bricks.

'What a dump,' breathed Tiger as we trotted into the entrance lobby.

'We can't really afford to bring it back to a decent state. Mr Zambini bought it when he was still Great and could conjure up an oak tree from an acorn in under a fortnight.'

'That one there?' asked Tiger, pointing at a sprawling oak that had grown in the centre of the lobby, its gnarled roots and boughs elegantly wrapped around the old reception desk and partially obscuring the entrance to the abandoned Palm Court.

'No, that was Half Price's third-year dissertation.'

'Will he get rid of it?'

'Fourth-year dissertation.'

'Can't you just *wizard* the building back into shape or something?'

'It's too big, and they're saving themselves.'

'For what?'

I shrugged.

'To earn a crust. And what's more, I think they prefer it this way.'

We walked through the lobby, which was decorated with trophies, paintings and certificates of achievements long past.

'The shabbiness adds a sense of faded grandeur to the proceedings. And besides, when you don't want to draw attention to yourself, it's better to look a bit down at heel. Good morning, ladies.'

Two elderly women were on their way to the breakfast rooms. They were dressed in matching shell suits and cackled quietly to themselves.

'This is the new foundling, Tiger Prawns,' I said. 'Tiger, these are the Sisters Karamazov – Deirdre and Deirdre.'

'Why do they have the same name?'

'They had an unimaginative father.'

They looked very carefully at Tiger, and even prodded him several times with long bony fingers.

'Ha-ho,' said the least ugly of the two, 'will you scream when I stick you with a pin, you little piglet you?'

I caught Tiger's eye and shook my head, to convey they didn't mean anything.

'Prawns?' said Deirdre. 'Is that a Mother Zenobia name?'

'Yes, ma'am,' replied Tiger politely. 'The Blessed Ladies of the Lobster often use crustacean names for the foundlings.'

The sisters looked at me.

'You'll educate him well, Jennifer?'

'To the best of my ability.'

'We don't want another . . . *foundling incident.*'

'No, indeed.'

And they hobbled off, grumbling to one another about the problem with spaghetti.

'They used to earn good money on weather prediction,' I told Tiger as soon as they were out of earshot, 'a skill now relegated to little more than a hobby after the introduction of computerised weather mapping. Don't stand next to them out of doors. A lifetime's work in weather manipulation has made them very attractive to lightning. In fact, Deirdre has been struck by lightning so many times it has addled her brain and I fear she might be irredeemably insane.'

'Winsumpoop bibble bibble,' said Deirdre as they vanished into the dining room.

'What did she mean by a "foundling incident"?'

'You'll find out.'

'I don't think I'll be here long enough to.'

I was confident that he would. For all the shortage of funds, bad plumbing, peeling wallpaper, erratic incantations and dodgy spells, Kazam was *fun*. The sorcerers spent much of their time talking fondly about the good old days, and telling tales of past triumphs and disasters with equal enthusiasm. Of the days when magic was powerful, unregulated by government, and even the largest spell could be woven without filling out the spell release form B1-7G. When they weren't reminiscing they spent their time in silent contemplation or practising weird experimental stuff that I was happier not knowing about.

'I'll show you to your room.'

We walked down the corridor to where the elevators had once been. They had not worked for as long as anyone could remember, and the ornate bronze doors were wedged open, revealing a long drop to the sub-basements below.

'Shouldn't we take the stairs?' asked Tiger.

'You can if you want. It's quicker to just shout out loud the floor you want, and hop into the lift shaft.'

Tiger looked doubtful so I said 'TEN' and stepped into the void. I fell upwards to the tenth floor and stepped out as soon as the fall was over. I waited for a moment, then peered down the shaft. Far below I could see a small face staring up at me.

'Remember to shout "TEN",' I called down.

There was a terrified yell as he fell towards me, and this turned into a laugh as he stopped outside the elevator entrance. He struggled for a moment to get out, missed his moment and fell back to the ground floor again with a yell. He didn't get out there either, and fell back up to the tenth floor, where I grabbed his hand and pulled him in before he spent the afternoon falling backwards and forwards – as I had done when I first got here.

'That was fun,' he said, trembling with a mixture of fear and excitement. 'What if I change my mind halfway?'

'Then you go to whatever floor you want. It's falling fast today. Must be the dry air.'

'How does it work?'

'It's a standard Ambiguity enchantment – in this instance, the difference between "up" and "down". Carpathian Bob left it to us in his will. The last spell of a dying wizard. Powerful stuff. You'll be in Room 1039. It's got an echo but, on the plus side, it *is* self-cleaning.'

I opened the door to his room and we walked in. The room was large and light and, like most of Zambini Towers, shabby. The wallpaper was stained and torn, the woodwork warped and unsightly damp patches had appeared on the ceiling. I watched as Tiger's face relaxed into a smile, and he blinked away the tears. At the convent, he would have been used to sharing a dormitory with fifty other boys. To anyone else, Room 1039 would have been a hovel – to the foundlings of the Sisterhood, it was luxury. I walked across to the window and removed the cardboard covering a broken pane to let in some fresh air.

'The tenth floor is self-tidying,' I said, 'nothing is ever out of place.'

To demonstrate, I moved the blotter on the desk slightly off kilter, and a second or two later it realigned itself. I then dug a handkerchief from my pocket and threw it on the carpet. As soon as it hit the floor it fluttered off to the top drawer of the bureau like a butterfly, folding itself as it went.

'Don't ask me how it works or who cast it, but be warned: enchantments have no intelligence. They follow spell sub-routines without any form of discretion. If you were to fall over in here you'd find yourself tidied away into the wardrobe, as likely as not on a coat hanger.'

'I'll be careful.'

'Wise words. You can use the self-tidying feature, but don't *overuse* it. Every spell is a drain on the power that runs through the building. If *everyone* were untidy, the speed of magic would slow dramatically. A hand-kerchief would self-fold in an hour, and the perpetual

teapot would run dry. The same is true of the elevator.
Play with it for too long and it'll slow down and stop.
I was stuck between floors once when Wizard Moobin
was trying out one of his alchemy spells. Think of
Zambini Towers as a giant battery of wizidrical power,
constantly on trickle charge. If used a lot, it will soon
run out. Used sparingly, it can go on all day. Is this
room okay?'

'Do people knock when they want to use the bath?'
he asked, staring into the marble-and-faded-gilt bathroom.

'Every room has its own bathroom,' I told him.

He looked at me, astonished that such extravagance
not only existed, but would be offered to him.

'A bed, a window, a bedside light *and* a bathroom?'
he said with a grin, 'It's the best room I'll ever have!
I'm going to like it here, even with the weirdness and
the laundry.'

'Then I'll leave you to settle in. Come down to the
Avon Suite on the ground floor when you're ready
and I'll tell you what's what. Don't worry if you hear
odd noises at night, the floor may be covered with
toads from time to time, stay away from orbs and never,
never, ask to go to the thirteenth floor. Oh, and you
mustn't look back if ever you pass the Limping Man.
See you later.'

I was barely out of the door when I heard a cry
from Tiger. I put my head back into the room.

'I saw a figure over there,' he said, pointing a trembling finger in the direction of the bathroom. 'I think it was a ghost.'

'Impossible – phantasms are confined to the third floor. You've just seen the echo I told you about.'

'How can you see an echo?'

'It's not sound, it's *visual.*'

To demonstrate I walked to the other side of the room, paused for ten seconds and then walked back. Sure enough, a pale outline of myself appeared a few seconds later.

'The longer you stay in one place, the more powerful the echo. We think it's a redundant strand on the self-tidying spell. Do you want to change?'

'Are the other rooms any less weird?'

'Not really.'

'Then this is fine.'

'Good. I'll see you downstairs when you're ready.'

Tiger looked around the room nervously.

'Wait a moment while I unpack.'

He took from his pocket a folded necktie and placed it in one of the drawers.

'I'm done.'

And he followed me down the lift shaft, but this time with a little more confidence, and with a little less shouting.

Kevin Zipp

'Can *you* do any magic?' he asked as we walked past the shuttered ballroom on our way to the Avon Suite.

'Everyone can do a *bit*,' I said, wondering where Kevin Zipp had got to. 'If you are thinking of somebody and the phone rings and it's them, that's magic. If you get a curious feeling that you've been or done something before, then that's magic too. It's everywhere. It seeps into the fabric of the world and oozes out as coincidence, fate, chance, luck or what have you. The big problem is making it work for you in some useful manner.'

'Mother Zenobia used to say that magic was like the gold that is mingled in sand,' observed Tiger, 'worth a lot of money but useless since you can't extract it.'

She was right. If you have magic within you, were properly trained and the sort of person who could channel their mind, then it was possible a career in sorcery might be the thing for you.

'Were you tested?' I asked him.

'Yes, I was a 162.8.'

'I'm a 159.3,' I told him, 'so pretty useless the pair of us.'

You have to have a thousand or more before anyone gets interested. You've either got it or you haven't — a bit like being able to play a piano or go backwards on a unicycle while juggling seven clubs.

'You and me and Unstable Mabel,' I added, 'are the only non-magic ones in the building.'

'What about the Quarkbeast?'

'Magic through and through — one of a bunch of creatures created by the Mighty Shandar in the sixteenth century.'

He looked down at the beast, who was trotting beside us while thoughtfully sucking the chrome off a section of car bumper.

'He was made by Shandar?'

'So they say. Here we are.'

I opened the door to the Kazam offices and flicked on the light. The Avon Suite was large but seemed considerably smaller owing to a huge amount of clutter. There were filing cabinets, desks where once sat now-long-redundant agents, tables, piles of paperwork, back issues of *Spells* magazine, several worn-out sofas and, in the corner, a moose. It chewed softly on some grass and stared at us laconically.

'That's the Transient Moose,' I said, looking through the mail, 'an illusion that was left as a practical joke long before I got here. He moves randomly about the building appearing now and then, here and there to this one and that one. We're hoping he'll wear out soon.'

Tiger went up to the moose and placed a hand on its nose. His hand went through the creature as though it were smoke. I took the papers off a nearby desk and placed them on a third, pushed up a swivel chair and showed Tiger how to use the phone system.

'You can answer from anywhere in the hotel. If I don't pick up, then you should. Take a message and I'll call them back.'

'I've never had a desk,' said Tiger, looking at the desk fondly.

'You've got one now. See that teapot on the sideboard over there?'

He nodded.

'That's the perpetual teapot I mentioned earlier. It's always full of tea. The same goes for the biscuit tin. You can help yourself.'

Tiger got the subtle hint. I told him I liked my tea with half a sugar, and he trotted off to the steaming teapot to fetch some.

'There're only two biscuits left,' said Tiger in dismay, staring into the biscuit tin.

'We're on an economy drive. Instead of an enchanted biscuit tin that's always full, we've got an enchanted biscuit tin with always only two left. You'd be amazed at how much wizidrical energy we save.'

'Right,' said Tiger, taking out the two biscuits, closing

the lid and then finding two new biscuits when he opened it again.

'The economy drive explains why they're plain and not sweet, right?'

'Right.'

'Quark.'

'What is it?'

The Quarkbeast pointed one of its sharpened claws at a bundle of old clothes on one of the sofas. I went and had a closer look. It was the Remarkable Kevin Zipp. He was fast asleep and snoring quietly to himself.

'Good morning, Kevin,' I said cheerily. He blinked, stared at me, then sat up. 'How is the job in Leominster going?'

I was referring to some work I had found him in a flower nursery, predicting the colours of blooms in ungerminated bulbs. He was one of our better pre-cognitives, usually managing a strike rate of 72 per cent or more.

'Well, thank you,' muttered the small man. His clothes were shabby to the point of being little more than rags, but he was exceptionally well presented in spite of it. He was clean shaven, washed and his hair was fastidiously tidy. He looked like an accountant on his way to a fancy-dress party as a vagrant.

I could see that ungerminated bulbs were not the cause of his visit, and whenever a pre-cog acts unusual, it's time to head for the storm cellar.

'This is Tiger Prawns,' I said, 'the seventh foundling.'

Kevin took Tiger's hand in his and stared into his eyes.

'Don't get in a blue car on a Thursday.'

'Which Thursday?'

'Any Thursday.'

'What kind of car?'

'A blue one. On a Thursday.'

'Okay,' said Tiger.

'So what's this about a vision?' I asked, sorting through the mail.

'It was a biggie,' Kevin began nervously.

'Oh yes?' I returned nervously, having heard a lot of predictions that never came to anything, but also having heard some chilling ones that did.

'You know Maltcassion, the Dragon?' he asked.

'Not personally.'

'Of him, then.'

I knew of him, of course. Everybody did. The last of his kind, he lived up in the Dragonlands not far from here, although you'd be hard pressed to find anyone who could say they had caught a glimpse of the reclusive beast. I took the tea that Tiger handed me and placed it on my desk.

'What about him?'

Kevin took a deep breath.

'I saw him die. Die by the sword of a Dragonslayer.'

'When?'

He narrowed his eyes.

'Certainly within the next week.'

I stopped opening the mail – mostly junk anyway, or bills – and looked over to where Kevin Zipp was staring at me intently. The importance of the information wasn't lost on him, and it wasn't lost on me either. By ancient decree the Dragon's land belonged to whoever claimed it as soon as the Dragon died, so there was always an unseemly rush for real estate which eclipsed a Dragon's death. Within a day every square inch of land would be claimed. In the following months there would be legal wranglings, then the construction would begin. New roads, housing and power, retail parks and industrial units. All would cover the unspoilt lands in a smear of tarmac and concrete. A four-hundred-year-old wilderness gone for ever.

'I heard that when Dragon Dunwoody died twelve years ago,' said Tiger, 'the crowd surge resulted in forty-seven people dead in the stampede.'

Kevin and I exchanged glances. The death of the last Dragon would be a matter of some consequence, and not just on matters of public safety. I felt something inside me turn over. The last Dragon was a big deal. I didn't quite know how I knew, but I did.

'How strong was this?' I asked.

'On a scale of one to ten,' replied Zipp, 'it was a twelve. Most powerful premonition I've ever felt. It was as though the Mighty Shandar himself had called me up person-to-person *and* reversed the charges. I can detect it on low-alpha as well as the wider brain wavelengths. I doubt I'm the only person picking this up.'

I doubted it too. I phoned Randolph, 14th Earl of Pembridge, the only other pre-cog on our books. Randolph, or EP-14 as he was sometimes known, was not only minor Hereford aristocracy, but an industrial prophet who worked for Consolidated Useful Stuff (Steel) PLC, predicting failure rates on industrial welding.

'Randolph, it's Jennifer.'

'Jenny, D'girl! I thought you'd call.'

'I've got the Remarkable Kevin Zipp with me and I wondered if—'

He didn't need any prompting. He had picked up the same thing but had also furnished a time and date. Next Sunday at noon. I thanked him and replaced the phone.

'Anything else?'

'Yes,' replied Kevin, 'Two words: Big Magic.'

'Both capitalised?'

'Does it make any difference?' he asked.

'Certainly,' I replied, 'big magic is simply a feat of magic that's, well *big*. But Big Magic with capitals is something else entirely.'

'Like what?' asked Tiger.

'I'm not sure,' I replied, 'hence the "something else

entirely" comment. The sorcerers speak of it in hushed tones. I asked once but I got stared at.'

'By Lady Mawgon?' asked Kevin.

'Yes.'

'I hate it when she does that,' he murmured, and gazed at the worn lino, deep in thought. Being a pre-cog wasn't a huge barrel of laughs. Generally speaking you always got it in the neck for not being specific enough. By the time the vision had been figured out, people were already dying.

'Before I go,' he said, pulling a rumpled piece of paper from his pocket, 'these are for you.'

He handed the grubby piece of paper not to me, but to Tiger.

He read the note as I looked over his shoulder. It didn't seem to mean anything at all.

Smith
7, 11, and 13
Ulan Bator

'I don't understand,' said Tiger at length.

'Me neither.' Zipp shrugged. 'Isn't seeing the future a hoot?'

Tiger looked at me and I nodded to him that he should take it seriously.

'Thank you, sir,' said Tiger with a bow.

'Well, there you have it,' said Kevin, and he left in

a hurry as he had felt a good tip on Baron, a six-year-old mare running in the Hereford Gold Stakes Handicap.

The phone rang and I picked it up, listened for a few moments and scribbled a note on a standard form.

'This is a form B2-5C,' I told Tiger, 'for a minor spell of less than a thousand Shandars. I need you to take it up to the Mysterious X in Room 245 and tell them that I sent you and we need this job done as soon as possible.'

He took the form and stared at me nervously.

'Who, exactly, is the Mysterious X?'

'They're more of a *what* than a *who*. It won't be in a form you'll recognise, and there is something *other* about X that defies easy explanation. It's more of a sense than a person. A shroud, if you like, that confuses their true form. It also smells of unwashed socks and peanut butter. You'll be fine.'

Tiger looked at the note, then at the Quarkbeast, then at where the moose had been but suddenly wasn't, then back at me.

'This is a test, isn't it?'

He was smart, this one. I nodded.

'You can be back with the Sisterhood by teatime, and no one will have thought any the worse of you. I'll let you in on a secret. You weren't sent to me as a punishment, nor by chance. Mother Zenobia is an ex-sorceress herself, and only sends those she deems truly exceptional. Aside from the fifth foundling – the one we don't talk about – she's never been wrong.'

'So was all that stuff about the Limping Man, the thirteenth floor, staying away from orbs and being flown in a cardboard box also part of the test?'

'No, that was for real. And that's just the weird stuff I can remember right now. We haven't even got started on emergency procedures yet.'

'Right,' he said and, after taking a deep breath, he left the room. He was back again a few moments later.

'This job,' he said, waving the form B2-5C nervously, 'is it something to do with Dark Forces?'

'There's no such thing as the "Forces of Darkness", despite what you read in the storybooks. There are no "Dark Arts" or "wizards pulled to the dark side". There is only the Good or Bad that lurks in the heart of Man. Misguided men and women can use magic for evil, but it's them that's wicked, not the magic. Magic has no intelligence. The choice to use it for good or bad lies with us. All of us. And despite Zambini's absence, I will defend his goal to keep magic clean and uncorrupted!'

My voice had been rising, and Tiger, startled, had taken a step backward. A teacup shattered on the draining rack and I felt myself grow hot.

'Hang on,' said Tiger, 'I'm just the trainee.'

'Sorry,' I said, opening a window and taking a deep

breath of cool air, 'but doing Zambini's job isn't just about answering the phone and balancing the books.'

Tiger laid a small hand on my arm. Foundlings looked after foundlings.

'You miss him, don't you?'

'Like I miss my own father.'

I turned and blinked away the tears. Kevin's premonition about Dragondeath had rattled me more than I realised.

'I miss my father,' said Tiger, 'I don't know who he is, where he is, whether he's alive or even knows I'm here – but I miss him.'

'Me too,' I said, blowing my nose and thinking for a moment before clapping my hands together.

'Back to work. In answer to your question, Mysterious X's job is a cat stuck up a tree. He'll grumble, but he'll do it. Even inexplicable entities comprised of charged particles kept in order by a weak magnetic field need cash to survive.'

About the Mystical Arts

———

'It was kind of . . . well, *vague*. Sort of shapeless – but with pointy bits.'

'That's the Mysterious X all over,' I said. 'Did it show you its stamp collection?'

'It tried to,' said Tiger, 'but I was too quick for it. What exactly *is* the Mysterious X anyway?'

I shrugged. There was a very good reason X carried the accolade 'Mysterious'.

We were talking over a pre-bedtime cup of hot chocolate in the kitchens. Wizard Moobin, Lady Mawgon and Full Price had finished the rewiring job early and got the bus back into town. They were quite elated at the way the gig had gone, and even Lady Mawgon had permitted herself a small smile by way of celebration. Wizidrical power had been strong today – almost everyone had noticed it. I'd fielded a call from a journalist at the *Hereford Daily Eyestrain* with a pertinent question over Dragondeath. The premonition was getting about. I told her I knew nothing, and had hung up.

The rest of the afternoon had been spent explaining to Tiger how Kazam is run, and introducing him to the least insane residents. He had been particularly taken with Brother Gillingrex of Woodseaves, who had made speaking to birds something of a speciality. He could speak Quack so well that he knew all the eighty-two different words ducks use to describe water. He could also speak Coot, Goose, Wader and Chirrup – which is a sort of generic Pigeon/Sparrow language. He was working on Osprey, had a few useful sentences in Buzzard and the Owl word for 'mouse', which is tricky to pronounce if you don't have a beak. He was mostly employed by birdwatchers, especially useful when it was time for putting identification rings on their legs. Birds worry endlessly about their appearance – all that preening is not only about flying, as they might have you believe – and a softly spoken 'that looks *really* fetching and totally matches your plumage' works wonders.

'Does anyone else at Kazam have an accolade?' asked Tiger, who had soon realised there was a lot to learn, and the sooner he got started, the better.

'Two *Ladies*, one *Mysterious*, three *Wizards*, one *Remarkable*, two *Venerables* and a *Pointless*,' I murmured, counting them off on my fingers, 'but once upon a time, they *all* had an accolade – and higher than the ones I've just mentioned.'

'Who's the "Pointless"?'

'It would be impolite of me to reveal, but you'll probably figure it out for yourself.'

'So those accoladed "Wizard" are the most powerful, yes?'

'Not quite,' I replied. 'An accolade isn't simply based on performance, but on reliability. Wizard Moobin isn't the most powerful in the building, but he's the most consistent. And to complicate matters further, a status is different to an accolade. Two wizards might both be status *Spellmanager* but if one has turned a goat into a moped and the other hasn't, then they get to call themselves "Wizard".'

'*A goat into a moped?*'

'You couldn't do that. It's just an example.'

'Oh. So who decides who gets an accolade?'

'It's self-conferring,' I replied. 'The idea of any kind of organised higher authority – a "Grand Council of Wizards" or something – is wholly ridiculous once you get to know how scatty they can be. Getting three of them to spell together is possible – *just* – but asking them to agree on a new colour for the dining room almost impossible. Argumentative, infantile, passionate and temperamental, they need people like us to manage them and always have done. Two paces behind every great wizard there has always been their agent. They always took a back seat, but were always there, doing the deals, sorting out transport, hotel bookings, mopping up the mistakes and the broken hearts, that sort of thing.'

'Even the Mighty Shandar?'

'There is no *record* that he had one, but we're usually

the first to be written out of history. Yes, I'm almost certain of it. Imagine being the Mighty Shandar's agent. No percentage, but the fringe benefits would be colossal.'

'Would you get dental?'

'Tusks if you wanted them.'

'Do you enjoy it?' he asked, and I had to think for a moment.

'Doing your duty is perhaps not the same as *enjoyment*,' I said slowly, 'but who would look after them if not me?'

'If I can last the course I guess I will.'

I stared at him. I'd be gone from here in two years upon my eighteenth birthday, and already I was dreading it.

'Do you have to leave?' he asked.

'It's when my indentured servitude is up,' I said, 'and I get the freedom to do what I want.'

'What if what you want to do is work here?'

'Then I'll come back,' I said slowly, having thought about this a great deal, 'but I want the freedom to make that decision for *myself*.'

'I can't fault your logic,' said Tiger, 'tell me more about accolades.'

'Right. The one thing sorcerers are good at is honour. You'd not award yourself an accolade that you didn't deserve, nor shy from demoting yourself if your powers faded. They're good and honest people – just a bit weird, and hopeless at managing themselves.'

'So what about the one who accoladed themselves "Pointless"?'

'They have self-confidence issues.'

Tiger thought about this for a moment.

'So what could a sorcerer do on the Spellmanager level?'

I took a sip of hot chocolate.

'Levitation of light objects, stopping clocks, unblocking drains and simple washing and drying can all be handled pretty well at the Spellmanager level. There's no one below this status at Kazam except you, me, Unstable Mabel, the Quarkbeast and Hector.'

'Hector?'

'Transient Moose.'

I nodded in the direction of the moose, who was leaning against one of the fridge-freezers with a look of supreme boredom etched upon his features.

'Above this is a Sorcerer. They can conjure up light winds and start hedgehog migrations. Sparks may fly from their fingertips and they might manage to levitate a car. The next rank is that of Master Sorcerer. At this level you might be expected to be able to create objects from nothing. A light drizzle could be conjured up, but not on a clear day. Above this is the Grand Master Sorcerer. These gifted people can levitate several trucks at a time, change an object's colour permanently and start isolated thunderstorms. They might be able to squeeze out a lightning bolt but not very accurately. The final category is Super Grand Master Sorcerer who can do almost anything. He or she can whistle up storms, command the elements and stop the tide. They can create spells and incantations that are so strong that they stay on long after they have died. They are also, supremely, incredibly, thankfully, *rare*. I've never met one. There aren't any. Not now, anyway. The greatest of all the Super Grand Master Sorcerers was the Mighty Shandar. It was said that he had so much magic in him his footprints would spontaneously catch fire as he walked.'

'And the Mighty Shandar is where we get the base measurement of wizidrical power – the Shandar?'

'That's about the tune of it.'

'But there are others, surely? Out there, doing normal jobs, who have this power?'

'Several hundred, I imagine,' I replied, 'but without a licence to practise they'd have to be either very stupid or very desperate to start chucking spells around. To perform magic of any kind you have to have a Certificate of Conformity – a licence. Once that hurdle has been crossed you have to be accredited to a licensed "House of Enchantment". After that, each spell has to be logged on a form B2-5C for anything below a thousand Shandars, a B1-7G form for spells not exceeding ten thousand Shandars, and a form P4-7D for those in excess of ten thousand Shandars.'

'That would be a seriously big spell,' said Tiger.

'Bigger than you and I will ever see. The last P4-7D job was signed off in 1947, when they built the Thames Tidal Barrage. There was a lot more power about in those days, but even so it took a consortium of twenty-six sorcerers, and the wizidrical power peaked at 1.6 MegaShandars. It was said children's sandpits turned to glass within a twenty-mile radius. They evacuated the local area for a job that size, naturally.'

Tiger blinked at me in wonder. Magic wasn't generally talked about. Despite the obvious advantages, it was still regarded with suspicion by most people. Reinventing sorcery as a useful commodity akin to electricity or even the fourth emergency service was something Mr Zambini had been most keen on.

'What if someone did?' he asked. 'Commit an act of illegal sorcery, I mean?'

I took a deep breath and stared at him.

'It's about the only thing the twenty-eight nations of the Ununited Kingdoms agree upon. Any unlicensed act of sorcery done outside the boundaries of a House of Enchantment is punishable by . . . public burning.'

Tiger looked shocked.

'I know,' I said, 'an unwelcome legacy from the fourteenth century and reinforced by the Blix episode in 1878. *Highly* unpleasant. And that's why you, me, we, *everyone*, has to be extra diligent when filling out the forms. Miss something or forget to file it and you're responsible for a good friend's hideous punishment. We lost George Nash four years ago. A lovely man and a skilled practitioner. What he couldn't tell you about smoke manipulation wasn't worth knowing. He was doing a routine earthworm charming and his B1-7G form wasn't filled in. Someone's eye wasn't on the ball.'

Tiger tilted his head on one side.

'It was the fifth foundling, wasn't it?'

Tiger was smart. Mother Zenobia had sent us the best.

'Yes,' I said, 'the fifth foundling's name isn't spoken under this roof.'

We both sat in silence for a moment, the only sound the panting of the Quarkbeast, the chewing of the Transient Moose and the occasional sip, from us, of hot chocolate.

Tiger, I guessed, was probably thinking the same as me. About being a foundling. We were left outside the Convent of the Blessed Ladies of the Lobster before we were even old enough to talk. We didn't know our true birth dates, and our names weren't the ones we were born with. I think that's why Tiger had guessed that the fifth foundling was the one responsible for George Nash. There is no greater insult among foundlings than to refuse to acknowledge the one thing that you value more than anything else — your name.

'Did you ever try to find out?' asked Tiger.

He meant my parents.

'Not yet,' I replied. Some of us built them up and were disappointed, others built them down so they wouldn't be. All of us thought about them.

'Any clues?'

'My Volkswagen,' I replied. 'It was abandoned with me in it. I'm going to find out its previous owners when I get out of servitude. You?'

'My only clue was a weekday return to Carlisle and a medal,' replied Tiger, 'placed in my basket when I was left outside the convent. It was a Fourth Troll Wars campaign medal with a Valour clasp.'

We sat in silence for a moment.

'*Lots* of parents lost in the Troll Wars,' I said.

'Yes,' said Tiger in a quiet voice, 'lots.'

I stretched and stood up. It was getting late.

'Good first day, Tiger, thanks.'

'I didn't do much.'

'It's what you didn't do that matters.'

'And what didn't I do?'

'You didn't run away screaming, or try to fight me, or make peculiar demands.'

'I like to think the Prawns are like that,' he said with a smile, 'loyal and dedicated.'

'How about fearless?'

He looked at the Quarkbeast.

'We're working on that.'

I saw him up to his room and asked whether he needed anything, and he said he was just fine, and everything was 100 per cent faberoo as he had his own room and that was the best thing ever, even if it was enchanted. I went down to my own room and brushed my teeth, then climbed into my pyjamas and got into bed, taking the precaution of laying out a blanket on the floor with a pillow, just in case. I then had another thought and took down the poster of Sir Matt Grifflon as it made me seem a little undignified. I rolled up the picture of the Kingdom's premier heart-throb and placed it in the cupboard.

I had read for only a few minutes when the door opened and Tiger tiptoed in, snugged up in the blanket I had laid out and sighed deeply. He'd never slept on his own before.

'Goodnight, Tiger.'

'Goodnight, Jenny.'

I lay awake for a while, my head full of dragons, premonitions and, for some reason, destiny. But not the ultimate destiny of magic that everyone at Kazam worried about – the destiny that disturbed me was . . . mine.

The Magiclysm

I didn't sleep well that night. It wasn't my fault; there was something in the air. Sorcerers tend to transmit their emotions when excited, upset, anxious or confused, and it permeates through the building like smelly drains. I'd taken to sleeping under an aluminised eiderdown, but it hadn't helped.

Tiger had gone by the time I awoke. The Quarkbeast too, so I imagined it had managed to communicate to Tiger that it liked a walk – and possibly the route, in unused back alleys and the wasteground behind the papermill, where its fearsome appearance wouldn't send anyone into traumatic shock. I knew the Quarkbeast well, and it sometimes frightened even me. It is said that the only thing a Quarkbeast looks good to is another Quarkbeast, but they never gather in pairs, for a reason I wasn't quite sure about.

I had a quick bath, dressed, and stepped out of my room. I was on the third floor, sandwiched between the room shared by the Sisters Karamazov and Mr Zambini's suite. I walked down the corridor and noted a sharp sensation in the air, very similar to the tingling that precedes a spell. The lights flickered in the corridor and my bedroom door, which I had closed, slowly swung open. I felt the building shimmer and the tingling sensation grew stronger and then, one by one, the light bulbs fell from their fittings, bounced on the carpet and then rolled to the far end of the corridor. Beneath my feet I could feel the floorboards start to bend and several toads started to drop from nowhere. I needed no further warnings. Zambini had briefed me about a Magiclysm, although I had never witnessed one. Without hesitation I ran to the alarm positioned next to the lift, broke the glass and pressed the large red button.

The klaxon sounded in the building, warning all those within to use whatever countermeasures they could, and almost immediately the misters filled the entire hotel with the fine dampness of water, which felt like stepping inside a cloud. Water is an ideal moderator and is about the only thing that can naturally quench a spell that is about to go critical. I paused and a few seconds later there was a tremendous detonation from somewhere on the fifth floor. The tingling and vibrations abruptly stopped and I turned to see a cloud of plaster and dust descend the stairwell. I switched off the alarm and ran up the stairs – lifts, even enchanted ones, should never be used in an emergency. I found Wizard Moobin lying in a heap on the fifth-floor landing.

'Moobin!' I exclaimed as the dust began to settle. 'What on earth happened to you?'

He didn't answer. Instead, he clambered unsteadily to his feet and returned to his apartment, the door of which had been blown clean off its hinges and was now embedded in the wall opposite. I put my head around the door and stared at the devastation. A wizard's room is also their laboratory, as all sorcerers are inveterate tinkerers by nature, and entire lifetimes are spent in pursuit of a specific spell to do a specific job. Even something as inconsequential as the charm for finding a lost hammer had taken Grendell of Cleethorpes an entire lifetime to weave in the twelfth century. A destroyed workshop often indicated several decades of important work lost in one short blast of uncontrolled wizardry. Magic can be strong stuff and bite the unwary.

I followed Wizard Moobin into his room and trod carefully through the jumbled wreckage. Most of his books had been destroyed and all the carefully laid-out glassware, retorts and flasks had been reduced to shards. But about this, Moobin seemed curiously unconcerned, nor was he worried that his clothes had been blown off him, and he was now dressed only in a pair of underpants and a sock.

'Are you okay?' I asked, but the wizard was far too busy searching for something to answer. I exchanged glances with Half Price, who had arrived at the door.

Despite being identical twins born two weeks apart, they were hardly alike at all. One was thin and the other stout.

'Wow!' said the Youthful Perkins, who had also just arrived. 'I've never seen a spell go critical before. What were you doing?'

'I'm fine,' Moobin muttered, turning over a broken tabletop. I picked up a fire extinguisher and put out a small fire in one corner of the room.

'What happened?' I asked again, and Moobin suddenly stood up from where he had been searching in a pile of smouldering papers and with shaking hand passed me a small toy soldier. It had only one leg, carried a musket and was very heavy. It was made of pure gold.

'Yes?' I asked, still in the dark.

'Lead, used to be, was, like, at least. Then, well—' exclaimed the Wizard excitedly, trying to find a chair undamaged enough to sit on.

'You're babbling,' I told him.

'Lead – now . . . *gold*!' he said at last.

'Way to go!' said the Youthful Perkins enthusiastically. He had been joined by the Sisters Karamazov, who were jostling each other for the best view.

'Lead into gold!?' I repeated incredulously, knowing full well that such a spell requires a subatomic meddling that is almost unheard of below the status of Grand Master Sorcerer.

'How did you manage to do that?'

'That's the interesting thing,' replied Moobin, '*I have no idea*. Every morning I concentrate my mind on that lead soldier, summon up every Shandar in my body and let fly. For twenty-eight years nothing has happened; not a flicker. But this morning—'

'Big Magic!' yelled the younger Karamazov sister.

Wizard Moobin looked up abruptly.

'Do you think so?'

'Rubbish,' returned her sister, 'don't listen to her – she's one spell short of a curse.'

'I was more powerful in the rewiring job yesterday,' Moobin said thoughtfully. 'Perhaps the surge has sustained for a bit longer.'

This, I mused, was possible. The background wizidrical power was subject to periodical fluctuations. There were, however, more practical matters to consider.

'I hate to be a stickler for regulations,' I said, 'but you're going to have to fill out a form B2-5C for this. I know we're in the Towers, but we should stay on the safe side. We'd better do a P3-8F as well, just in case.'

'P3-8F?' queried Moobin. 'I haven't heard of *that* one before.'

'Experimental spells resulting in accidental damage of a physical nature,' put in the younger Karamazov sister, who, despite the repeated lightning strikes, could still have moments of lucidity.

'I see,' replied Moobin, turning to me. 'If you fill them in, I'll sign them.'

I left him to tidy up and walked downstairs to the ground floor, where I met Tiger and the Quarkbeast as they returned. Tiger had a graze on his nose, his clothes were scuffed and he had some twigs in his hair.

'If he starts to run you have to drop his leash as soon as possible.'

'I know that now.'

'Did he drag you far?'

'It wasn't the distance,' replied Tiger, 'it was the terrain. What's going on?'

'Wizard Moobin experienced a surge,' I said as we entered the offices in the Avon Suite. I sat down at my desk and pulled the *Codex Magicalis* towards me to make sure I didn't need to fill out any more paperwork. 'Something's going on. Yesterday they finished the rewiring in record time, and this morning Moobin turned lead into gold.'

'I thought the power of magic was diminishing?'

'It is, in general. But every now and again it surges upwards and they can all do things they haven't been able to do for years. The problem is that surges usually herald a slump, and if you couple this with what Kevin Zipp told us yesterday, we could find ourselves without magic at all, come next Sunday.'

'You think Dragons have something to do with magic?'

'It was one of Zambini's many theories,' I replied. 'He said there must be a reason Kazam is based in the Kingdom of Hereford. We're twenty miles away from the Dragonlands, and while a link between Dragons and magic has never been proved, there's more than enough anecdotal evidence to link the two. In any event,' I added, 'if we're to try and preserve the mystery and majesty of magic, we need to find out more.'

We stood in silence for a moment.

'By the way,' said Tiger, 'is the Quarkbeast allowed to chew corrugated iron before breakfast?'

'Only galvanised,' I replied without looking up, 'the zinc keeps his scales shiny.'

After the excited buzz about Moobin's accident had died down and everyone had tried the lead-into-gold thing themselves without any success, I got down to the day-to-day running of Kazam. I had a job for Full Price to divine the position of a wedding ring that had been flushed accidentally down the loo, and another tree-moving job that the Green Man and Patrick of Ludlow could handle. I sorted through the mail. There were a few cheques so at least I could speak to the bank manager again. There was also a letter that carried the official seal of the Hereford City Council, and it informed me that our contract to clean the city's drains would not be renewed. I called my contact at the council to try to find out why.

'The fact is,' said Tim Brody, who was acting assistant deputy head of drains, 'that Blok-U-Gon, the well-known and TV-advertised industrial drain unblockers, have undercut your price, and we have a budget to think of.'

'I'm sure we can come to some arrangement,' I said, trying to act how Mr Zambini might. Some work we did at a loss, either simply to keep the sorcerers busy, or to give us a presence in the marketplace. We needed the public to see us working in order to gain their trust and promote wizardry as simply a way of life. The last thing we needed was for the fifteenth-century view of sorcerers to spring to the fore, and for the citizenry to regard those at Kazam with loathing and mistrust.

'Listen,' I said, 'a drain cleared by magic is the best way. It doesn't smell, no fuss, you don't have to be embarrassed by what you blocked it up with, and besides, I offer a good guarantee. If it blocks again within twenty-four hours we redo the job for free and charm the moles from your garden – or your face: the choice is yours. I even do the form B1-7Gs for you. Besides, it's *traditional*.'

'It's not just the cost, Jennifer. My mother used to be a sorceress so I've always tried to use you guys. The problem is that King Snodd's useless brother has recently bought a five per cent share in Blok-U-Gon, and, well, you see?'

'Oh,' I said, realising that this was bigger than both of us, 'right. Thanks for your time, Tim. I'm sure you did your best.'

I hung up. Although King Snodd IV was in general a fair and just ruler who seldom put people to death without good reason, he was not averse to making edicts that were of financial benefit to him and his immediate family. There was nothing I could do. He was the King, after all, and, indentured servitude or not, I and all those who held Hereford nationality were loyal subjects of the Crown.

'We just lost the drain unblocking contract to King Snodd's useless brother,' I said.

'I don't know about his useless brother, but Mother Zenobia took us all to see King Snodd on Military Hardware Parade Day,' remarked Tiger thoughtfully.

'What did you think?'

'The landships were impressive.'

'I meant about the King.'

He thought for a moment.

'Shorter than he looks during the weekly TV address.'

'He does the address sitting down.'

'Even so.'

But Tiger was right.

'The six-foot-tall Queen Mimosa doesn't help him,' I observed. 'She used to work here thirty years ago when she was plain Miss Mimosa Jones. Mr

Zambini said she could pollinate plants over seven times more efficiently than bees. A good little earner, he said, given Hereford's fruit exports. But then Prince Snodd took an interest, proclaimed his undying love and she renounced her calling to be the princess, later Queen. Mr Zambini was sad to lose her, but the bees were relieved to be back to full employment.'

'She's very beautiful,' said Tiger.

'And witty and wise,' I added, 'what with all the stand-up comedy she does, and the Troll Wars Widows charity.'

'Quark.'

The door to the office cracked open and a large man with a sharp suit and a fedora put his head round the door. He soon noticed the Quarkbeast. Hard not to, really.

'Does he, er . . . bite?'

'Never deeper than the bone.'

He jumped.

'My joke, Mr . . . ?'

The large man looked relieved and entered. He removed his hat and sat in the chair I offered him while Tiger was dispatched to fetch a cup of tea.

'My name is Mr Trimble,' announced the man, 'of Trimble, Trimble, Trimble, Trimble and Trimble, attorneys-at-law.'

He handed me a card.

'That's me there,' he said, helpfully pointing to the third Trimble from the left.

'Jennifer Strange,' I replied, handing him a brochure and rate-card.

There was a pause.

'Can I speak to someone in charge?'

'That's me.'

'Oh!' he said apologetically. 'You seemed a little young.'

'I'm sixteen in two weeks,' I said, 'and I've been at Kazam for four years, acting manager for six months. You can talk to me.'

'Commendable, Miss Strange, but I usually speak to Mr Zambini.'

'Mr Zambini is regrettably . . . unavailable right now.'

'Where is he?'

'*Indisposed*,' I replied firmly. 'How can I help?'

'Very well,' said Mr Trimble, once he could see I would not be moved. 'I represent the Consolidated Useful Stuff Land Development Corporation.'

'I'm sorry to hear that,' I replied. 'But unless *you* really want to change, there's not a lot we can do.'

'I don't regard it as a problem, Miss Strange,' he replied testily.

'Oh,' I said, 'sorry.'

'Never mind. Do you have any reliable pre-cogs on your books?'

'I have two,' I answered happily, glad for the additional work, and from someone who could pay their bills – the Consolidated Useful Stuff Land Development Corporation was the property arm of Consolidated Useful Stuff, and there wasn't much that ConStuff didn't do and own. They even had their own kingdom in the chain of islands to the east of Trollvania, which used a large foundling labour force to make cheap and shabby goods far more cheaply and shabbily than anyone else – a clear advantage that allowed them to dominate the Ununited Kingdoms' cheap and shabby goods market. It was said that of every pound, spondoolip, dollop, acker or moolah spent, one in six went into ConStuff's pocket. No one much liked them, but few didn't shop there. ConWearStuff had recently introduced an 'all you can wear for five moolah' section, and on my miserable allowance, I couldn't afford to shop anywhere else. To my credit, I *did* feel guilty afterwards.

'Two pre-cogs?' said Trimble, taking a chequebook from his pocket. 'That's excellent news. I wonder if any of them have predicted the death of the loathsome Maltcassion recently?'

I hope he didn't see me flinch.

'Why?'

'Well,' continued Mr Trimble genially, 'it's just that my aunt had a vision last night of the Dragon's death.'

'Did she say when?'

'No; this year, tomorrow, who knows? She's only

rated a 629.8, so her predictions are a bit wild. But I can't ignore it. All that land ripe for claiming. The precise time of the Dragon's death would be invaluable to a property developer, if you get my meaning. Land is so much better managed when there is only one company administering it. Having the general public own dribs and drabs here and there and everywhere can be highly irksome, wouldn't you agree?'

He smiled and handed me a cheque. I gasped. It was for two million Herefordian moolah. I'd never seen so many zeros in one place without 'overdrawn' written next to them.

'If you can tell me the precise time and date I will return and sign that cheque. But *only* for the correct time and date. Do you understand?'

'You . . . want to cash in on the death of the last Dragon?'

'*Precisely* what I mean,' he said happily, mistaking my sense of annoyance for one of agreement, 'I'm so glad we understand one another.'

Before I could say another word he had shaken my hand and walked out of the door, leaving me staring at the cheque. His offer would clear our overdraft and quite possibly see all of the wizards into a cosy retirement – always a possibility, given the diminishing power of magic.

'By the way,' he said, popping his head round the door again, 'there seems to be a moose in the corridor.'

'That would be Hector,' said Tiger, 'he's transient.'

'Perhaps so,' replied Trimble, 'but he's blocking the way.'

'Just walk through him,' I said, still deep in thought, 'and if you've ever wanted to know how a moose works, stop halfway and have a good look round.'

'Right,' said Mr Trimble, and left.

I leaned back in my chair. The apparent word of Maltcassion's demise was getting about. The death of a Dragon was a matter of some consequence, and such things are not to be treated lightly. And when I'm in need of advice, there is only one place to go: Mother Zenobia.

Mother Zenobia

The Convent of the Sacred Order of the Blessed Ladies of the Lobster was once a dank and dark medieval castle but was now, after a lick of paint and the introduction of a few scatter cushions, a dank and dark convent. The building overlooked the River Wye, which was pleasant, and was right on the edge of the demilitarised zone, which wasn't. Successive King Snodds had looked upon the Duke of Brecon's neighbouring duchy with envious eyes, and a garrison from each had faced one another across the ten-mile strip of land which was their only shared border. The upshot of this was that King Snodd's artillery was *behind* the convent, and used to fire a daily shell across the building to fall harmlessly into the demilitarised zone beyond. The Duke of Brecon, whose sabre-rattling had been reduced to dagger-rattling recently due to a cut in his defence budget, had his artillerymen yell 'bang' in unison by way of a returned salvo, and reserved live shells for special occasions, such as birthdays.

Despite the stand-off on their doorstep, the Sisterhood grew and supplied vegetables, fruit, honey and foundlings in exchange for cash, which allowed them to continue to bring up orphans like myself and Tiger. To us, the artillery camped out in the orchard was a matter of singular unimportance, except that you could tell the time by the single shot, which was always at 8.04 precisely.

I parked my car outside the convent and the Quarkbeast and I walked silently through the old gatehouse in an attempt to surprise Mother Zenobia, who was dozing in a large chair on the lawn. She was well over one hundred and fifty, but still remarkably active. She was a Troll War widow herself and had taken to the Lobsterhood soon after the loss of her husband. There were hushed rumours of a former riotous life, but all I knew for certain was that she had held the 1927 air-racing record in a Napier-engined Percival Plover at 208.72 m.p.h. I can be specific because the trophy commemorating the feat was kept in her small room – even Ladies of the Lobster are permitted one small vanity.

'Jennifer?' she asked, reaching out a hand for me to touch. 'I saw you drive up. Was your car orange?'

'It was, Mother,' I replied.

'And you are wearing blue, I think?'

'Right again,' I replied, amazed at her observations. She had been totally blind for nearly half a century.

She clapped her hands twice and bade me sit next to her. A novice ran up and Mother Zenobia ordered some tea and cake. She tickled the Quarkbeast under the chin and gave it a tin of dog food to crunch, which is a bit like waving your hand near an open food blender with your eyes closed. The Quarkbeast had never given me any trouble, but the sight of his knife-like fangs still unnerved me.

'How is young Prawns settling in?'

'Very well. He's answering the phones as we speak.'

'A special one, that,' remarked Mother Zenobia, 'and destined for great things, even if a bit troublesome. He managed to pick the lock of the food cupboard no matter how many times we improved security.'

'I didn't see him as a thief.'

'Oh, he never stole anything – he just did it to demonstrate that he could. He'd read the entire library by the time he was nine.'

She thought for a moment.

'Tiger's father was Third Engineer on a landship in the Fourth Troll Wars. Vanished during the Stirling Offensive.'

It had simply been one more campaign against the Trolls in order to push them back into the far north. For this, the Ununited Kingdoms had put aside their differences and assembled eighty-seven landships, vast tracked war machines as big as a five-storey building. Powered by four powerful diesel engines and built of riveted iron, their wide tracks could propel them through a town, flatten a forest and cross the widest river without so much as pausing for breath. The landships had passed the first Troll Wall at Stirling and arrived at the second Troll Wall eighteen hours later. The last radio contact was shortly after they had opened the Troll Gates, and then – nothing. The generals ordered the infantry to advance rapidly to the front to 'assist where possible' and not one of them was ever seen again.

The final toll of those 'lost or eaten in action' was close to a quarter of a million men and women. The first Troll Wall was rebuilt, and plans for the invasion of the Trolls' territory postponed.

'But,' continued Mother Zenobia, 'only tell Tiger when he asks.'

'I'll be sure to.'

'Is this a social visit?' she asked.

'No,' I confessed, having learned long ago that you never lie to Mother Zenobia.

'Then it's about the Dragondeath.'

'You can feel it too?'

'Given the power of the transmission, there won't be anyone who hasn't by the end of the week. Has anyone mentioned Big Magic recently?'

'They have. What is it?'

'All in good time. What is your interest in Dragons, young Jennifer?'

'I'm not sure,' I shrugged, 'but something's not right.'

Mother Zenobia chuckled enigmatically. It sounded like she knew more than she let on.

'It is time,' she said in a grand manner. 'Master Prawns isn't the only one destined for great things. You are too. And to that end, you need to know more about Dragons.'

I frowned. I didn't see how Dragons could have anything to do with me. Zambini thought they were linked to magic, but I wasn't. I didn't do magic, I *managed* it, and there's a big difference. But I knew better than to argue with Mother Zenobia. I settled comfortably in a chair as Mother Zenobia took a sip of her tea, and began:

'Dragons, like four o'clock tea, crumpets, marmalade and zip-up cardigans, are a peculiarity of the Ununited Kingdoms. They were fierce fire-breathing creatures of great intelligence, dignity and sensitivity who could and did converse on matters of great importance. It was said that a Dragon named Janus was the first to suggest that the Earth went round the sun, and that the pinpoints of light to be seen at night were not holes in a velvet blanket, but stars like our sun. It was also rumoured – although man's deceit prevents it from being anything more than a legend – that it was Dimwiddy, a small Dragon from the island of what is now ConStuffia, who first discovered the mathematical law of differential calculus. It is also said that "Bubbles" Beezley, the fabled pink Dragon of Trollvania, was a very good comedian who would capture victims and bombard them with jokes

74

until their hair was turned snowy white by the experience. But for all their intelligence, wit and social graces, Dragons still had one habit that made them impossible to ignore.'

'And that is . . . ?'

'They liked to eat people.'

'I thought that was just a story to frighten children?'

'Oh no, it's true all right,' replied Mother Zenobia sadly, 'they did. And don't interrupt. For centuries the population of these islands maintained an uneasy peace with the Dragons. Since Dragons didn't like crowds and favoured feeding at night, it was best to stay indoors and avoid going for long walks on your own. If you did then it was a wise precaution to wear a large spiked helmet of copper, something Dragons find highly unpalatable. But for all these precautions, Dragons *did* still eat people, and the country lived in fear. Before the Dragonpact, knights were the only method of Dragonslaying, and many a fearless young knight, driven by the promise of a king's daughter's hand in marriage, would boldly sally forth to attempt to kill a Dragon, returning – he hoped – with the jewel that a Dragon had in its forehead as proof of the conquest.'

'And?' I asked, as Mother Zenobia seemed to have fallen asleep. She hadn't, of course; she was just gathering her thoughts.

'The problem was, not many managed to kill a Dragon. Indeed, out of a recorded 8,128 attempts by knights, only twelve managed to succeed, mostly due to a lucky charge with a brave horse and a providential jab in the unarmoured section just beneath the throat. After two hundred years of this, the interest in becoming a knight and marrying a princess started to wane, and following the time when five knights tried a multi-pronged attack and were all returned impaled on a lance like a giant kebab, knights were forbidden to Dragonslay, which caused a great deal of relief, but generally only among the knights.'

'What happened then?'

'For two hundred years, not very much. Even the discovery of gunpowder failed to make a dent on the Dragon population. Cannonballs just bounced off a Dragon's hide, giving it nothing more than indigestion and a sore temper. Many a thatched village was set on fire in the middle of the night by a Dragon who had been much annoyed at being shelled when he was sunning himself quietly in the afternoon. The only solution to the Dragon Problem seemed to be in the use of magic. But since Dragons are fine practitioners of the sacred arts themselves, it required the arrival of a magician so utterly powerful that it was said his footprints spontaneously caught fire as he walked—'

'The Mighty Shandar?'

'Have I told you this story before?'

Mother Zenobia was suspicious that I was

humouring an old person with a flaky memory; she would have narrowed her eyes if she had any.

'Not at all. It's just that the sorcerers back at Zambini Towers often speak of him.'

'He is the yardstick for magicians everywhere,' replied Mother Zenobia solemnly. 'That is why we measure magical power in Shandars.'

Making a toad burp requires about two hundred Shandars; boiling an egg can use over a thousand. My own power had been rated at 159.3, which is not far from the national average of 150, which gives you a good idea of how bad I was at it.

'Where were we?' asked Mother Zenobia, who had lost track of the conversation.

'You were telling me about the Mighty Shandar.'

'Right. No one knew where he came from, nobody knew where he went, and few people even know what he looked like or what he liked to eat. But in one respect everyone was agreed: the Mighty Shandar was the most powerful magician the planet had ever known. Greater than Mu'shad Waseed, the Persian wizard who could command the winds, more powerful than Garance de Povoire, the French wizard of Bayeux, or even Angus McFerguson, the Scottish sorcerer who made the Isle of Wight a floating isle, which could be towed by tugs to the Azores for the winter, and to the best of my knowledge, still is.'

'I think they have engines attached to it now,' I

mentioned, as Mother Zenobia rarely kept up with the times. 'Did . . . did the Mighty Shandar have an agent?'

'History does not record one. Why do you ask?'

'No reason. What happened next?'

She paused for thought and took another sip of tea.

'It was in June 1591. As soon as the Mighty Shandar arrived in England, he decided to demonstrate his awesome powers and promptly built the Great Castle at Snodhill, which has housed the ruling Kings of Hereford ever since. He sat in his castle and waited for the word to spread. And spread it did. Within a week ambassadors from the then seventy-eight different kingdoms of Britain descended on the Great Palace, all to offer him employment. The point was this: the most powerful kingdom in those days before the invention of modern weapons was the kingdom with the most powerful wizard. But the Mighty Shandar was not a man to side with the most wealthy or help the bullies overcome the weak. No, he told the assembled ambassadors that he would work for none of them, but *all* of them. So the seventy-eight ambassadors went away and had consultations with their leaders and one another and reported back to the Mighty Shandar that the greatest thing he could do would be to deal with the Dragon Problem. Shandar put his great fingers to his great forehead and thought great thoughts; he agreed to the great task but because of the great difficulty and the great amount of time it would take, he would require a great deal of money; eighteen dray-weights of gold.

'"*Eighteen dray-weights of gold?*" the ambassadors said to one another, shocked at so high a price. "Are you nuts? Mu'shad Waseed offered to rid us of the Dragons for only seven dray-weights!"'

'The Mighty Shandar *definitely* had an agent,' I said with a smile, 'and better than Mu'shad Waseed's.'

'Didn't I tell you not to interrupt?'

'Sorry.'

Mother Zenobia continued.

'"But Mu'shad Waseed," replied Shandar in answer to the ambassadors, "fine magician as he is, does not have in his entire body one hundredth the power I have in my smallest toe."

'"I heard that!" said Mu'shad Waseed, throwing off his disguise and stepping forward. He had secretly arrived at Shandar's palace the day before, having heard of Shandar's demands. "Let's see this mighty toe of yours!"'

'But instead of showing Mu'shad Waseed his toe, the Mighty Shandar bowed low, so low in fact that his forehead touched the ground, and he said, in a voice toned deep with respect and reverence:

'"Welcome to my humble palace, most noble Wizard of the Persian Empire, controller of the winds and tides and known locally as *He who can quell the Tamsin*."'

'Don't you mean Khamsin?' I asked. 'The hot and dusty wind that blows through the Arabian peninsula?'

'If I *meant* Khamsin I would have *said* Khamsin,' replied Mother Zenobia. 'Tamsin was Mu'shad Waseed's second wife. Frightful, *frightful* woman. Her love of glittery things, fine robes and bathing in rabbit's milk set feminism back four centuries. And since you interrupted again, I'm going to ask Sister Assumpta to finish the story.'

'Please don't.'

Personally, I liked Sister Assumpta, but she had an annoying habit of telling stories using cricket as a metaphor. I'd be hearing the story in the context of a match, with the knights using the Mighty Shandar as their last man in, and fifty to make in failing light.

'Very well,' said Mother Zenobia, who didn't like cricket metaphors either. 'Last chance.'

'"Great Mu'shad Waseed," continued Shandar, "I read of your work in *Sorcerers Monthly*. Your control of the thunderstorm and the winds is quite awe-inspiring."

'But Mu'shad Waseed, who was the combustible product of a Persian father and a Welsh mother, was too angry to return Shandar's politeness and instead caused a massive rainstorm to move in from the west, and as all the ambassadors of the seventy-eight kingdoms of the Ununited Kingdoms ran for cover, Mu'shad Waseed and Shandar faced each other. Their eyes narrowed and a Super Grand Master Sorcerers' contest seemed ready to begin. But Shandar, whose turn it was by the sorcerer's code to begin the contest, did nothing.

'"Very well," said Shandar slowly, a smile gathering on his lips, "you may deal with the Dragon Problem. I shall return when you fail." And so saying, he vanished.

'Mu'shad Waseed gulped. In reality he knew that his power was puny compared to that of the Mighty Shandar; when he had built a castle in Alexandria it had taken him not one night, but a month, and although he had, on occasion, built palaces in a lunch break, none of them had included – as Shandar's had – a four-acre heated swimming pool, a library containing every book ever published and a zoo that apart from most of the world's animals, also included a few that the Mighty Shandar had made up himself – the Quarkbeast amongst them.

'Whoops,' thought Mu'shad Waseed, as the seventy-eight ambassadors of the Ununited Kingdoms emerged from their carriages wearing raincoats and galoshes, eager to know how Mu'shad Waseed was going to deal with the Dragon Problem.

The Dragon Problem

'Despite his own misgivings, Mu'shad Waseed accepted the task and threw himself into the project heartily. His first act was the instigation of a class of warriors known as the Dragonslayers, men and women who were bold in heart and soft in the head, who would be sworn into the service after a five-year apprenticeship. To each Dragonslayer he gave a horse blessed with intelligence and courage, and finally a sword and a lance, both of which were made of the finest steel, and sharpened still by spells that looped and twirled and with loose ends not tied but *joined*, as any incantation can be undone if the spell has any loose ends, in the same way that even the most difficult knot can be untied.

'Mu'shad Waseed made one hundred each of these lances and swords, and trained one hundred Dragonslayers. To each of these one hundred Dragonslayers was given an apprentice to learn from his master. All seemed well, and after eight years, Mu'shad Waseed sent his Dragonslayers forth to slay the Dragons.

'Initially, things seemed to go pretty well. Reports

came flooding in of defeated Dragons; even "Bubbles" Beezley, the fabled pink comedic Dragon of Troll-vania, fell to a Dragonslayer with the words:

'"Is there anyone here from Newcastle?"'

'The number of jewels plucked from the foreheads of the Dragons rose quickly. Since the Dragon census of the day listed forty-seven active Dragons, the ambassadors of the Ununited Kingdoms wanted to see that many jewels as proof the Dragon Problem had been solved. Mu'shad Waseed was not the only person eager to see the seven dray-weights of gold. Besieging the Persian wizard's camp were representatives of hoteliers and restaurateurs, laundry companies and tailors, who had all given Mu'shad Waseed eight years of credit and now wanted their money. As reports of fallen Dragons came pouring in, parties were planned throughout the islands by the grateful inhabitants; a land without Dragons meant their harvest wouldn't be burnt, their livestock wouldn't be eaten, and they could walk around at night without wearing an uncomfortable copper helmet. So everyone, for the moment at least, was happy.

'The seventy-eight ambassadors came to see Mu'shad Waseed when he announced that all the Dragons had been slain and, in return, they brought the gold to pay him in many stout carts drawn by oxen. There was a big banquet in honour of Mu'shad Waseed with twenty-nine courses and fifty-two different wines. There were dancing girls and acrobats and fire-eaters and Lobster knows what else. And at the head of the table, sitting on the glittering heap of head-jewels, was Mu'shad Waseed himself. But then, after the speeches but before the liqueurs, a fierce whooshing, beating of wings and growling came from the north. In the dying light of the day the party guests could see the sky darken with the approach of the Dragons. Small Dragons, large Dragons, grey ones, blue ones; keen on the wing and lively in claw and breathing fire while howling an agonising war-cry. The party ceased, the musicians stopped playing. The milk turned sour and the wine turned to vinegar. There could be no doubt where the Dragons were heading: they were all converging on the feast of Mu'shad Waseed. The terrified ambassadors turned to the great and powerful wizard:

'"Great Mu'shad Waseed; there were forty-seven Dragons in the country and you claimed to have killed them all; tell us now, who are these Dragons and where do they come from?"

'"I think," answered the wizard with a resigned sigh, "that reports of Dragon death have been greatly exaggerated."

'The revenge of the Dragons was quick, terrible and absolute. Mu'shad Waseed, his magic weakened by the eight years of toil, could do nothing, and the terrible screams of the lizards and their victims were heard twenty miles away.'

I wanted to ask a question, but with the threat of Sister Assumpta looming, I thought better not to.

'Only one person was spared to relate the story,' said Mother Zenobia. 'It was said that Mu'shad Waseed was enveloped with a thunderous blast of fire so intense that he was turned to charcoal where he stood. The Dragons razed Mu'shad Waseed's headquarters to the ground until all that was left of the carts, horses, ambassadors, musicians and guests was a fine grey ash. Then the Dragons vanished back to where they had come from, leaving behind a blackened patch of earth and a lot of disgruntled hotel owners and restaurateurs who, as far as we know, never got paid.

'Mu'shad Waseed had failed. The Dragons carried on as before. Unsurprisingly, they reacted badly to the attempted extermination, and caused much trouble on the islands; the Dragonslayers could do little. By the time the year was out and snow once more blanketed the land, only three Dragons had been slain to seven lost Dragonslayers. It was a disaster, and the seventy-eight kings, emperors, queens, presidents, dictators, dukes and elected representatives who paid Mu'shad Waseed for not very much fiercely regretted not spending the extra eleven dray-weights of gold and employing the Mighty Shandar instead.'

'That's quite a story,' I said as Mother Zenobia stopped for breath, 'but if there were still dozens of dragons, where did all the forehead-jewels come from?'

'No one knows,' replied Mother Zenobia. 'Perhaps the Dragon census was inaccurate, or Waseed decided to claim his reward by making false jewels. How am I meant to know? But that's not the best bit.'

She paused for a moment, produced a pair of pliers from the air and plunged them into the Quarkbeast's open mouth.

'Sister Angeline had a Quarkbeast,' she said in explanation and, panting slightly with exertion, added, 'A pair of pliers, a corkscrew and an angle-grinder should be included in the grooming kit. Ah – got it!'

She withdrew the pliers as the Quarkbeast shut his jaws with a snap. In the pliers was a piece of twisted metal.

'Piece of a tin can. Just behind the fifth canific molarcisor. Common problem. Where was I?'

'You were about to tell me the best bit.'

Mother Zenobia smiled.

'This: the Mighty Shandar did not return that winter. He did not return that spring. Summer turned to autumn, turned back to summer and then to spring again. And then one day, the following summer after *that*, Shandar reappeared.

'"Sorry I'm late," he said once all the ambassadors had gathered before him, "I had one or two things to attend to."

'"You *must* help us," begged the ambassadors, all hastily replaced but one, "Mu'shad Waseed tried to create Dragonslayers, but now the Dragon Problem is worse than ever—"

"'I know, I know," said the Mighty Shandar, interrupting them, "I read all about it in the papers. Frightful business. My price for peace with the Dragons is now *twenty* dray-weights of gold. Do you accept?"

'After a brief conversation, the seventy-eight ambassadors accepted unconditionally, and Shandar got to work.

'In the first year he learned to speak Dragon. In the second year he learned where the Dragons held their annual general meeting. In the third and fourth year he attended the meetings, and in the fifth, he spoke.

"'Oh, Dragons wise and bountiful," he said, although we have only his word for what happened, as no one accompanied him. "The humans seek my help in destroying you, and I could do precisely that . . ."

'Here he turned the Dragon next to him to stone to demonstrate what he could do.

"'Paltry human!" scoffed Earthwise, the elected head of the Dragon Council. "Watch this!"

'But try as he might, not even the finest magic of the strongest Dragon could turn their comrade back from stone again. Nor could they even attack Shandar, as he had woven a force of electricity between himself and the Dragons, and anyone who came close got their claws zapped. When they had calmed down,

Shandar changed the stone Dragon back to flesh again and said:

'"You have seen my word of death. With it you know that my word of life will be true also. Men will not be puny mortals for ever. I can see a time when the cannonballs they annoy you with now will be even more powerful; great land creatures made of iron will crawl up to your lairs and blast you with cannons more powerful than you can possibly imagine. After that I see winged creatures of steel flying faster than sound itself. I can see all this in the future and I say to you now that peace needs to be made with the humans."

'Earthwise looked at him, a wisp of smoke escaping out of his nostrils and floating to the roof of the cave. Earthwise could see parts of the future too, and he knew that Shandar spoke the truth. They talked long into the night and then, the following morning, Earthwise bore Shandar to the seventy-eight ambassadors, who, much fearful of such close proximity to the Dragon, listened eagerly to the plan that had been drawn up. It was very simple. The Dragons were to have lands given over to them and they would be kept stocked with sheep and cows for the Dragons to eat. Each Dragonland would be surrounded by boundary stones protected by a strong magic that would vaporise a human if he or she tried to pass. For their part the Dragons agreed to give up eating people, stop torching villages and to leave townsfolk's cattle and sheep well alone. The sole remaining Dragonslayer would be retained to keep an eye on things to ensure fairness, and if a Dragon transgressed the laws, the Dragonslayer would mete out any punishment.

'And so it was agreed. The Dragonlands were established, stocked with livestock and marked with boundary stones. The last Dragonslayer was re-educated in her new role as peacemaker, Shandar took his twenty dray-weights of gold, and vanished. And that,' concluded Mother Zenobia with a dramatic flourish, 'was the story of the Dragonpact.'

'And what about the Mighty Shandar?' I asked, never having believed that any story really had an end.

'That was four hundred years ago. The Mighty Shandar retired to Crete with twenty dray-weights of gold, and spent the rest of his days in comfortable retirement. The Dragons' numbers have been diminishing ever since. In the intervening years all but one have died of old age. Since Dragon M'foszki died eleven years ago, Maltcassion, who still resides in the Dragonlands not ten miles from here, is the last of his breed. When he goes, the Dragon will be no more.'

'What about—?'

But Mother Zenobia had vanished into a grey mist; abrupt teleportation was just one of her many skills. I looked behind me and could see her rematerialise inside the dining room. It must have been sausages, her favourite.

'Did you log that as a B1-7G, Bernice?' I asked her novice, who had been sitting close by. 'We wouldn't want to have an *incident*.'

She smiled.

'I keep a close eye on the old sorceress, Jenny, don't you worry.'

With my mind full of Dragons and pacts and Shandars and slayers and marker stones and lunch, which I had forgotten to eat, I drove up to the Dragonlands near a picnic spot I knew at Dorstone. I parked up and walked across the turf to the humming marker stones that encircled the lands at twenty-foot intervals and looked about. On the Dragonlands side of the marker stones the countryside was pristine unspoiled moorland, yet on the human side it was quite a different story – tents and caravans had sprung up everywhere as word had got about that Maltcassion was about to go belly-up. Small groups of people talked to each other while seated on folding chairs, sipping tea from thermos flasks. Everyone seemed to have a good supply of tent pegs and string with which to make their claim, and with the Dragonlands covering an area of almost 350 square miles, a lot was at stake. Several enterprising souls had even parked their Land Rovers pointing in towards the lands, ready to bounce into the interior and claim as large an area as they could before anyone else.

As Mother Zenobia had said, the last Dragon to die had been M'foszki, the Great Serpent of Bedwyn, whose lair was on what was then the Marlborough Downs. Quite suddenly the marker stones stopped humming and a daring lad named Bors stepped across into the Dragonlands, walked the empty hills until he entered the Dragon's lair, a deep underground cave worn smooth by M'foszki's hard skin. There he found a lot of cattle and sheep bones, some jewels and gold and a very large and dead Dragon. Bors took the Dragon's head-jewel and swapped it for a handsome townhouse. As for the Marlborough Dragonlands, every square inch was claimed within twenty-four hours; a rare pair of Lesser-spotted Bworks were shot and stuffed by a passing hunter, and the land is now used for farming.

I stared into the empty Dragonlands, then at the people who were still arriving, following the call of cash as if in some deep-rooted herding instinct. The milk of human kindness was turning sour, and it was wrong.

Patrick and the Childcatcher

Tiger was in the lobby when I got back, and I asked him why he wasn't manning the telephone as he had been told.

'Very funny,' he said.

'I see you've met Patrick of Ludlow,' I replied, trying to stifle a giggle, for Tiger was thirty feet up in the shabby atrium, perched high upon the chandelier. 'How long have you been up there?'

'Half an hour,' he answered crossly, 'with only a lot of dust and Transient Moose for company.'

'You'll have to suffer a few jokes in good humour,' I told him, 'and consider yourself lucky that you have witnessed both passive and active levitation in the same week.'

'Which was which?'

'Carpeteering is *active*; heavy lifting is *passive*. Could you feel the difference?'

He crossed his arms sulkily.

'No.'

'Did your metal fillings ache when he lifted you?'

Jasper Fforde

'My fillings are Marzicrete,' he replied grumpily, 'they were cheaper.'

'Never mind,' I said as I walked off towards the Kazam offices. 'I'll ask Patrick to get you down.'

Our heavy lifter was eating biscuits in the Avon Suite when I arrived. Patrick of Ludlow was a year shy of his fortieth birthday, was amiable if a little simple, and quite odd looking: like most sorcerers who made their living using passive levitation, he had muscles mainly where he shouldn't – that is to say, grouped around his ankles, wrists, toes, fingers and the back of his head.

'How did the clamping removals go?' I asked.

'Eight, Miss Jennifer, which brings my score to four thousand, seven hundred and four. The most popular car colour for people who don't care where they park is silver; the least popular, black.'

'Was it Wizard Moobin who told you to put Tiger up there?'

I knew he wouldn't have done it on his own.

'Yes, Miss Jennifer. Was that wrong of me?'

'No, it was just a joke. But get him down now, yes?'

He waved his hand in the direction of the lobby, and a minute or two later Tiger walked back into the office with a scowl etched upon his forehead.

'Patrick, this is Tiger Prawns. Tiger is the seventh foundling, here to help me run the place. Tiger, this is Patrick of Ludlow, our heavy lifter, who was told to put you up there by a wizard or wizards unknown, and is thus blameless. You will be friends and not hold a grudge.'

Patrick jumped up politely, said how happy he was to meet him and thrust out a hand for him to shake. Tiger blinked. The hand looked like a joint of boiled ham with fingertips poking out of the end, and I watched to see what Tiger would do faced with an appendage so misshapen. To his credit, he didn't flinch and instead held one of the fingertips and shook that. The lack of any reticence pleased Patrick, who grinned broadly – although he'd come to terms with the way he looked, he'd never really got used to it.

'Sorry about putting you up there,' he said.

'No problem,' replied Tiger, who had become more cheery now he knew the prank wasn't malicious. 'The view was very pleasant. How do you hold things with hands like that?'

'I don't need to,' replied Patrick, and demonstrated by raising his tea to his lips by thought power alone.

'Useful,' said Tiger. 'Who was the person on the *other* chandelier?'

'What?'

Tiger repeated himself and I went out to the lobby to check. Tiger had been right, and when I saw who it was, I had to bite my lip to avoid giggling.

'Patrick,' I shouted down the corridor, 'would you let the Childcatcher down, please?'

Patrick reluctantly let the man down, but not so lightly as he had Tiger, and the truant officer landed heavily on the carpet.

'Sorry about that,' I said, even though I wasn't, 'but Patrick has a long memory, and you and he didn't get along, now did you?'

'It's an unpopular profession,' said the Childcatcher, brushing himself down, 'but someone must do it.'

The Childcatcher had a weaselly face covered in unsightly pustules which was framed between two curtains of lifeless black hair.

'He should show greater respect to a servant of the Crown.'

'And he will,' I assured him. 'We take any disrespect to King Snodd's representatives most seriously.'

'Good,' said the Childcatcher, although I could tell he wasn't wholly convinced. 'I understand you have a new foundling, and I want to know why he has not been enrolled into any schools.'

Tiger and I exchanged glances. He'd be too busy for school, and working at Kazam was education enough. Besides, if he *did* need to learn anything truly academic, we could always get one of the wizards to help. A book hidden under an enchanted pillow at night to seep up into the head works wonders. Sadly, the school board didn't see it that way.

'Unless I have a very good reason for Master Prawn's non-attendance, we shall be forced to send him to school against his will.'

I didn't know what to say. Mr Zambini had bribed the Childcatcher when he came for me, but that had been a different Childcatcher – one that had eventually gone to prison for taking bribes. Luckily for me, school was optional at age fourteen for foundlings – I think it was something to do with economics and the cheap labour supply. I wasn't sure bribery would work with this one even if we had some money, which we didn't, and using sorcery to bend the will of a civil servant was not just a one-way ticket to the pyre, but unethical.

'I don't need to go to school,' said Tiger confidently, 'because I already know everything.'

I frowned at his sweeping statement, but the Childcatcher laughed.

'Then answer me this: what did the "S" stand for in General George S. Patton?'

'Was it "Smith"?'

'Hmm,' said the Childcatcher suspiciously, 'probably a lucky guess. What are the prime factors of 1001?'

'Easy – 7, 11, and 13.'

I stifled a laugh and attempted to look serious as Tiger reeled off the answers that the Remarkable Kevin Zipp had given him the previous day. It was just as well he had memorised them.

'Okay, that was quite impressive,' said the Child-catcher. 'Final question: what is the capital of Mongolia?'

'Is it Ulan Bator?'

'It is,' replied the Childcatcher uneasily. 'Looks like you are what you say you are. Good afternoon, Master Prawns, good afternoon, Miss Strange.'

And he stomped angrily from the hotel.

'Well,' said Tiger, 'I know now why Kevin Zipp carries the accolade Remarkable. How does he do at the races? I expect he makes a fortune.'

'He's lost every penny he ever owned,' I replied, 'and the shirt off his back. Soothsayers are like that. They see many futures, but never their own.'

Norton and Villiers

I shut up the office at five after completing the form P3-8F for Wizard Moobin's accident and all the B1-7Gs for the day's work. Once they were signed by the magician they related to, my day was done. But as I walked along the corridor towards the lobby the Quarkbeast's hackles rose and he made growly Quarky noises deep in his throat. It was easy to see why. There were two men waiting for me beneath the spreading boughs of the oak tree.

'Call the Quarkbeast off, Miss Strange,' said one of the men. 'We're not here to harm you or it.'

The two men were well dressed and very familiar. They were Royal Police, and were always the ones assigned to investigate any possible deviation from the Magical Powers (amended 1966) Act. I'd known them for as long as I had been here, and two things were certain: one, they would go away empty handed, and two: they always began with the same introduction, even though they knew exactly who I was – and I them.

'I'm Detective Norton,' said the taller and thinner of the two, 'and this is Sergeant Villiers. We work for the King and we would like you to help us with our inquiries.'

Sergeant Villiers was a good deal heavier in body and face than Norton, and we often joked that the pair of them looked like the 'Before and After' in a slimming advertisement.

The Quarkbeast sniffed Villiers' trouser leg excitedly, and wagged his tail.

'You have a new prosthetic leg, Sergeant,' I observed, 'made of magnesium alloy.'

'How did you know?'

'Magnesium is catnip to a Quarkbeast. If you still have your old one, I'd wear it next time you come round.'

'I'll remember that,' he said, peering nervously at the Quarkbeast, who was in turn staring intently at his leg, his razor-sharp fangs dripping with saliva. He'd have eaten the leg in under a second if I'd allowed him, but Quarkbeasts, for all their fearsome looks, were obedient to a fault. They were nine tenths velociraptor and kitchen blender and one tenth Labrador. It was the Labrador tenth that I valued most.

'So, gentlemen,' I said, 'how can I help?'

'Is Mr Zambini back yet?'

'I'm afraid not.'

'I see. You have a few soothsayers and pre-cogs on yours books, I understand?'

'You know I have,' I answered, 'and they both hold Class IV Premonition Certificates.'

'Quark,' said the Quarkbeast.

'Have any of your pre-cogs mentioned the death of Maltcassion?' asked Norton.

'It doesn't take any special skills, Detective. Take a look up at the Dragonlands. Besides, doesn't the King have a seer of his own?'

Villiers nodded in agreement. 'He certainly does. The Inconsistent Sage O'Neons has predicted the death of the Dragon, but also mentioned that the Dragon was to be killed by a Dragonslayer. Does this sound correct?'

'No one can enter the Dragonlands *but* a Dragon-slayer, Villiers. I think perhaps Sage O'Neons is less astounding than you think.'

'Insulting the King's advisers is an offence, Miss Strange.'

I'd had enough of all the beating-around-the-bush stuff.

'What do you want, Norton? This isn't a social call.'

Villiers and Norton exchanged glances. The door to the Palm Court on the other side of the lobby opened and the Sisters Karamazov popped their heads out.

'I'm fine, sisters, thank you.'

They nodded and withdrew. It was Villiers who spoke next.

'Sage O'Neons said a young woman named Strange would be involved in the Dragondeath.'

'There must be hundreds in the phone book.'

'Perhaps, but only one has a Quarkbeast.'

The Quarkbeast looked up quizzically.

'Quark,' he said.

They both stared at me as though I was somehow meant to account for myself appearing in one of the royal seer's visions. In any other set of circumstances I could safely have ignored them, but with everything that was going on, I was beginning to wonder if I *was* somehow connected – no matter how impossible that sounded.

'Pre-cogs,' I began, not wanting to give anything away, 'even *royal* ones, don't always get it right. Any seer worth his salt will tell you a premonition is seven-tenths interpretation. And remember, Strange isn't just a name, it's an adjective.'

Villiers and Norton shuffled uneasily. It didn't make a whole lot of sense to them either, interviewing someone on the basis of a vision, but when the King speaks, they have to do his bidding.

'We're just following a number of leads, Miss Strange. I hope you would consider your allegiance to His Majesty King Snodd IV (may he live for ever) above all else?'

'Of course.'

Villiers nodded.

'Then I would expect a call if you knew anything?'

'Goes without saying.'

They knew I didn't mean it, and I knew they knew.

They bade me good afternoon and left, purposefully leaving the front door open.

I went up to my room and switched on the television. It was as I had feared: the news about the potential Dragondeath was going national. The Ununited Kingdoms Broadcasting Corporation was running a live feed from the Dragonlands – they had even sent their star anchorwoman.

'This is Sophie Trotter of the UKBC,' announced the reporter, 'speaking live from the Maltcassion Dragonlands, here in the Black Mountains. A wave of premonitions about the death of the last Dragon has given rise to a gathering in the Marcher Kingdom of Hereford. No one can say for sure when this event will happen, but as soon as the repulsive old lizard kicks the bucket you can be sure that there will be a wild race to claim as much land as possible. When he dies, the good people of the Ununited Kingdoms can finally sleep easily in their beds, secure in the knowledge that the last of these loathsome worms has been eradicated from the world. The question that is on everyone's lips is: when? An answer that we, as yet, do not know. But when the Dragon finally croaks you can be sure that UKBC will be in with the first wave of new claimants. Next up, an exclusive interview with leading Herefordian knight Sir Matt Crifflon, who explains why the dragon needs to die, and performs his latest hit song: "A Horse, a Sword, and Me".'

'Makes you sick, doesn't it?' said a voice from the door. It was Wizard Moobin, none the worse for the explosion that morning.

'Sir Matt Grifflon's new song?' I asked. 'No, I thought it was quite good – if you like that kind of thing.'

'The Dragonlands. If I had my way I'd make them a national park, a safe haven for wild Quarkbeasts. Isn't that right, lad?'

'Quark,' said the Quarkbeast happily. I gave him two unopened tins of dog food. He crunched them up happily, can and all.

'We agree on that,' I replied, 'but if you're going to play jokes on the new boy, can you please not ask Patrick of Ludlow to help out? He's very impressionable.'

'I don't know what you mean. Watch this.'

And so saying, he put out his hand and narrowed his eyes. There was a crackle in the air and a vase displaced itself from my dresser and flew across the room to his outstretched hand. The Quarkbeast Quarked excitedly; there was now a bunch of flowers in the vase as well.

'These are for you,' said the Wizard gallantly, presenting the roses with a flourish.

I took the flowers carefully, for they were not real in any sense of the word, just images conjured up by the wizard. They twinkled with small sparks of electricity in the dimness of the room, and changed colour slowly, like the setting sun. They were beautiful, but wholly out of Moobin's league.

'They're fantastic!' I muttered, adding: 'Don't think me rude, but . . . ?'

'I'm as surprised as you are,' he confessed, pulling a small device from his pocket. It was a portable Shandarmeter – a device for measuring wizidrical power. He turned the gadget on and handed it to me. I pointed the meter at him as he levitated the vase.

'What did I get?'

'3000 Shandars.'

'Last week I could barely manage 1500,' said Moobin excitedly. 'Even if we discount the lead/gold switcheroo as a surge, I'm still twice as powerful as I was two days ago.'

'You think it's connected with the Dragondeath?'

'A definite link between Dragons and magic was never proved, but the nearer I am to the Dragonlands, the stronger my powers. The same jobs I might try in London take a lot more effort. I rarely like to work much farther than Yorkshire, yet my father was powerful as far away as the Great Troll Wall.'

'The Great Zambini always thought it was due to Dragons,' I observed. 'More Dragons, more magic, fewer Dragons, less magic.'

'We often spoke of it,' said Moobin thoughtfully. 'When Maltcassion dies, does magic go with him? All this might be the last knockings – the brief surge an engine will give before it runs out of fuel.'

'Sister Karamazov mentioned Big Magic,' I said, 'what did she mean?'

Moobin thought for a moment.

'It's an old wizard's legend – of a massive burst of wizidrical power that changes everything.'

'Good or bad?'

'Either, neither or both. No one knows.'

We stood in silence for a moment. I needed to know more.

'Perhaps if I were to talk to the Dragonslayer?' I ventured.

'Is there one?'

'There *has* to be, doesn't there? It was part of the Dragonpact.'

'You could try. It's possible that the Dragon may not die. After all, seers and pre-cogs only see a *version* of the future. There are few premonitions – if any – that can't be altered.'

Wizard Moobin left soon after and I gazed at the roses as they twinkled and faded as the magic wore off.

Soon after, Owen of Rhayder knocked on my door. He was our second carpeteer. Owen had defected to Hereford from the ramshackle Cambrian Potentate in Mid Wales about ten years previously, which wasn't hard to do if your particular skill was carpet.

'Look at this, Jennifer, girl,' he said crossly, unfurling the carpet and letting it hover in the middle of the room.

'There's mangy for you.'

He waved a table light under the carpet and the light gleamed through the threadbare old rug.

'As soon as a hole opens up I'm going to retire. I don't want to go the way of Brother Velobius.'

Brother Velobius had run a magic carpet taxi service about thirty years ago, in the days before all sorts of regulations seriously hampered the carpet business. On a high-speed trip to Norwich Brother Velobius and both his passengers died when his Turkmen Mk18-C 'Bukhara' carpet broke up in mid-air. The Air Accident Investigation Department painstakingly rebuilt the carpet, and eventually concluded that the break-up was caused by rug fatigue. All carpets were vigorously tested after that and none passed the stringent safety rules for passenger carrying, and they were relegated to solo operation and delivery duties. But that wasn't all: operators were told to carry licences, a registration number, navigation lights for night flying and a mandatory upper speed limit of 100 knots. It was like selling someone a Ferrari and telling the new owner not to change out of first gear.

'It looks like we're going to lose the live organ transportation contract,' I told him.

His face fell and he lowered the carpet to the floor, where it rolled itself automatically and hopped into the corner, startling the Quarkbeast, who dived under the table in fright.

'So it's pizza and curry deliveries, then?' he asked bitterly.

'We're in negotiations with FedEx to make up the shortfall.'

'Deliveries aren't the *spirit* of carpeting, Jenny, *bach*,' he said sadly. 'Organ delivery made us *relevant*.'

'I'm really doing my best, Owen.'

'Well, perhaps your best is not good enough.'

He glared at me, unfurled his carpet and was off out of the window, streaking back towards Benny's Pizzas to do some deliveries.

Mutiny

'I'm not paying,' announced Mr Digby angrily, waving the bill I had hurriedly written out for the rewiring and replumbing job. 'I specifically said *plastic* piping.'

It was the following morning, and Mr Digby had turned up as soon as Tiger and I had opened the office.

'We don't work in plastic,' announced Full Price.

'We don't work in plastic,' I repeated.

'Listen,' said the man, whose patience was deserting him rapidly, 'if I ask a plumber to replumb the house and I specify plastic, then that's what you'll use. I pay the bills, I call the shots.'

'If you understood how sorcery works, you would know that long-chain polymers do not react as well—'

'Don't try to blind me with your voodoo science!'

'Very well,' I said with a sigh, 'I'll instruct my people to remove all the plumbing immediately.'

'No you won't!' said Mr Digby angrily. 'If I catch you on my property I'll call the police!'

I stared up at the red-faced individual and wondered

whether the sorcerer's code of ethics couldn't be relaxed for just a moment; I thought our irate customer would make a fine warthog.

'I'll meet you halfway.'

He grumbled for a bit as Price rose in disgust and walked out of the door.

'The more you do this,' I said, altering the total on the bill and recalculating the VAT, 'the fewer sorcerers there will be to do this sort of work. The next time you want any plumbing done you'll have to get a builder in and tear all the plaster off the wall.'

'What do I care?' sneered Mr Digby selfishly. 'The job is done.'

He stormed out and Price came back in. He wasn't very happy.

'It took us only half a day to do his house, Jennifer. An army of plumbers couldn't do it that fast and I got a splitting headache to boot. We should have taken him to court.'

I got up and placed the cheque he had written in the cash tin.

'You know as well as I do the courts rarely side with the Mystical Arts. All he has to do is invoke the 1739 Bewitching Act and you could end up on a ducking stool – or something worse. Is that what you want?'

Full Price sighed.

'I'm sorry, Jennifer. It just makes me so mad.'

The phone rang and Tiger picked it up.

'Hello,' he said, 'Kazam Mystical Arts Management, can I help you?'

There was a pause.

'No, I'm sorry, madam, we can't turn people into toads. It's usually permanent and highly unethical . . . no, not even for cash. Thank you.'

At that moment, Lady Mawgon strode in with Moobin close behind. She didn't look too happy – furious, actually.

'I've explained about Mr Digby to Full Price,' I said, feeling mildly nervous. Mr Zambini had been gone six months, and although I had so far avoided any arguments, they would eventually happen, I knew it – and, as likely as not, they would come from Mawgon.

'We're not here about that,' said Lady Mawgon, and I noticed several other Zambini Tower residents at the door. Some were on the active list, like Kevin Zipp, and others not, like the Sisters Karamazov. There were also ones I hadn't seen for a while, such as Monty Vanguard the Sound Manipulator, and an old and very craggy sorceress who looked as though she were half tortoise – long-retired eleventh-floorers, the pair of them.

'What can I help you with, then?'

'Am I to understand,' began Lady Mawgon, trembling with indignation, 'that Mr Trimble of the ConStuff Land Development Agency offered Kazam two million moolah for the precise time of the Dragondeath?'

'He did, and I said I'd think about it.'

'Isn't that the sort of decision that we should *all* make in the absence of Mr Zambini?' asked Lady Mawgon.

'Two million moolah is a lot of moolah,' added Price.

'And could pay for *all* our retirements,' put in Monty Vanguard.

'I'm not sure the deal is still on the table,' I said, trying to stall for time.

'Mr Trimble just called me,' said Lady Mawgon. 'The deal is *definitely* still on.'

'Listen,' I said, suddenly feeling hot all over, 'we don't know for sure the Dragondeath is going to happen. The link between magic and Dragons is not proven, but there's not a sorcerer in the building who doesn't believe it's there. There's a whiff of Big Magic in the air, and I don't think we should be cashing in on the Dragondeath – it's just not what we do.'

'Who are you to decide what it is we do?' demanded Lady Mawgon imperiously. 'Try as you might, you cannot be Mr Zambini, and never will be – you are simply a foundling who got lucky.'

Several of the other sorcerers winced. None of them would have gone *that* far. Lady Mawgon was making it personal, which it wasn't.

'If he's going to die anyway it's free cash,' remarked

Full Price, trying to calm the situation down, 'and if the Big Magic goes the wrong way we'll have lost out completely – no magic, no cash. And if the enchantment holding up this building unravels, no home either.'

'The way through is clear,' announced Lady Mawgon, even though it wasn't. 'We want Mr Trimble's cheque and the time and date of the Dragondeath.'

But I wasn't yet done.

'We all know how premonitions work,' I said, swallowing down my anger at the 'foundling got lucky' jibe, 'and they'll sometimes come true only by the burden of our expectation. If we sell the time and date, then the Dragon may die whether he was meant to or not. If Big Magic goes the wrong way, as Price suggests, then we may have exchanged magic for cash. I'm not sold on that, and I think many of you will agree. Everyone is here at Zambini Towers because of what they are or what they have been. And I think that counts for something.'

There was a pause. Sorcerers liked cash as much as the next person, but they liked honour and their calling better. Ask a wizard if they'd swap their powers for a stack of cash, and they'd choose magic every time.

'This is all conjecture,' remarked Monty Vanguard.

'What in sorcery isn't?' added Half Price. 'I'm with Jennifer on this one.'

'There's no conjecture in a cosy retirement guaranteed,' said the half-tortoise from the eleventh floor, speaking for the first time.

We all stood there in silence for a moment, so I thought I should act. I took Trimble's unsigned cheque from the cash tin and laid it on the desk.

'Dragondeath Sunday at noon,' I said, feeling a thumping pulse in my temples. 'As Lady Mawgon has so graphically pointed out, you don't need me to make the decision for you, and no, I'm not Mr Zambini and we don't know when or if he's coming back. But as long as my name is Jennifer Strange I won't help ConStuff profit by Maltcassion's death. And what's more,' I went on, my anger suddenly making me impetuous, 'you can find a new acting head of Kazam if you do. I'll work out the rest of my servitude helping Unstable Mabel and mucking out the Mysterious X when he has another one of his episodes.'

There was silence when I'd finished, and they all looked at one another uneasily.

'I think we should put it to a vote,' said Moobin.

'There won't be a vote,' said Lady Mawgon, reaching for the cheque. 'Our path has never been so clear.'

'Touch that cheque without a vote and I'll newt you,' said Moobin.

It was quite a threat. Being changed into a newt was a spell a wizard would only use as a last resort. It was irreversible and technically murder. But Lady

Mawgon thought he was bluffing. After all, it took a lot of power to newt someone.

'Your days of newting were over long ago,' she said.

'Lead into gold, Lady Mawgon, lead into gold.'

Wizard Moobin and Lady Mawgon stared at each other. Spells were never instantaneous, and required a modicum of hand movements. The thing was, whoever made the first move was the aggressor. If you moved first and newted someone, you were a murderer. Move last and it was self-defence. There was silence in the room as the two of them continued to stare at one another, hardly daring to blink. A week ago this would have been a hollow threat, and even though neither of them had newted anyone for decades, the increased background wizidrical energy and the fact that it was early morning meant that such a thing was possible.

The Remarkable Kevin Zipp broke the stand-off.

'No one's going to newt anyone.'

Mawgon and Moobin looked mildly relieved at Zipp's pronouncement. After all, neither of them wanted to be a murderer – the punishment is particularly nasty.

'How strong was the premonition?' I asked.

'Oh, it wasn't a premonition,' he confessed with a grin. 'I was just listening in to Master Prawn's phone conversation.'

We all turned to look at Tiger as he placed the handset back on its cradle.

'That was the news desk at the UKBC,' he said. 'I just told them the time and date of the Dragondeath.'

'You did *what*?'

He repeated himself to a shocked silence in the room, and then added: 'The information is out in the public domain, so ConStuff have no advantage. The deal is dead.'

'You shouldn't have done that,' remarked Wizard Moobin.

'Well, I did,' he said, taking a deep breath. 'You can newt me if you like, but Jenny is right: Dragons are noble creatures, and as likely as not the source of your power. It would be like selling your index fingers. My conscience is clear.'

'I'll make you wish you'd never been born!' screeched Lady Mawgon, and pointed a long bony finger in his direction. Tiger didn't even blink.

'I'm a foundling,' he said simply, 'I often wish I'd never been born.'

Lady Mawgon paused, lowered her finger and then strode from the room with a loud cry of 'Foundlings, bah!'

The others filed out soon after as there was nothing more to be done, and they all glared daggers at Tiger as they went, until only he and I were left.

'That was a stupid thing to do,' I said, 'stupid, but brave.'

'You and me both, Miss Strange. You were going to resign over it, and I wasn't going to let that happen.'

He stared up at me with a look of hot indignation, and a clear sense of right and wrong. Mother Zenobia had been right. This one was special. But I couldn't be angry with him, and couldn't go without punishing him either – it should have been put to a vote, despite my personal viewpoint. I shrugged. It would have to wait. Events were beginning to mount up, and it was confusing me. I'm not a person well disposed to being confused. If events were unfolding, I needed to be with them, and not *behind* them.

'I'll deal with you when I get back,' I said, picking up my car keys and whistling for the Quarkbeast. 'Keep an eye on the phones and stay away from Lady Mawgon.'

'Where are you going?'

'To find out what's going on.'

'You're going to investigate ConStuff?'

'They're just after profit. To get to bottom of this I need to speak to the real player – the Dragon himself.'

I paused dramatically.

'Hmm,' said Tiger, 'It *sounds* like a good idea, but how in heck do you get to Maltcassion? Put a toe between the marker stones and you're hot dust. And even if you do make it through, there's nothing to say he won't incinerate you for your impudence.'

I smiled.

'There's someone who can help me. A foundling like you and I, he is a fountain of encyclopaedic knowledge that not only puts the reference section of the Kingdom's central library in the shade, but also ensures he has won every pub quiz in the land.'

'You mean——?'

'Right,' I said, 'William of Anorak.'

William of Anorak

I stopped off at the local library to get some background information. William of Anorak was expensive,
and notoriously dull – even the hardiest soul can barely
last twelve minutes in his company. I read as much
about Dragons as I could, which wasn't much. No
one had ever done a study, and apart from one blurred
photograph of a Dragon in flight taken in 1922, no
one had any idea what one looked like. I thumbed
through a book of zoology and discovered that they
weren't a protected species; indeed, no one had even
bothered to classify them at all. According to natu-
ralists the Dragon belonged to the animal kingdom
for certain, almost definitely to the vertebrates, and
was as likely as not a reptile. Other than that –
nothing.

But from my reading I also learned one singular
fact: according to the Dragonpact there *had* to be a
last Dragonslayer. Only he or she could mete out
punishment as only they could pass the marker stones
unharmed. And, I reasoned, they had to be living close
by. Armed with this intelligence, I headed to the one

place where I knew William would almost certainly be hanging out: Hereford's main railway station. I was in luck. He was on platform six, staring at the coal wagons.

He was about fifty and dressed in a hooded cloak of a rough material, tied at the waist with baling twine. He was nearly bald and peered out at me through thick pebble spectacles. I noticed that he wore sandals carved from old car tyres and a duffel coat that was so worn and threadbare that only the buttons remained.

I hailed him and he looked up, gave a wan smile and replied to my greeting:

'*The Audio chameleon changes sound to fit in with its surroundings. On a busy street it sounds like a road drill, but in the front room it makes a noise like a ticking clock.* Good day!'

'My name is Jennifer Strange,' I said, 'I have need of your services.'

'William of Anorak,' said William of Anorak, offering a grubby hand and adding quickly: '*The Magna Carta was signed in 1215 at the bottom, just below where it says: "All who think this is a groovy idea, sign here".*'

He turned back to a coal truck and started to scribble a number in a dirty notebook held open by an elastic band.

'I need to know where to find the last Dragonslayer,' I said following him down the row of coal wagons.

'I was last asked that question twenty-three years, two months and six hours ago. *The only fish that begins and ends with a "K" other than the Killer Shark is the King-sized portion of haddock.*'

'And what was your answer?'

'*The record number of pockets in a single pair of trousers is nine hundred and seventy-two. Only three had zippers, and the combined loose change was enough to buy a goat at 1766 prices.* Four hundred moolah, please.'

'Four hundred?' I repeated incredulously. My only possession was my Volkswagen Beetle, and it was barely worth a tenth of what he was asking.

'Four hundred moolah,' replied William of Anorak firmly, 'in cash. *There are three types of Shridloo: Desert, Desiree, and Dessert. The Desert Shridloo is remarkable for not living in a desert. The Desiree Shridloo is indistinguishable from a potato, and the Dessert Shridloo is the edible variety.*'

'Do you have to keep on reeling off useless facts?'

'Unfortunately so,' replied William of Anorak, adjusting his glasses, 'I have over seven million facts in my head and if I don't repeat them to myself in order I run the risk of forgetting them completely. *Milton wrote* Samson Agonistes. Would you like to hear it?'

'No thanks,' I said hurriedly. 'Who said: "Never commit anything to memory you can't look up?"'

'It was Albert Einstein and I see your point, yet I am as much a victim of my own powers as those who have the misfortune to stay in my company. You have been here over two minutes; that is better than most. *Most people prefer carpooling when other people do it, and the average number of pips in a tangerine is 5.368.*'

'I have no money,' I implored, 'not even a twenty-moolah note. But to know the answer to my question I will gladly give you everything I possess.'

'Which is? *An anagram of Moonlight is thin gloom, and the average Troll can eat fifteen legs at one sitting.*'

'A 1958 Volkswagen Beetle with an MOT that expires next week, a few books and half a piano.'

William of Anorak looked up and stopped scribbling in his pad.

'*The most favourite boy's name is James; the least favourite is Gzxkls.* How can you have half a piano?'

'It's a long story, but basically I'm a musical duet penfriend with another foundling in San Mateo.'

He continued to stare at me.

'*A red setter is so stupid even the other dogs notice, and cats aren't really friendly, they're just cosying up to the dominant life-form as a hedge against extinction.* You're a foundling? From where?'

'The Lobsterhood.'

A smile crossed his grubby unshaven features.

'You're *that* Jennifer Strange? The one at Kazam with the Quarkbeast?'

I nodded and pointed at the Quarkbeast, who was sitting in the car. He had once idly chewed his way through a locomotive's drive wheel, and hadn't been allowed on railway property since.

'*In the first photograph ever taken,*' said William, staring at me thoughtfully, '*someone blinked, and they had to begin again from scratch. It set the industry back two decades, and the problem has still not been properly rectified.* You were left in that Beetle when a foundling, yet you would give it to me?'

'I would.'

'Then I will tell you the answer to your question for free. You will find Brian Spalding, worshipful Dragonslayer, appointed by the Mighty Shandar himself and holder of the sacred sword Exhorbitus—'

'Yes, yes?'

'Probably at the Duck and Ferret in Wimpole Street.'

I thanked him profusely and shook his hand so hard I could hear his teeth rattle.

'There's one other thing!'

He beckoned me to lean closer. I did so and he whispered:

'*The largest deposit of natural marzipan ever discovered is a two-metre-thick seam lying beneath Cumbria. The so-called "Carlisle Drift" is worth a potential 1.8 trillion moolah, and may provide light and heat for two million homes when it comes on stream in 2010.* Not a lot of people know that. Good luck, Miss Strange, and may you always walk in the shadow of the Lobster.'

Brian Spalding

I thanked William of Anorak and hurried off towards
the Duck and Ferret. It was shut due to King Snodd's
strict licensing laws that dictated bars should be shut
when you wanted a drink. So I sat down on a bench,
next to a very old man who had skin like a pickled
walnut and eyes sunk deep in his head. He wore a neat
blue suit and homburg hat, and carried a cane with a
silver top. He looked at me with great interest.

'Good afternoon, young lady,' said the old man in
a chirpy voice, tipping his head back to allow the
warmth of the sun to fall upon his face.

'Good afternoon, sir,' I replied, always meeting
politeness with politeness as Mother Zenobia had
taught me.

'Is that your Quarkbeast?' he asked, his eyes following
the creature as it sniffed suspiciously at a statue of St
Grunk the Probably Fictitious.

'He's totally harmless,' I replied. 'All that stuff about
Quarkbeasts eating babies is just fear-mongering by
the papers.'

'I know,' he replied, 'I used to have a Quarkbeast

myself. Fiercely loyal creatures. Where did you find him?'

'It was in Starbucks,' I replied, 'about two years ago. The manager said to me: "Your Quarkbeast is making the customers pass out in shock" and I turned round and *Quark*, there he was, staring at me. So I said he wasn't mine, and they went to call the Beastcatcher, and I know what they do with Quarkbeasts, so I said he was mine after all and took him home. He's been with me ever since.'

The old man nodded thoughtfully.

'I rescued mine from a Quarkbaiting ring,' he said, shuddering at the thought. 'Frightfully cruel sport. He could chew his way through a London bus *lengthwise* in under eight seconds. A good friend. Does yours speak?'

'Not that I'm aware of. I'm not even sure if he's a boy or a girl. I wouldn't know how to tell, and quite frankly, it might be undignified to try and find out.'

'They don't procreate in the usual manner,' said the old man, 'they utilise quantum reproduction – they are just suddenly there, seemingly out of nothing.'

I didn't know this, and told him so.

'Quarkbeasts always arrive in pairs,' added the old man knowledgeably, 'somewhere there will be an anti-Quarkbeast – a mirror image of your own. If paired Quarkbeasts come together they disappear in a flash of energy. Remember the explosion last year in Hythe, which they claimed was a gas explosion?'

'Yes?' I said slowly, for the explosion had left a crater twelve metres deep in a housing estate, and fourteen dead.

'It was an unlucky *confluence* of Quarkbeasts. A separated pair came together quite by chance. They're lonely creatures – they have to be. Misunderstood, too.'

This was indeed true. I'd owned mine for six months before the lingering suspicion that I might be eaten alive gave way to genuine affection.

The old man paused to give a coin to a beggar-lady collecting for the Troll Wars Widows, then added: 'Are you waiting for something?'

'I'm waiting for *someone*.'

'Ah!' he replied. 'Me also.' He sighed deeply and looked at his watch. 'I wait for many years, but still Jennifer Strange does not appear.'

'I'm sorry?' I said with a start. 'Who did you say you were waiting for?'

'Jennifer Strange.'

'But I'm Jennifer Strange!'

'Then,' replied the old man with the ghost of a smile, 'my wait is over!'

By the time I had recovered from this shock, the old man had jumped to his feet and was walking swiftly along the pavement.

'Quickly, quickly,' he muttered. 'I wondered when you were going to turn up!'

'Who *are* you?' I asked, somewhat perplexed. 'And how in the world did you know my name?'

'I,' said the old man, stopping and turning so suddenly that I almost ran into him, 'am Brian Spalding!'

'The Dragonslayer?'

'At your service.'

'Then I must ask you—' I began, but the old man interrupted me again and crossed the road in front of a bus that had to swerve to avoid him.

'You've taken your time in getting here, young lady. I thought you would arrive when I was about sixty to give me a bit of a retirement, but no – look here.'

He stopped and showed me his face, which was wrinkled and soft like a prune.

'Look at me now! I am over a hundred and twelve!'

He strode towards the opposite pavement and waved his cane angrily at a taxi that had to do an emergency stop just inches from his shins.

'Confound you, sir!' he shouted at the cabby. 'Driving like a madman!'

'But how do you know my name?' I asked again, still confused.

'Simplicity itself,' he replied. 'The Mighty Shandar wrote a list of all the Dragonslayers that were to come, so the outgoing Dragonslayer would know the new apprentices and not employ some twerp who would bring dishonour to the craft. You were chosen for your calling over four centuries ago, my girl, and rightly or wrongly, you will take your vows.'

'But my name's not *actually* Jennifer Strange,' I said, 'I'm a foundling – I don't know what my name is!'

'It's Jennifer Strange enough for the Mighty Shandar,' he said cheerily.

'I'm going to be a Dragonslayer?'

'Goodness me, no!' chuckled the old man. 'You are to be an *apprentice* Dragonslayer.'

'But I only started looking for you this morning—'

The old man stopped again and fixed me with his bright blue eyes.

'Think of a huge feat of magic.'

I thought of moving Hereford's cathedral two feet to the left.

I nodded.

'Good. Then double it. Double it again, multiply by four and then double *that*. The answer is one tenth the size of the Old Magic involved here.'

I leaned against a lamp-post for support and tried to get my breath. This was all too confusing. I was half expecting myself to be involved *somewhere* in all this – but not at the thick of it. I didn't do magic, I managed it.

'Wait,' I said, as uncertainty and a mild panic suddenly washed over me, 'I'm not sure I want to be a Dragonslayer's apprentice.'

'Sometimes choice is a luxury that fate does not afford us, Miss Strange. We're here.'

He was pointing across the road to a small house which was only one of many in a row of ordinary-looking terraced dwellings. The building had two large green garage doors and painted on the road outside was a faded yellow hatched box with the words 'Dragonslayer, No Parking' in large letters. The old man opened the front door and beckoned me in.

He turned on the lights and I looked around. The Dragonstation was large and airy and seemed to be living quarters and garage all rolled into one. At one side of the room was a kitchenette and living area with a large table, sofa and TV, and in the other half, parked in front of the double doors, was an old Rolls-Royce armoured car. The car was of heavy riveted construction and had emergency lights like a police car. Two twin-tone sirens were bolted to the turret and all over the vehicle were sharp copper spikes, protruding in every direction like a large metallic porcupine's, and which reminded me of the armour that Dragonslayers and their steeds donned all those years ago.

'A Rolls!' I exclaimed.

'It is *never* a Rolls, young lady,' admonished the old man. 'Neither is it a Roller. The Slayermobile is a Rolls-Royce, and don't you forget it.'

'Sorry.'

'Times have moved on a bit, you know,' he went

on. 'I started with a horse but changed to the Rolls-Royce when they demolished the stables to make way for the shopping precinct. I've never used it although it remains in tip-top mechanical condition. This is the hotline.'

He pointed to a red telephone, which was covered by a glass dome much like those you see in bakers to keep the cakes fresh.

'If it rings, it means there's a Dragon attack going on somewhere. That's where we get the phrase "hotline" – Dragons incinerating stuff.'

'So *that's* where it comes from,' I said, then added, more relevantly, 'has it ever rung?'

'Not once in four centuries for any Dragon-related business, although we have recently been getting calls for Benny's Pizzas in error – the numbers are quite similar. This way.'

I followed the old man over to the far wall, upon which hung a long lance, whose sharpened tip glistened dangerously, and on a table beneath it lay an exquisite sword whose long blade ended in a large hilt, bound with leather and adorned with a ruby the size of an orange.

'Exhorbitus,' said the old man in a soft, reverential voice. 'The sword of a Dragonslayer. Only a Dragonslayer or his apprentice may touch it. One finger of an unauthorised hand and "Voof!"'

'Voof?' I queried.

'Voof,' repeated the old man.

'Quark,' said the Quarkbeast, who understood something important when he heard it.

'Someone tried to steal it once,' continued the Dragonslayer. 'Broke in at the back. Touched the ruby and was carbonised in less time than it takes to wink.'

I withdrew my hands quickly and the old man smiled.

'Watch this,' he said, picking up the sword with a deftness that belied his old age. He swished it about elegantly and then made a swipe in the direction of a chair. I thought he had missed, but he hadn't. He prodded at the chair and it fell into two pieces, neatly cleaved by the keen blade.

'As sharp as nothing else on this earth. It will cut through carbide steel as though it were a wet paper bag.'

'Why is it called Exhorbitus?'

'Probably because it was very expensive.'

He replaced Exhorbitus on the desk whilst I looked around. All over the walls were lurid paintings of Dragons showing how they attacked, how they drank, how they fed and the best way to sneak up on them.

I pointed to a large oil painting of an armoured Dragonslayer doing battle with a flame-breathing Dragon. It was quite graphic and very exciting. You could almost sense the heat and the danger, the sharpness of the talons and the clanking of armour.

'You?'

The old man laughed.

'Dear me, no! That painting is of Augustus of Delft doing battle with Janus during Mu'shad Waseed's failed Dragon campaign. He was doing frightfully well right up until the moment he was sliced into eight more or less equal parts.'

He turned to me more seriously.

'I've been the Dragonslayer for ninety-one years, and only the seventh since the Mighty Shandar finalised the Dragonpact. None of us have ever set foot inside a Dragonland. But that's not to say we don't know a thing or two about Dragons.'

He tapped his head.

'All the knowledge since the first Dragonslayer went to do battle is up here. Every plan, every attack, every outcome, every failure. All this information has been here ready and waiting just in case. *But it has never been needed!* Not one Dragon has ever transgressed the Dragonpact. Not one single burnt village, one stolen cow or an eaten farmer. I'm sure you'll agree that the Mighty Shandar has done a pretty good job.'

'But that's all changed.'

His face fell.

'Indeed. Events, I fear, are soon to come to fruition. There is a prophecy in the air. It's like cordite and paraffin. Can you smell it?'

'I'm afraid not.'

'Must be the drains, then. The pre-cogs say I am

to kill the last Dragon, and I will not falter in the face of my destiny. Shortly I am to do battle with Maltcassion, but I cannot do it alone. I need an apprentice. That person is *you*. Next Sunday at noon I'm to go and destroy him, and you must help me prepare.'

'But there's no reason for you to go up there,' I pointed out. 'He has not transgressed the Dragonpact in any way.'

The Dragonslayer shrugged.

'There are still four days left; much can and will happen. This is bigger than me and bigger than you. Whether we like it or not, we will play our parts. Few of us understand the reason we are placed here; be grateful that you have so clear an objective.'

I digested his words carefully. I still did not hold that the Dragon had to die, nor that premonitions are certain to come true. But on the other hand it struck me that the Dragonslayer's apprentice might be well placed to ensure the Dragon's survival. If I was to be anything other than a passive observer in the next few days I was going to have to move fast.

'How do I become your apprentice?'

'I was beginning to think you'd never ask,' he replied, looking at the clock nervously. 'It usually takes ten years of study, commitment, deep learning and the attainment of a spiritual oneness, but since we are in a bit of a hurry I can give you the accelerated course.'

'And how long does that take?'

'About a minute. Place your hand on this book.'

He had taken a battered volume entitled *The Dragonslayer's Manual* from a small cupboard. I placed my hand on the worn leather and felt a feeling like electricity tremble in my fingers, run up my arm and tingle along my spine. As I closed my eyes images of battle entered my head, memories of Dragonslayers long dead, passing on their wisdom of centuries to me. I could see the Dragons in front of me, their faces, their ways, their habits; I felt the beat of a wing and heard the whoosh of fire as a Dragon set fire to a village. I was upon a horse, galloping across a grassy plain, a Dragon bellowing a fearful yell and igniting an oak tree, which burst into fire like a bomb. Then I was in an underground cavern, listening to a Dragon telling me stories of long ago, of a home far from here, a land with three moons and a violet sky. He spoke of a hope that humans and Dragons could live together, of old things passing away and a new life without strife. Then we were on the coast, running along the beach with a Dragon splashing beyond the surf line. I could see the images, and smell them and almost taste them . . . when, abruptly, it all stopped.

'Time's up!' said the old man, grinning. 'Did you get it all?'

'I'm not sure.'

'Then answer me this: who was the second Dragonslayer?'

'Octavius of Dewchurch,' I said without thinking.

'And the name of the last horse in my service?'

'Tornado.'

'Correct. You have the knowledge. Now swear on the name of the Mighty Shandar and the Old Magic that ties you to your calling, that you will uphold every rule of the Dragonpact until you are less than dust.'

'I swear,' said I.

There was a crackle of electricity and a fierce wind blew up inside the building. Overhead I heard a peal of thunder and somewhere a horse whinnied. The Quarkbeast Quarked loudly and ran under the table as a globe of ball lightning flew down the chimney, floated across the room and evaporated with a bright flash and the pungent smell of ozone.

As the wind subsided, the old man became unsteady and sat on a nearby chair.

'Is anything the matter?' I asked him.

'I am sorry if I have deceived you, my child,' he murmured softly, the brisk energy with which he seemed imbued not more than two minutes ago having left him entirely.

'What do you mean?' I asked, anxious not to leave my new friend and master.

'I have been economical with the truth,' he answered sadly. 'Sometimes it is necessary for the greater good.

You are not an apprentice, you are the Dragonslayer proper. I will not be joining you on Sunday; you will go alone.'

'No—!'

'I'm afraid so. You were late in arriving, my child; Old Magic kept me from the ravages of nature. I am not a hundred and twelve but almost one hundred and fifty – and I can feel the years advancing by the second. Good luck, my child, in whatever you do and however you do it. Fear not for me because I fear not for myself. The keys to the Rolls-Royce are in that drawer over there; always check the oil and water daily, and . . .'

Here his voice started to falter.

'. . . you will find living accommodation up those stairs. The sheets were clean on this morning. I have prepared for your arrival every morning for thirty years.'

If his face had been wrinkled when I met him, it was twice as wrinkled as the years poured on to his ancient body.

'Wait!' I urged him. 'You cannot go now! Who is to follow me?'

'No one, my child. Your name was the last on Shandar's list. Maltcassion will die in your tenure. You are the last Dragonslayer.'

'But I have much to ask you—!'

'You are a clever girl.' He coughed, his voice growing weak. 'You will do well of your own accord. Be true to yourself and you will not fail. But please, do one thing for me.'

'Anything.'

He handed me a scrap of paper.

'I gave my watch to be repaired last Tuesday. Would you fetch it and give it to the serving lady named Eliza at the Dog and Ferret, with my love?'

'Of course,' I replied, my eyes growing misty as my new friend aged rapidly in front of me.

'And it is prepaid, the repair,' he added, 'so don't let the cheeky monkey charge you twice.'

'I understand.'

'One last thing,' he murmured. 'Will you fetch me a glass of water?'

I left him and went across to the sink.

'I must just ask you,' I said as I filled a glass, 'about the link between magic and Dragons. My mentor the Great Zambini was of the opinion that—'

I stopped as I returned with the glass. He must have been wanting to spare my feelings, for when I got back there was nothing left of him but his suit, hat and silver-topped cane lying in a heap on the floor among a fine smattering of grey powder. I'd never gained and lost a friend so quickly, and I hoped he would have thought the same about me.

Thus it was that I, Jennifer Strange, sixteen years next month and loyal subject of King Snodd IV in the Kingdom of Hereford, took on the rights and responsibilities of the last Dragonslayer. It hadn't been what I had expected, but then I don't know *what* I had been expecting. That's the thing about destiny: it can't be predicted, and it's usually pretty odd.

'Quark,' said the Quarkbeast.

'Shh,' I said, sitting on the sofa, my mind in a whirl, 'I'm thinking.'

The Dragonlands

I looked around my new home. Upstairs was a bedroom with a good supply of books, and downstairs was a kitchen with a well-stocked larder. My friend, the previous Dragonslayer, had been a meticulous housekeeper. There was barely a speck of dust anywhere. I called Tiger.

'It's Jenny,' I told him, 'is everything all right?'

'Everyone's glaring at me and mumbling in low tones.'

'You're going to have to deal with that for a while.'

'How did you get on with finding out about Dragons?'

'Quite well, actually,' I replied slowly. 'I think I'm the last Dragonslayer.'

There was silence on the other end of the phone.

'I said I think—'

'I heard what you said. I just don't think it's very funny. I put my neck on the block as a kind of "foundling solidarity" thing and you don't take any of it seriously.'

'I'm not kidding. I'm the last Dragonslayer. I'm at

the Dragonstation now and have the sword and everything.'

There was another pause.

'This kind of changes things,' said Tiger. 'You'll be famous and asked what you're going to do and who you're going out with and what food you eat and opinions and asked to endorse rubbish products and stuff.'

'I'm not looking forward to it, nor the possibility of killing a dragon. But at least I get to actually find something out about Maltcassion – and with the sword Exhorbitus, I'll finally be able to trim the Quarkbeast's claws.'

'That would be helpful,' admitted Tiger, 'all that click-click-click upon the floor is a bit annoying.'

He paused again.

'Does this mean I have to run Kazam?'

I told him that I was sure I could do both, and that I would try to smooth things over with Lady Mawgon and Moobin and the others. This seemed to satisfy him, and after telling him to go and hide in a wardrobe if things got bad, I added I would be home as soon as I had 'sorted a few things out'.

I replaced the phone slowly. My life had taken a sudden turn and I wasn't really used to it yet. I walked around the apartment a few times, touched Exhorbitus and was relieved to find I didn't go voof, then had a poke around in the Slayermobile, which smelled of leather and warm oil. I called Mother Zenobia, who couldn't be disturbed as she was taking her nap, then made a cup of tea while I walked nervously about the room some more, fervently wishing Mr Zambini were here. *He* would know what to do.

'Quark,' said the Quarkbeast, pointing a claw at a painting of the Dragonlands.

'You're right,' I said, taking a deep breath. I wasn't going to learn anything sitting around in the Dragonstation drinking tea, so I mounted the lance on the side of the Rolls-Royce and clipped Exhorbitus on to the bracket next to the riveted iron door. The doors to the garage opened easily on well-oiled hinges and the Rolls-Royce whispered into life. I paused for breath, and then, with the Quarkbeast riding shotgun, I edged the Slayermobile out into the traffic.

It was busy on the streets, yet the traffic peeled out of my way as I approached. Although no one had seen the Slayermobile before, most could guess what it was, especially as it had 'Dragonslayer On Call' written on the side in big letters. It was tricky to drive, the steering heavy, and I misjudged a corner once and hit a bollard, but the sharp spikes on the Rolls-Royce simply sliced through the iron as if it were butter. Children pointed, grown-ups stared and even drunks saluted me with their half-nibbled blocks of industrial-grade marzipan. Cars stopped at lights to let me cross unhindered, and several times a confused policeman, thinking I must be a new secret weapon of King Snodd's or something, halted traffic and waved me through a red light, saluting as I passed.

I reached the Dragonlands in under forty minutes and drove carefully through the caravans and tents that had increased in number dramatically since the previous night. Word had got about and people were travelling to the Kingdom of Hereford from all over the Ununited Kingdoms. I even noted that several catering vans had turned up, eager to turn a profit wherever crowds gathered. The mass of people waved excitedly as I entered, running for their balls of string and claiming-stakes in case this was the end of the Dragon. They would have to be disappointed. I took a deep breath and drove between the marker stones. There was a crackle and a rumble. If I had tried the same thing an hour ago I would have been vaporised. I parked the Rolls-Royce and waved cheerfully to the crowd on the other side of the marker stones, who gaped back like fish.

'New Dragonslayer,' I shouted by way of explanation, 'just going to go and do . . . my . . . *thing*.'

I turned back and jumped, for there in front of me, here in the Dragonlands, was a man. He was quite unlike any man I have ever seen before. He was tall and graceful with a shock of white hair, craggy complexion and gleaming eyes that sparkled and danced. He was dressed in a black suit and cape, wore a large amethyst ring on his finger and carried a staff of willow. I had never seen this man before, yet I knew instantly who he was.

'The Mighty Shandar!' I gasped, and dropped to my knees.

'Quark, *quark*,' said the Quarkbeast, and explosively shed several steel-tipped scales in his excitement, one of which embedded itself in a nearby tree with a *twong*.

'You must be a Dragonslayer or their apprentice,' said a warm voice that sounded like how I hoped my father would speak, 'For only they may pass the marker stones.'

'I am, sir,' I muttered, unsure of how to address the most powerful wizard the world had ever known.

'I expect you have many questions,' continued the Mighty Shandar.

'Well, yes, I do,' I replied, looking up, 'in particular, how the whole Dragon/magic deal—'

'—questions that I cannot hope to answer.'

I got to my feet. 'How's that?' I asked, but the Wizard ignored me.

'This is a recording, by the way,' answered Shandar, who now that I looked more closely seemed almost translucent, like a spectre. The image flickered and rocked as he spoke, and I was surprised to find that a sorcery recording is not a lot better than a poor video recording. I waved a hand in front of his eyes, but he didn't react. The Mighty Shandar continued:

'You are the first Dragonslayer to venture on to the lands and you are here for one of two reasons: one, you are curious, or two, the Dragon violated the Dragonpact. If the reason is the former, then look and see and leave as soon as you can. If the reason is the latter, then look very carefully at the evidence of the suspected crime. There is much deceit in this world, and if there is even the slightest doubt in your mind, let the Dragon live. One more point. Dragons can be deceitful too. They often have a separate agenda and will manipulate the weak-minded for their own purposes. I wish you the best of luck. If you want to hear the message again, clap your hands once. If you want to delete this message, clap your hands twice. If you want to save this message then . . . oh, never mind.'

He smiled, the image flickered twice and then faded from view, leaving me to mull over his words. Shandar's support of Dragons seemed unequivocal, yet he didn't appear to think you could trust them. Confused, and with his warnings about deceit filling me with unease, I began my walk into the Dragonlands, the Quarkbeast at my heels.

The hill was mostly scrubby moorland of heather and bracken. It was full of wildlife, which had learned to live without the fear of man. Rabbits sniffed at my

ankles and the now feral cows and sheep paid me
little or no heed as I walked past them in the warm
summer air. After an hour's climb across the empty
moorland I came across a small lake. I walked around
the water's edge, peering at the fish in the clear waters
and wondering what a loss this vast natural wildlife
park would be when Maltcassion had gone. I knew
from my geography classes that the lands covered an
area of 350 square miles, slap bang in the disputed
borderlands between the Kingdom of Hereford to the
east and the Duchy of Brecon to the west. I reached
the far side of the lake, walked through a spinney of
silver birches and then climbed another hill from
where I could see deep into the Dragonlands. It was
a landscape without electricity pylons, buildings or
telegraph poles. There were no roads, no railways, and
no people. The vegetation had grown unchecked for
centuries, and large oaks were interspersed amongst
beech and elder. The land was free and clear and
seemed to stretch away for ever. It would take me a
long time to explore it but I was in no hurry. In fact,
if I were lost for a week it would be to Maltcassion's
distinct advantage.

I ran down the short slope and walked by a stream
whose clear waters babbled excitedly about the rocks.
Presently I came across a crashed aircraft. The loss of
this particular aeroplane in fog one snowy night ten
years previously had shown that the force-field was

shaped like a dome with its highest extremity at five thousand feet. Only the very brave or the very stupid would dare to fly above the lands, as an engine failure would spell certain death. I looked into the plane; it was empty. The pilot and passengers would have been vaporised as the small craft came within the marker stones' influence.

I forded a river, stopped for a drink and then followed the watercourse into a forest of Douglas fir. As I did so I noticed an eerie silence fall upon the land. The soft and lush undergrowth absorbed the sound, so even my boots splashing through the brook seemed to make very little noise. After a few hundred yards I noticed that old animal bones were scattered in the stream, so I guessed I was nearing my quarry. A little farther on I found a ruby the size of a man's fist lying on the bed of the stream and several gold doubloons. Within a few hundred yards more we came across a large clearing in the forest.

'Quark,' said the Quarkbeast as we stood on the smooth compacted earth. In the centre of the clearing was a large stone, not unlike the boundary stones that ringed the Dragonlands. It was humming audibly in the still air, and above us a light wind moved the uppermost branches of the trees. Hidden in the compacted earth were glimpses of gold and the flash of a jewel from where the riches of the Dragon lay hidden. Here indeed was the lair of a Dragon. His food, his gold,

his jewels. Everything, in fact, except a Dragon. There
was no cave of any sort. Indeed, apart from a pile of
rubble on one side of the clearing, there was nothing
here at all. I guessed that Maltcassion had either flown
out or was elsewhere on the lands. I turned to go
when suddenly, in a clear and patient voice, came the
words:

'Well, look what we have here: a *Dragonslayer*!'

Maltcassion

I turned but saw no one.

'Who's there?' I asked, my voice trembling. I thought I was the only one allowed in the Dragon-lands. I looked around but still could see no one, and was just thinking of climbing the odd pile of stones to get a better look when I noticed, lying in the rubble, a fine red jewel about the size of a tennis ball. I reached out to touch it but then froze as the jewel looked me up and down, and Maltcassion spoke again:

'Bit young for a Dragonslayer, aren't you?'

The pile of rubble moved as he spoke and I felt the ground shiver. He unwrapped his tail and stretched it out, then, using it as a back-scratcher, rubbed his back just above where two wings were folded tightly against his spine.

'I'm sixteen,' I muttered indignantly.

'Sixteen?'

'In two weeks. Actually, since I don't know precisely *when* I was born I might already be sixteen. I may have been two weeks old when I was abandoned, but birthdays are always taken from the date you were left at the convent for a foundling so—'

'—you're gabbling, whoever you are.'

'I am, aren't I? Sorry. I'm not well acquainted with Dragons.'

'Few are,' he said with a soft chuckle, 'are you here to slay me?'

'No.'

He raised his massive head from where he had been hiding it between his two front claws and looked at me curiously. Then he opened his mouth wide and yawned. Two large rows of teeth about the size of milk bottles presented themselves to me. The teeth were old and brown and several had broken off. My eyes started to water at the smell of his breath, which was a powerful concoction of rotting animal, vegetation, fish and methane gas. He raised his head and coughed a large ball of fire into the air before looking at me again.

'Excuse me,' he muttered apologetically, 'the body grows old. What's that?'

'It's a Quarkbeast.'

Maltcassion moved closer to the Quarkbeast and studied it at length. 'Does it change colour?'

'Only when there's too much silicon in its diet.'

'Ah.'

The Dragon then dug his two front claws into the hard-packed soil and pushed with his hind legs to stretch. The power of his rear easily overcame the anchoring properties of his front, and his claws pushed through the solid earth like twin ploughshares. There was a large *crack* from his back and he relaxed.

'Ooh!' he muttered. 'That's better.'

This done, his wings snapped open like a spring-loaded umbrella and he beat them furiously, setting up a dust storm that made me cough. I noticed that one wing was badly tattered; the membrane covering was ripped in several places. After a minute or two of this he folded them delicately across his back, then turned his attention back to me. He came closer and sniffed at me delicately. Oddly, I felt no fear of him. Perhaps that was my training; I didn't suppose I would have dared stand next to forty tons of fire-breathing dragon twenty-four hours ago without feeling at least some anxiety. I could feel the sharp inrush of air tug violently at me as he inhaled. He seemed satisfied at last and put his head down again, so once more his scaly skin looked like nothing more than a huge pile of rubble.

'So, Dragonslayer,' he asked loftily, 'you have a name?'

'My name is Jennifer Strange,' I announced as grandly as I could, 'with two N's.'

'In "Strange" or "Jennifer"?'

'Jennifer.'

'Oh,' said the Dragon. 'Just checking.'

'I present myself to you by way of introduction,' I

continued, 'I sincerely hope that I have no need of my calling, and that you and the citizenry—'

'Claptrap,' said Maltcassion, 'pure claptrap. But I thank you anyway. Before you go, could you do me a favour?'

'Certainly.'

He rolled on to his side and lifted a front leg, pointing with the other to an area just behind his shoulder blade.

'Old wound. Would you mind?'

I clambered on to his chest and looked at the area he indicated. Just behind a leathery scale was a rusty object protruding from a wound that had obviously been trying to heal for a while. I grasped the object with both hands and then, pressing my feet against his rough hide, pulled with all my might. I was just beginning to think that it would never come out when I was suddenly on my back in the dust. In my hands was a very rusted and very bent sword.

'Thank you!' said Maltcassion, reaching round to lick the wound with a tongue the size of a mattress. 'That's been annoying me for about four centuries.'

I threw the rusty sword away.

'You may help yourself to some gold or jewels by way of payment, Miss Strange.'

'I require no payment, sir.'

'Really? I thought all mankind gravitated towards things that were shiny? I'm not saying it's *necessarily* a bad thing, but when it comes to species development, it could be limiting.'

'I'm not here for money. I'm here to do the right thing.'

'Principled as well as fearless!' murmured Maltcassion with a chuckle. '*Quite* a Dragonslayer! My name is Maltcassion, Miss Strange. You have a good heart. We were right to wait for you. You may leave now.'

'*Wait* for me?' I asked. 'What do you mean?'

But he had finished speaking. He closed his jewel-like eyes and shuffled to get more comfortable. I couldn't think of anything more to say so I just stared at this huge untidy heap that was the rarest animal on the entire planet. Considering the amount of time and effort spent on the protection of endangered species such as pandas, snow-leopards and Buzonjis, I suddenly became perplexed and not a little angry that here was a creature of extraordinary nobility and intelligence that everyone actually *wanted* to die so they could grab some land.

'It's a PR thing,' said the Dragon, half to itself.

'Sorry?'

'It's a public relations thing,' he said again, opening his eyes and staring at me. 'Why do people spend millions trying to save dolphins, yet eat tuna by the bucketful. Isn't that what you were thinking of?'

'You can read my thoughts?'

'Only when someone feels passionately about

something. Ordinary thoughts are pretty dull. Powerful ideas have a life of their own, they carry on, unshakeable, from person to person. Wouldn't you agree?'

He didn't wait for an answer, but carried on.

'Elephants, gorillas, Buzonjis, dolphins, snowleopards, Shridloos, tigers, lions, cheetahs, whales, seals, manatees, orang-utans, pandas – what have all these got in common?'

'They're all endangered.'

'*Apart* from that.'

'They're all pretty big?' I hazarded.

'They're all *mammals*,' said Maltcassion contemptuously. 'You seem to be making this planet into an exclusive mammals-only club. If seal cubs were as ugly as the average reptile, I wonder if you'd bother with them at all. But those big eyes and the cute barking and the soft fur, well, they just melt your little mammalian heart, don't they?'

'There are other non-mammals that are protected,' I argued, but Maltcassion wasn't impressed.

'Window dressing, nothing more. No one much cares about the reptiles, bugs or fishes, unless, of course, they look nice. Seems a pretty crummy method of selecting species for survival, doesn't it to you? If you want to redress your overtly mammal supremacist attitudes, I should ban the words "cuddly", "cute" and "fluffy", for a start. There are six great apes — all of which you merit of special attention — but over six hundred different varieties of the floon beetle alone.'

'Floon beetle?' I queried. 'I've never even *heard* of a floon beetle.'

'And that's my point,' said Maltcassion triumphantly. 'You lot haven't even discovered *one*, let alone the other five hundred and ninety-nine. And a floon beetle is a *fascinating* creature. One variety turns itself inside out purely for kicks and giggles, and another has the power of invisibility. A third secretes an enzyme that will convert raw marzipan to usable Almondoleum without the need for vast distillation plants. They are the most singular creatures on this planet, and yet mankind knows nothing about them at all. Do you see what I mean?'

'Floon beetle, eh?' I mused.

'You know,' he went on, after lapsing into silence for a few moments, 'if someone asked me to sum up all complex life on Earth in two words, do you know what I'd say?'

I shook my head.

'Mainly insects.'

I couldn't think of much to say about this, so I asked instead:

'Can I come and see you again?'

'Why?'

'To ask you some questions.'

'Why?'

'So we might know more about Dragons.'

'Humans,' he scoffed. 'Always so *inquiring* about stuff. Never satisfied with the status quo. It will be your downfall, but oddly enough, it's also one of your more endearing features.'

'Do we have any others?'

'Oh yes, plenty.'

'Such as?'

'Well, counting in base ten is pretty wild, for a start,' he said after giving the subject a moment's thought. 'Base twelve is *far* superior. You also have extraordinary technical abilities, a terrific sense of humour, thumbs, being built inside out—'

'Wait! Being built inside out?'

'Of course. As far as the average lobster is concerned, mammals – with the possible exception of the armadillo – are built inside out. Any crab worth his claws will tell you the soft stuff should *definitely* be on the inside. Bones in the middle? Whoever designed you was having a serious off day. Put it this way: if you lost a limb, would it grow back?'

'No.'

'Mine neither, but if we were a member of the crustacean family we could expect a new limb the following year. Mind you, if we're talking about regeneration we could go a step farther and take a leaf out of the sponge book. There are sponges you can chop to pieces, whizz up in the blender and then press through a sieve, and they'll *still* regenerate.'

'Useful, maybe,' I replied, 'but I think there is a limit to the amount of fun you could have as a sponge.'

'I think you have something there,' conceded the Dragon, 'when it comes to comedy, crabs are king.'

'I never thought about crabs having a sense of humour.'

'Well, they do. You wouldn't walk sideways for any other reason, would you?'

'I guess not.'

'Lobsters are more serious and cultured. Hermit crabs don't say much but think a great deal. Horseshoe crabs are frankly a bit dim, but shrimps and prawns, well, they just love to party.'

'You seem to know a lot about animals.'

'I'm always surprised that you lot don't take more interest in other creatures. It's like living in a street and not knowing your next-door neighbour. If I were human I'd start investing in a little kindness. When the arthropods rule the planet all those lobster dishes and crab sticks could well be a cause of some regret.'

'I don't think mammals are on the way out, Maltcassion.'

'That's what the giant reptiles said. What are they now? Birds. One moment you're tearing a Stegosaurus to bits with rows of razor-sharp fangs, next thing your name's Joey and you're sharing a cage with a bell, a ladder and a dried cuttlefish. Bit of a come-down for a mighty thunder lizard, don't you think?'

'So what are you saying?'

'Well, Darwin got it very nearly completely right. A remarkable brain for a human. But he overlooked one thing. Natural selection is also governed by a sense of humour. You would see it yourself if only your lifespan were long enough. Over ninety million years ago there was a small, brightly coloured beetle named a Sklhrrg beetle. It was beautiful. I mean *really* beautiful. Even the most brainless toad would stop and gaze adoringly. It strutted around the forest, preening and primping itself, being admired by all. A few thousand years of this and it had evolved into one of the most vain and obnoxious creatures you could possibly meet. It was all "me, me, me". Other beetles avoided it, and party invitations simply dried up. But nature adores a joke. Thirty million years later and what has it evolved into?'

'I don't know.'

'The dung beetle. Dull coloured and innocuous, it pushes dung around. Lives in it, eats it, lays its eggs in it. Don't tell me nature doesn't have a sense of humour!'

Maltcassion grunted out a short burst of fire that I took to be a laugh, then muttered something about chameleons telling jokes in colours before he settled down, shut his eyes and started to snore. Since he didn't specifically say I wasn't to return, I supposed he wouldn't mind me coming back, so I stared at the heap of rubble for a while, delighted at my good fortune so far. His tattered wing led me to suppose that he couldn't fly, and if that was the case I couldn't see him actually getting out to break the Dragonpact. I waited until I was sure he was truly asleep, then crept from the clearing and retraced my steps back towards the marker stones and the Rolls-Royce.

As I walked over the last rise I was surprised to see that a large group of people had gathered at the spot where I had entered the Dragonlands six hours previously. The potential claimants had alerted the press and TV stations; the last Dragonslayer was news indeed. I walked down to the marker stones and stepped through the force-field.

'Auster Old-Spott of *The Daily Whelk*,' said one man in a shabby suit. 'Can I ask your name?' He thrust a microphone in my face as another equally shabby newsman said:

'Paul Tamworth of *The Clam*. Have you seen Malt-cassion?'

'When do you expect to kill the Dragon?' asked a third.

'How did you get to be a Dragonslayer?' asked another. A man in a suit elbowed his way through the crowd and showed me a contract. 'My name is Oscar Pooch,' he announced, 'I represent Yummy-Flakes breakfast cereals and I'd like you to endorse our product. Ten thousand moolah a year. Do we agree? Sign here please.'

'Don't listen to him!' said another man in a pinstripe suit. 'Our company will offer you *twenty* thousand moolah for exclusive rights to represent Fizzi-Pop soft drinks. Sign here—!'

'Wait!' I shouted.

The whole crowd went silent. All one hundred, two hundred, I don't know how many there were, but there were a lot. The cameramen from the TV stations trained their cameras on me, waiting for whatever I had to say. I took a deep breath and swallowed down my nervousness.

'My name is Jennifer Strange,' I began, to the sound of frantic scribbling from the newspapermen's pens. 'I am the new Dragonslayer. Charged by the Mighty Shandar himself, I will uphold the rules of the Drag-onpact and protect the people from the Dragon, and the Dragon from the people. I will issue a full state-ment in due course. That is all.'

I was impressed by the speech, but then I had been bound to pick up a thing or two during Brian Spalding's one-minute accelerated Dragonslaying course. I retrieved the Rolls-Royce and headed back into town, the crush of journalists and photographers following me as best as they could. Brian Spalding had never alerted me to this sort of media attention, although the sound of twenty thousand moolah just to endorse Fizzi-Pop sounded like some very easy money indeed.

Gordon van Gordon

I returned to the Dragonslayer's office to find the whole street crowded with even more journalists, TV crews and onlookers. The police had thoughtfully closed the road, erected barriers and kept the public to the far side of the street. I parked outside and jumped out of the Slayermobile to the rattle of cameras and popping of flashbulbs. I ignored them. I was more concerned with a small man dressed in a brown suit and matching derby hat. He was aged about forty and tipped his hat respectfully as I placed the key in the lock.

'Miss Strange?' enquired the small man. 'I've come about the job.'

'Job?' I asked. 'What job?'

'Why, the job as apprentice Dragonslayer, of course.'

He waved a copy of the *Hereford Daily Eyestrain* at me.

'On the *Situations Vacant* page. "Wanted—"'

'Let me see.'

I took the paper and, sure enough, there it was in black and white: 'Wanted, Dragonslayer's apprentice.

Must be discreet, valiant and trustworthy. Apply in person to number 12, Slayer's Way.'

'I don't need an assistant,' I told him.

'Everyone needs an assistant,' said the small man in a jovial tone. 'A Dragonslayer more than anyone. To deal with the fan mail, if nothing else.'

I looked past the small man to where there were perhaps thirty other people who had also replied to the advert. They all smiled cheerily and waved a copy of the paper at me. I looked back at the small man, who raised an eyebrow quizzically.

'You're hired,' I snapped. 'First job, get rid of this little lot.' I jerked my head in the direction of the wannabe apprentices and went inside. I shut the door and wondered quite what to do next. On an impulse I called Mother Zenobia. She seemed even more pleased to hear from me than usual.

'Jennifer, darling!' she gushed. 'I've just heard the news and we are *so* proud! Just think, a daughter of the Great Lobster becoming a Dragonslayer!'

I was slightly suspicious.

'How did you hear, Mother?'

'We've had some charming people around here asking all kinds of questions about you!'

'You didn't tell them anything, did you?'

I had no real desire to have my rather dull childhood splashed all over the tabloids. There was a pause on the other end of the phone, which answered my question.

'Was that wrong?' asked Mother Zenobia at length.

I sighed. Mother Zenobia had taken over the role of my real mother almost perfectly, even that unique motherly quality of being able to acutely embarrass me.

'It doesn't matter,' I replied with a trace of annoyance in my voice, a trace that she obviously didn't pick up.

'Jolly good!' she said brightly. 'I've already accepted on your behalf an invitation to talk on the *Yogi Baird Radio Show.*'

'Why would you do something like that?'

'They agreed to take on four foundlings as juniors in their office.'

'Well, in that case, okay.'

'*Excellent.* And if I may say so, I think Fizzi-Pop is a fine product. I have a jolly pleasant young man who is very keen to talk to you.'

I thanked her and rang off. The doors to the garage opened and the small man in the brown suit expertly reversed in the Rolls-Royce. He hopped down from the armoured car, put the sword and lance away – he could without being vaporised, since I had employed him – and offered me a small hand to shake.

'Gordon's the name,' he said brightly, pumping my arm vigorously. 'Gordon van Gordon.'

'That means "Son of Gordon", doesn't it?'

He nodded enthusiastically.

'I come from a long line of Gordons. My full name is: Gordon van Gordon Gordon-son ap Gordon-Gordon of Gordon.'

'I'll stick to "Gordon",' I said.

'It may save some time.'

'Jennifer Strange,' I announced, 'pleased to meet you.'

'And you.'

He didn't stop shaking my hand. He seemed so happy to be here he wanted everything he did to last as long as possible so he could savour it to the full.

'I don't know who put the ad in the paper but it wasn't me,' I told him.

'That's easily explained,' he said with a grin. 'It was me!'

'You? Why?'

'I wanted to be first in the queue. Dragonslayers *always* need an apprentice so I thought I would save you the trouble of advertising.'

'Very enterprising,' I said slowly.

He raised his hat again. 'Thank you. A Dragonslayer's apprentice has to be discreet, valiant, trustworthy *and* enterprising.'

'Gordon?'

'Yes?'

'Can I have my hand back?'

He apologised and let go.

'So,' he said, 'what's our first move, chief?'

'Nothing yet. I'll be living over at Zambini Towers

as usual but it might help to have some food in the house. The Quarkbeast likes to rest in a dustbin; you'll have to buy one from the hardware store but make sure it's painted and not galvanished as he will chew it. He eats dog food but isn't particular as to the brand. He needs a link of heavy anchor chain to gnaw on a week and a spoonful of fish oil in his water dish every day – it keeps his scales from chipping. Do you cook?'

'Yes.'

'Well, I'm vegetarian but not particularly militant – you can eat what you want.'

He had been scribbling down notes on his cuff. I swore him to secrecy and told him about the prophecy regarding next Sunday. This filled him with greater enthusiasm than cooking, dustbins or the Quarkbeast's peculiar eating habits.

'Great!' he enthused. 'I'll change the oil on the Slayermobile so when you come to do some slaying we'll be ready and—'

'Wait a minute!' I interrupted hurriedly, grabbing his lapel between finger and thumb as he tried to hurry off. 'I want to make this *very* clear. I don't ever intend to actually kill a Dragon.'

'So why are you a Dragonslayer?' he asked with blinding directness.

'Because . . . because . . . well, that's the way Old Magic made it happen.'

'Old Magic?' he said uneasily. 'Wait a minute. You

never mentioned anything about Old Magic in the advertisement.'

'Didn't I?'

'No. We're going to have to discuss new terms if Old Magic is involved.'

I thought for a second.

'Hang on. Gordon, *you* wrote the advertisement!'

He paused for thought.

'I did, didn't I?' he said at length. 'Well, I'll let it go this once, then.'

He looked crestfallen, but soon perked up when I told him he could be my press officer, and he dashed off to get some paper and crayons from the dresser to draft a quick press release.

It was by now early evening and I needed to get back to Zambini Towers. But I hadn't got more than one pace from the door before a scrum of people ran quickly towards me.

The first to talk to me was a businessman wearing a very large hat and an expensive suit.

'Jethro Ballscombe,' he said, passing me a business card the size of a roofing slate. 'I want to make YOU a very rich young woman.'

He grinned at me, showing a ridiculously large gold tooth that must have made metal detectors in airports throw an electronic fit. He thought that my silence indicated assent rather than a curious interest in his dentition, so he continued:

'Do you know how much people will pay to come and see a real live Dragon?'

He grinned wildly, expecting me to leap up and down or something.

'You want to put Maltcassion in a zoo?'

He put an arm around my shoulder and hugged me as though I were a long-lost niece.

'Not so much a zoo but his own special one-species family-entertainment exclusive themed adventure park.'

He waved a hand in the air and stared into the middle distance to make his point.

'DragonWorld™,' he gasped, hardly daring to say the word owing to the size and breathtaking audacity of the project. 'You and me, partners, fifty-fifty. What do you say?'

He smirked at me expectantly, moolah signs in his eyes, waiting for my reply.

'I'll mention it to him,' I said coldly, 'but he'll probably say no.'

'Mention it to who?' he asked, genuinely confused.

'Why, Maltcassion, of course!'

He slapped me on the back and laughed so loudly I thought he would surely choke.

'I like a girl with a sense of humour! Well, that's agreed, then. You won't regret it!'

He shook my hand heartily and bade me goodbye, climbed into a waiting limousine and was gone, convinced that his project was a certainty.

Another man tried to collar me about licensing a range of collectible ornamental plates entitled *The World of the Dragonslayer* and there was even another offer from Fizzi-Pop, this time for forty thousand moolah. I told them I wasn't interested and then, with the press clamouring for a further statement, I nipped back inside. I found Gordon van Gordon vacuuming up the grey ash that had once been Brian Spalding.

'I know, I know,' he said when I remonstrated with him. 'I'm going to put him in this empty syrup tin. You can take him up to the Dragonlands next time you go.'

It was fair enough. I looked for a back door to the building and opened it on to an alleyway that was thankfully empty. I made my way quickly to the Dog and Ferret, where I had left my Volkswagen, and drove from there back to Zambini Towers.

The Truth about Mr Zambini

'Hello,' I said to Tiger as I walked into the Kazam offices, 'how are things?'

'These are for you,' he said, handing me a stack of messages that didn't relate to Kazam at all, but to me.

'The *Mollusc on Sunday* want to do a feature on me,' I said, flicking through the messages, 'and this one's an offer of marriage.'

'There are another five of those. Did you see Lady Mawgon on your way in?'

I looked up.

'No.'

'She's been looking at me in a funny way. I think she's scheming.'

'She's *always* scheming,' I replied, dropping the messages in the wastepaper bin. 'I'm not sure she can even see an applecart without wanting to overturn it.'

I walked across to the Quarkbeast's snack cupboard and tossed him a tin of sardines which he crunched up gratefully. I spent the next hour explaining what had happened that morning. About Brian Spalding, the accelerated Dragonslaying course, the Dragonlands, Maltcassion and talking to the press on the way out.

'I was going to bring Exhorbitus to show you,' I concluded, 'but I didn't want to arouse any suspicion.'

'I think it's a bit late for that. Have you seen the TV recently?'

He switched on the set. UKBC were now covering the drama unfolding on our doorsteps with almost constant coverage. The screen showed Sophie Trotter again, this time up by the marker stones.

'. . . there are an estimated eight hundred thousand people gathered around the Dragonlands,' she said, looking behind her at the chaotic scrum that seemed to be developing. 'There have been reports of jostling that sent one man through the boundary where he was vaporised in a bright blue flash. The police are worried that there might be a bigger disaster, so are attempting to move the crowds back from the marker stones.'

There was a bright flash behind her.

'Whoops, there goes another one. I must just see if we can ask a grieving relative how they feel . . .'

I switched off the television and looked at my watch.

'It's time for you to go home.'

'I am home.'

'Me too,' I replied. 'I mean it's time to stop work.'

'I knew what you meant,' returned Tiger, 'it's just that even with everyone in the building except you hating me—'

'Quark.'

'Sorry, everyone except you *and* the Quarkbeast hating me, I just wanted you to know that I've never been happier. But can I ask you something?'

'Sure.'

'What *did* happen to Mr Zambini?'

I looked across at him. If I couldn't trust him now, I couldn't trust him ever.

'Okay, here it is, but you must promise not to tell any of the others. You should know that the Great Zambini was once one of the best. I use his redundant accolade out of respect. When he was young and powerful he held the magicians' world teleport record of eighty-five miles, although unofficially he had managed well over a hundred. He could conjure up showers of fish, and manipulate matter to a level that would make Moobin's lead-into-gold escapade seem like kitchen chemistry. He paid for the Towers personally, and gathered together the sorcerers within to try to keep the *spirit* of the Mystical Arts alive, even when he knew that wizidrical powers were fading. He gave everything he had to Kazam. He would work every hour of the day and night, and I with him. He was like a father to me. Kind, generous, hard working, and utterly committed not just to his calling, but to protecting and supporting those within it.'

'It sounds like he was an honourable man.'

'He was. But *still* money was short, and he was

forced to do the one thing that sorcerers should never do. An act of such gross betrayal of his art that if it was made common knowledge his reputation would be destroyed for ever and he would die a broken man, humiliated and shunned by his peers.'

'You mean—?'

'Right. He did children's parties.'

Tiger put his hand over his mouth.

'He lowered himself, for *them*? For Lady Mawgon and Moobin and those batty sisters whose name I can't remember?'

'All of them. He used to do the events out of town, of course, and in disguise. Simple stuff: rabbits out of hats, card tricks, minor levitation. But one afternoon he must have had a surge. He vanished in a puff of green smoke during his finale. Hasn't come back.'

'So when you said he'd disappeared, you really meant it.'

'Totally. But I've not given up hope. He spontaneously rematerialises every now and again, and although Kevin Zipp can give me a time or a place for a reappearance he can't give me both – it's easy to be in the right place, but a week late, or at the right time, but in the wrong village. There's a lot of countryside out there.'

'And a lot of Now.'

'Tons. And I can't get the others to help because I'd have to reveal what he'd been up to, and I can't see the old man humiliated. On the plus side, the kids thought he was great, and a standing ovation from five-year-olds is not to be sniffed at.'

'But that's not the whole story, is it?' said Tiger, holding up a battered copy of *Simpkin's Foundling Law.*

'No,' I replied. 'Until he comes back or is declared dead or lost, he can't sign us out of our indentured servitude. Technically speaking, we're here until we die.'

Tiger closed the book.

'That's what I thought.'

'He'll come back,' I assured him, 'or failing that, I'll confess everything and we'll have him declared lost and have our servitude assigned to his successor. In any event, I've still got two years to run, and you've got six. Lots can happen.'

I smiled at him and he smiled back. It was my way of telling him not to worry, and his way of agreeing that he shouldn't.

'I'm going to go and see Moobin,' I told him. 'I need to know how the wizards are doing. Keep well away from Lady Mawgon and I'll see you later.'

Big Magic

I found Wizard Moobin in his room. He had repaired the door, but was still busy tidying up his room after the explosion. There was almost nothing unbroken. The power of magic can be devastating when uncontrolled, and ever since the Blix episode, incantations were intentionally kept below the half-a-MegaShandar level for individual practitioners. Blix had made use of a loophole to store wizidrical power and use it on a spree of subjugation. The six-GigaShandar blast that heralded the end of Blix's brief reign had taken out not just him, but two kingdoms and an estimated half a million people.

Moobin was there with the Prices, Full and Half, and they were having a meeting of sorts. There was someone else in the room, too, someone I didn't recognise.

'Ah,' said Moobin when he saw me, 'it's you. This is Mr Stamford, a lapsed sorcerer from Mercia. He'll be staying with me for a few days. Mr Stamford, this is Jennifer Strange.'

Stamford was a sallow man with greasy hair. He peered at me cautiously and shook my hand.

'You're here because of the Dragondeath?' I asked.

'I think so,' he replied after a moment's thought. 'You know that feeling when you go into a room and then can't remember what it is you're there for?'

'Yes.'

'It's *exactly* like that. I don't know why I'm here, I just feel that I should be.'

And he fell silent.

'He's the third to arrive since this morning,' said Wizard Moobin. He paused for a moment. 'Tiger Prawns was out of order going public and sabotaging the ConStuff deal, you know.'

'I know. He was doing it to stop me resigning.'

'It was noble, I grant you that. And we respect honour, sacrifice, nobility and ethical stances. Sadly, Lady Mawgon doesn't. She wanted to have you both replaced and asked Mother Zenobia to send a short-list of new foundlings so we could start interviewing.'

'That's not how it works.'

'It's how Lady Mawgon works.'

'What happened?'

'Mother Zenobia told her they'd run out.'

I smiled. Mother Zenobia had hundreds of foundlings ready to take up servitude. It must have made Mawgon even *more* angry.

'So what's she doing now?'

'Lady Mawgon? Marching around the corridors

gnashing her teeth and seething, I imagine. But that's not the biggest issue right now, is it?'

'You saw the news on the TV?'

'It was hard to miss it. It surprised us all, I must say. How did you get to be the last Dragonslayer?'

I told him briefly how it all came about, and he nodded sagely. I added that it wouldn't alter my commitment to Kazam, but that I might be busy on Sunday, about noon.

'We all wish you the best, of course,' he said, then added: 'except Lady Mawgon perhaps, who would probably be delighted to see you eaten. I should ignore her.'

'I plan to.'

Moobin thought for a moment.

'You're no longer a bystander, Jennifer, you're a player. And not just in the world of Dragonslaying – but magic.'

'I figured that,' I said slowly, 'perhaps this is a good time to tell me what a Big Magic is, and where you get one?'

Brother Stamford and Moobin exchanged glances and nodded to one another.

'There was a time before magic,' said Brother Stamford, 'and there will be a time when magic has gone. In between those times the power of magic will ebb and flow like the tide. But unlike the tide, it is entirely possible that the power of magic, aided by the destructive agencies of distrust, denial and disuse, will recede for ever and *never* return.'

'That's unthinkable.'

'We are all agreed on *that* score,' said Moobin, 'but the news isn't all bad. There is always an opportunity to rekindle that spark and bring the tide of power back into flood – and with the flood brings on renewal. Renewal of the power of magic.'

'And that opportunity is a Big Magic?' I asked.

'A chance to recharge the batteries, so to speak,' continued Wizard Moobin. 'But at times of low power, sorcerers are less likely to see the signs of a Big Magic. We never know when it will be, or what form it will take. The last time Big Magic took place was two hundred and thirty years ago, with the appearance of the star Aleutius in the evening sky. If Brother Thassos of Crete had not seen it as the sign it was, magic might have vanished for good.'

'But where does magic come from?' I asked, 'and where does it go?'

'Explaining magic is like explaining lightning or rainbows a thousand years ago, inexplicable and wonderful but seemingly impossible. Today they are little more than equations in a science textbook. Magic is the fifth fundamental force, and even more mysterious than gravity, which is *really* saying something. Magic is a power lurking in all of us, an emotional energy that can be used to move objects and manipulate matter. But it doesn't follow any physical laws that we can, as yet, understand; it exists only in our hearts and minds.'

'And the Dragonlands? What do they have to do with it?'

'I wish we knew. But one thing is crucial. With the way that the power of magic has been deteriorating over the past thirty years, this happening – whatever it is – might be the last chance to regather the power before it goes completely.'

'What are the chances it will happen?'

'A renewal is a risky undertaking. Chances are twenty per cent, at best.'

And on that note, Moobin returned to his tidying.

I looked at Brother Stamford, who fired a shimmering globe from his fingertip that buzzed round the room before vanishing. He held up a hand-held Shandarmeter and I looked over his shoulder as the small needle bobbed against the scale.

'The background wizidrical radiation has risen almost tenfold since yesterday,' he mused. 'I've never seen anything quite like it.'

'Is that why you're here?' I asked Brother Stamford, 'like moths to a light?'

I wandered up to my room soon after, deep in thought. My window faced west and I watched the deep orange sun sink slowly behind the marzipan refinery at Sugwas, the heat from the refinery's gas flares making the air wobble and distorting the image. I sat down on the bed.

'Do you want some pizza, Tiger?'

'Yes, please,' came a small voice from inside the cupboard. It seemed Tiger still wasn't happy sleeping on his own. 'Hey,' he added, 'is this a Matt Grifflon poster you've hidden in here?'

'I'm looking after it for a friend,' I said hurriedly.

'Right.'

His Majesty King Snodd IV

I left Zambini Towers as soon as it was dark enough to move around without being spotted and spent the rest of the night at the Dragonslayer's apartment. The crowds of press hadn't gone by the morning, and pretty soon I had to leave the phone off the hook after two radio stations, the lifestyles section of *The Daily Mollusc*, the features editor of *The Clam* and a representative from Fizzi-Pop all called me within the space of forty-seven seconds. All was not bad news, however. Gordon had excelled himself at breakfast, and I was soon tucking into a massive stack of pancakes. I was just reading in the paper about a border skirmish between the Kingdom of Hereford and the Duke of Brecon when there was a knock at the door.

'If it's that idiot from Yummy-Flakes tell him I'm dead,' I said, not looking up from the newspaper. It wasn't the Yummy-Flakes man. It wasn't even the theme park guy. It was a royal footman in full livery who ignored Gordon and approached me at the breakfast table. He had a pomaded wig, scarlet tunic and breeches. His shirt had deep frilly cuffs and his starched collar was so stiff he could barely move his head.

'Miss Strange?' he asked in a thin voice.

'Yes?'

'Dragonslayer?'

'Yes, yes?'

'I am commanded by His Majesty King Snodd to convey you to the castle.'

'The castle? Me? You're joking!'

The footman looked at me coldly.

'The King doesn't make jokes, Miss Strange. On the rare occasion that he does he circulates a memo beforehand to avoid any misunderstandings. He has sent his own car.'

The footman and chauffeur looked at me dubiously as the Quarkbeast joined me on the Buzonji-hide upholstered rear seat of the King's Hispano-Suiza K6 limousine, but otherwise didn't say a word as we drove out of Hereford towards Snodd Hill, traditionally the place of residence of the Monarch of Hereford since the Dragonpact, as it nestled comfortably – and strategically – against the eastern edge of the Dragonland and was thus completely free from attack in at least one direction. The high ramparts and curtain walls grew larger as we rattled over drawbridges on our way to the inner bailey. I didn't have time to ponder much as the car pulled up outside the keep and the door was opened by another footman in impeccable dress. He beckoned me to follow and I almost had to run to keep up as we negotiated the winding stairs of the old castle. After a brief sprint he stopped outside two large wooden doors, knocked and then flung them open with a flourish.

The doors led into a large medieval hall. The high ceilings were decorated with heraldic shields and from the massive oak beams hung tapestries depicting the Kingdom's dubiously won military triumphs over the centuries. At the far end of the room was a large fireplace, in front of which were two sofas which seated six men. They were all watching a short man who was outlining something on a blackboard. None of them seemed to take the least notice of me so I walked closer, listening intently to what was going on.

'. . . the trouble is,' said the man at the blackboard, who I recognised instantly as His Gracious Majesty King Snodd IV, 'that I have no idea what that rascal Brecon is up to. My sources tell me . . .'

His voice trailed off as he noticed me. I suddenly felt very small and naked as all the High Lords of the Kingdom swivelled their heads to stare at me. I knew most of them by sight, of course – they quite liked to get on TV. There was one in particular who was on our screens more than the rest – Sir Matt Grifflon, who was Hereford's most eligible bachelor and about as handsome as any man could be. He smiled at me and I felt my heart flutter. Despite this, there was an uneasy silence. The other men on the sofas were all clearly military men, although the only one I recognised for sure was the Earl of Shobdon; Kazam had once charmed all the moles off his estate.

'Who are you?' demanded the King.

'Your servant, Sire,' I stammered, curtsying clumsily. 'My name is Jennifer Strange; I am the Dragonslayer.'

'The Dragonslayer?' echoed the King. 'The Dragonslayer is a *girl*?'

I watched silently as he started chortling with small grunty coughs. I have to say I had taken a dislike to my King already. The others started to laugh too and I felt a hot flush of anger rising under my skin. The King raised a hand and the laughter stopped. But before he could continue, his eyes opened wide and he yelled out in alarm.

'What in Snodd's name is *that*?'

It was the Quarkbeast. Bored with hiding behind a pillar, it had trotted out to sniff at the bronze leg of a table. The King quickly recovered himself and clapped his hands in delight. 'My goodness! A real live Quarkbeast!' He snapped his fingers and a footman appeared.

'Some meat for the Quarkbeast,' he said without turning. 'A *most* unusual pet, Miss Strange. Where did you find him?'

'Well, it was more of a case of him—'

'How *fascinating*!' replied the King, cutting me dead. 'You are loyal to the Crown?'

'Yes, Sire.'

'That's a relief. Tell me, Miss Dragonslayer, do you have an apprentice yet?'

'Yes, sir, I do.'

The King moved closer to me and I found myself backing away. I had to stop when I came up against a pillar, and he took the opportunity to regard me minutely through a monocle that he had screwed into his eye.

'Hmm,' he said at last. 'You will fire your apprentice and hire the man I send to you. That is all. You are dismissed.'

I started to leave but then stopped as I realised my sixty-second accelerated Dragonslayer course had furnished me with one or two snippets about despots and how to deal with them. Instead of hurrying off, tail between legs and heartily intimidated, I stood my ground.

'Are you deaf, girl?' he repeated. 'I said dismiss! Away with you! Shoo!'

'My Lord,' said I, my voice cracking as I stared into the beetroot-red face of the monarch, 'I wish only to serve my King and will do anything that he reasonably expects of me. But I must point out that by the Mighty Shandar's decree and ancient law, the concerns of the Dragonslayer are of no consequence to my noble King.'

There was a deathly hush. One of his advisers started

to giggle but wisely changed it into a cough. The King's monocle dropped from his face. He turned to his advisers and asked in an exasperated tone:

'Was that a refusal?'

His aides all muttered to one another, nodded their heads and generally made noises of assent. The King turned back to me and wagged a slender index finger in my face.

'You dare to speak of a higher authority than I? Where, might I ask, is this so-called Mighty Shandar? He has not been seen for a hundred and sixty-one years, yet you tell me that he is the last word on Dragons? You are in big trouble, young lady.'

'No, Sire, I think she does you greater honour by her refusal.'

The voice was raw and gravelly and sounded like that of the janitor from the convent. It was one of the King's advisers. He rose from his sofa, disturbing one of a pair of greyhounds that had been asleep at his feet, and approached us both.

'What is the meaning of this, Lord Chief Adviser?'

The Lord Chief Adviser was a tall man of advancing years. His hair and beard were snow white and he walked with a limp. He smiled at me and I breathed a sigh of relief. It stood to reason that a king had others to advise him who were, well, *smarter*.

'I remember the last Dragonslayer, my Lord, perhaps you do not.'

'*Previous* Dragonslayer,' I said, interrupting without thinking.

'What?' said the King.

'Previous Dragonslayer. *I'm* the last Dragonslayer, so if you mean Mr Spalding you should say "previous Dragonslayer".'

The King and Lord Chief Advisor stared at me in disbelief. I don't think anyone ever spoke out of turn in the King's presence. Or at least, not until now.

'I could have said: "*last* last Dragonslayer",' said the King.

'But it doesn't quite *sound* right, does it?'

The King stared at me for a long time, as likely as not contemplating execution.

'Perhaps,' he said at last, 'but what is beyond doubt is that you, like the previous Dragonslayer, are grossly impertinent.'

'There is a reason for that,' intervened the Lord Chief Advisor in his most diplomatic voice. 'A Dragonslayer has a position quite unique. They are answerable not to one leader, but to all of them. The independence of the Dragonslayer should not be compromised, and never coerced.'

'Speak English, damn you! Besides, who's coercing?' asked the King in a shocked tone. 'I am ordering her to employ an apprentice of my choosing. It is *quite* a different matter. Guards, lock this Dragonslayer up in the most frightful room of the highest tower and feed her on powdered mouse until she agrees.'

'You cannot, Sire.'

'Cannot?' asked the King, his face growing red with anger. '*Cannot*? I am the King. I WILL BE OBEYED!'

'As powerful as my Lord is, not even your finest squadron of super-dreadnought landships can come close to the power of magic.'

'Magic? Pah!' scoffed the King. 'This is the twenty-first century, Lord Chief Adviser. I think you accord too much relevance to antiquated notions.'

But the Lord Chief Adviser was not going to be defeated.

'Your father never dismissed magic so readily, and neither should you.'

The King bit his lip and looked at me. The Lord Chief Adviser continued:

'I do not advise you to hold a Dragonslayer against their will, Sire. I also think you should apologise to Miss Strange and welcome her to the court.'

'What?!' said the King, his monocle popping out of his eye again. 'Outrageous!'

At that moment the footman arrived with a small plate of meat for the Quarkbeast.

'What's that for?' asked the King, who had forgotten all about it.

'Quark,' said the Quarkbeast, who hadn't.

The King took the plate and placed it on the floor

next to the Quarkbeast, who looked at me obediently. I nodded my assent and he demolished the food, then chewed the pewter plate for a bit before spitting it out in such a mangled and ugly state that one of the ladies-in-waiting fainted and had to be carried out.

'Goodness,' said the King, who had never seen a Quarkbeast eat before. The greyhounds saw it too and wisely scurried away to hide.

The Lord Chief Adviser took advantage of the distraction and leaned forward to the King's ear and whispered something for about thirty seconds. The King's face gradually broke into a smile.

'Oh, I see. Of course. Will do.'

He turned to me again but his manner had abruptly changed.

'I am so sorry, my dear. Please accept my apologies for my brusque behaviour. No doubt you will have heard about the border skirmishes with the Duke of Brecon early this morning. Intelligence sources tell me that since your surprise appointment yesterday and the realisation that this Dragon chappie will soon be dead, Lord Brecon is considering moving his troops forward to capture as much of the Dragonlands as he can. I fully appreciate your position in all this and I hope I can trust in your loyalty to Hereford?'

I was suspicious about his rapid about-face but decided not to show it.

'You can, Sire.'

'Perhaps you would consider a small request that I have in mind, then?'

'And that is . . . ?'

He shook his head sadly.

'No no no. I am the King. You say yes, *then* ask me what I require. Your upbringing has not been good, girl.'

'Very well,' I replied, 'I will consider very carefully any request my King might make of me.'

'A *bit* better,' conceded the King doubtfully, 'You realise that only you can get into the Dragonlands?'

I nodded.

'Good. I should like you to stake the claim of this crown all over the Dragonlands. So when the good Dragon dies, your monarch and state will be in a more powerful position to better serve its citizens. In return for this I offer you one hundred acres of the Dragonlands and the title Lady Jennifer, First Marchioness of Craswall. Am I not the most generous king ever?'

'I will consider what you have said most carefully, my Lord.'

'That's all agreed then. Lord Chief Adviser, would you show this good lady to my car?'

The royal adviser took me by the arm and we backed away together for a respectable distance before turning our backs on the King and leaving the room.

'I am Lord Tenbury, Miss Strange,' announced the adviser in a kindly tone. 'You may call me Tenbury. I was an adviser to the King's father. You will forgive King Snodd's quick temper.'

We continued to walk along the corridor, the Quarkbeast at our heels.

'You have trouble with the Duke of Brecon?' I asked him.

'As usual.' He sighed. 'Brecon would dearly love to expand into the Dragonlands as soon as Maltcassion dies and I'm afraid we can't allow that to happen. You and your apprentice have the only access to the Dragonlands and that is very useful to us. I beg you to consider the King's request most carefully.'

He stopped and looked into my eyes with an earnest expression.

'Remember you are a subject of King Snodd, Jennifer, and that your duty as a Dragonslayer is second only to your duty as a loyal defender of this crown.'

'All I want is what's best for the Dragon, Tenbury.'

The adviser smiled.

'Things are never as simple as they appear, Miss Strange. By taking on the mantle of Dragonslayer you have inherited a political position every bit as delicate as that of the skilled court adviser. I hope in all this you will make the right decisions.'

We had reached the front door, where the mute driver with the Hispano-Suiza awaited me.

'There is one other thing I would ask of you,' said Tenbury, looking about nervously and moving closer.

'I respect your candour, sir,' I replied. 'What do you wish?'

'That you think very carefully about merchandising.'

'What?'

'Merchandising. Dragonslayer toys, games and so forth. It's big business these days; the King's useless brother and myself are regional representatives of Consolidated Useful Stuff and have been authorised to offer you twenty per cent of everything sold. We think that plastic swords are probably worth a half million in sales alone.'

He smiled and gave me his card.

'Promise me you'll think about it?'

'I will promise you that.'

Up until that point, I had almost liked him. I sighed deeply. King Snodd's rapid about-face meant only one thing: I hadn't heard the last from him.

Yogi Baird

'What did the King have to say?' asked Gordon van Gordon, who was doing the washing up in a flowery pinny. He had taken off his suit jacket and rolled up his sleeves, but was still wearing his brown derby hat.

'My elevation yesterday to Dragonslayer has removed any doubt that Maltcassion isn't long for this world. Brecon is looking to increase his lands and the King is unwilling to let him do so. They want us to lay out the Crown's claims on the Dragonlands before he dies, thus allowing the land to cede painlessly into Snodd's hands.'

'I see,' said Gordon, 'and what are your opinions on these matters?'

'I'm a Dragonslayer,' I replied, 'not an estate agent. It won't make me very popular with the King, though.'

'I agree with that. But you must do what you feel is right. Fancy a cup of tea?'

I nodded gratefully.

'I had another call from Fizzi-Pop,' said Gordon.

'Oh yes?'

'They upped their offer to fifty thousand for your endorsement.'

'What about Yummy-Flakes?'

'They only went as far as forty. ConStuff want to talk some more about merchandising rights, Cheap & Cheerful want to launch a line of Jennifer Strange sporting clothes, and ToyStuff want a licence to release a model of the Slayermobile. The bookies won't take any bets for you to win but they are offering the Dragon three hundred to one, and a tie at five hundred to one.'

'Is that all?'

Gordon smiled, finished filling the kettle and plugged it in.

'No. MolluscTV want to do a documentary about you and the UKBC's wildlife department is interested in you taking a camera into the Dragonlands. I've had three producers wanting to buy the exclusive rights to your story and one even said that Sandy O'Cute was very big on the idea of playing you in the movie.'

'I bet she was.'

'In your mail, ninety-seven per cent want you to kill the Dragon and three per cent want you to leave it alone. Fifty-eight people have written in with offers of marriage, and two have claimed they are the real Dragonslayer. One little old lady in Chepstow wants you to use your sword to dispose of a particularly invasive thorn tree, and another in Cirencester wants you to appear at a fund-raiser for the Troll Wars Orphans appeal. And finally, the Wessex Rolls-Royce club want you to bring the Slayermobile on a rally next month.'

'And this is just the beginning,' I murmured.

Gordon poured the boiling water into the teapot.

'It'll calm down, as soon as there's no more news.'

'I hope. Milk, please, and half a sugar. Mind you, I'm not averse to appearing for the Troll Wars Orphans appeal.'

The doorbell rang. Gordon looked at his watch and pulled off his pinny.

'Who's that?' I asked.

'The *Yogi Baird Daytime TV Show*. Mother Zenobia arranged for you to talk to them.'

'She did, didn't she?'

He opened the door and Yogi Baird strode in, shook my hand, grinned wildly and said how *wonderful* it was to meet me and how he simply *knew* it would be a great show. As he was telling me this he was being dabbed at by a make-up woman. They were joined by a cameraman, an engineer, two electricians, a producer, three assistants and someone who wore black whose function it was to requisition our telephone and then make lots of calls about nothing in particular. Within a short time they had the camera set up and a live uplink to a local transmitter. The same make-up person faffed over me as they set up two chairs in front of the spiky Rolls-Royce and a sound engineer fixed me with a microphone.

While all this was going on I had placed a paper bag over the head of the Quarkbeast with a single hole for him to see out of. It wouldn't do to unnecessarily frighten the crew, and if the Quarkbeast went on live TV, he might cause a panic and small children to start crying, something neither of us wanted.

The floor manager counted Mr Baird in with his fingers and pointed at him as the red 'live' light mounted on top of the camera flicked on. The TV presenter grinned broadly.

'Good afternoon. This is Yogi Baird, speaking to you live from the Dragonslayer's office in Hereford, capital city of the Kingdom by the same name. In just a minute we'll be talking to our very special guest, Dragonslayer Jennifer Strange. But before all that, a word from our sponsors. Has your get-up-and-go got up and went? Need a pick-me-up for a hard morning's work?'

He produced a packet of breakfast cereal.

'Then you need to try Yummy-Flakes for that extra *vavoom!*'

He put down the packet as the jingle played briefly, then he smiled into the camera and continued:

'Listen, everyone's been talking about Dragons these last few days. Dragon this, Dragon that, seems like a bit of a *drag* to me. That joke will *slay* me, but listen, folks . . .'

He didn't seem so funny live. The audience back at the studio were doubtlessly holding their sides, but I was feeling uncomfortable. Like almost everyone in the Kingdoms I had watched the Yogi Baird show all my life, but was beginning to feel as though I was being used – and that Dragonslayers should perhaps show more dignity. I stayed for Mother Zenobia's sake. I knew she would be watching – or listening, anyway.

'. . . have you noticed just how many people have converged on the Dragonlands? Biggest show in town. Maltcassion will soon have his own TV station.'

The cameraman zoomed out to include me in the shot as the floor manager waved frantically at me to be ready.

'. . . but all kidding aside, for the past few days the small Kingdom of Hereford has been alive with speculation over the death of the world's last Dragon. With rumours of his demise imminent, this four-hundred-year-old Dragonland may very well soon be passed to any number of lucky claimants. I have with me the one person who could be battling with the Dragon some time in the next week. Ladies and gentlemen, Jennifer Strange.'

I looked across at Gordon, who gave me the thumbs-up through the glare of the lights. I was being beamed live into the homes of over thirty million people. Two days ago no one had heard of me, yet today you would be hard pressed to find someone who hadn't. The power of the media.

'Welcome to the show, Jennifer.'

'Thank you.'

'Miss Strange, have you met with Maltcassion today?'

'Yesterday,' I replied.

'And was he as horribly grotesque as you had thought?'

'No; on the contrary. I found him a highly intelligent creature.'

'But ugly, of course? And potentially a maneater with nothing on his mind but death and destruction?'

'Not in the least.'

Yogi Baird abandoned that line of questioning.

'O . . . kay. Even pre-cogs as low as B-3 are receiving visions that he is shortly to be killed at your hands. What's your reaction to that?'

'I can't say. Maltcassion has not transgressed the Dragonpact, and so long as he doesn't, I am not required or empowered to do anything at all. In fact,' I added, 'I think the name Dragonslayer is a misnomer. I see myself more as a keeper, who has to weigh the interests of the Dragon against dangerous outside influences. Besides, we know very little about these noble creatures. I am in a good position to change all that. I aim to study Maltcassion.'

'Ah yes. Some newspapers have criticised you for your

pro-Dragon stance. Our researchers have uncovered the truth about Dragons and they are, I quote: *Dangerous fire-breathing and evil-smelling loathsome vermin who would think nothing of torching an entire village and eating all the babies were it not for the magic of the Dragonpact.'*

'Where did you read *that*?'

'My researchers have sources.'

'Well,' I conceded, 'it *is* the populist view, although after my short meeting with Maltcassion I was more inclined to think him a gentleman of considerable learning.'

'So, loathsome worm or learned gentleman? Let's see what the callers have to say. I have Millie Barnes on line one. Hello, Millie, what is your question, please?'

A little girl's voice came over the loudspeaker. She couldn't have been older than five.

'Hello, Jennifer. What's a Dragon like?'

'He looks like a huge pile of stones, Millie. Rough and shapeless. You wouldn't know he was there unless he spoke. As for character, he is noble and fearless and has much that he could teach us—'

'Thank you for your question, Millie,' said Mr Baird dismissively. 'I have Colonel Baggsum-Gayme on three. Go ahead, Colonel.'

'Jennifer, m'girl,' said the colonel gruffly, 'best not to try and attack the blighter on your own, what with you being a girlie and all. Allow me to offer my services as the finest hunter of big game, advice absolutely free as long as I can stuff the ruffian and put him in the trophy room. I'll even have one of his legs made into an umbrella stand for you. Deal?'

'Next caller?' I asked.

'Hello, yes, I think what you're doing is absolutely right and you should follow your own obviously high moral code in this most difficult of situations.'

I liked this caller better.

'Thank you, Mister . . . ?'

'Strange. Or at least it will be. I think that I should adopt *your* name when we are married. Do you like Chinese food?'

'Thank you, caller. I have Mr Savage from Worthing on line six. Hello, caller, go ahead.'

'Hello, Miss Strange.'

'Hello, Mr Savage. What's your question?'

'You call yourself a Dragonslayer, Miss Strange, but I have irrefutable evidence shown to me by a man in the pub that it is I who am the true Dragonslayer. I see you as an usurper, keeping me from my true calling.'

'Well, Mr Savage,' I began, thinking how wrong I was to suppose that I would get only one nutter on the phone-in, 'perhaps you and I should discuss this *inside* the Dragonlands. As you know, only a true—'

But the line had gone dead.

'Our next caller is Mrs Shue from the Corporate Kingdom of Financia. Hello, caller, go ahead.'

'Hello, yes. My husband is up at the Dragonlands, waiting for this creature to die, and we wanted to claim a small hill overlooking a stream. I wonder if you can tell us the best place to go once the force-field is down?'

'My advice to you,' I began slowly, 'is the same as for every person who might be waiting up at the Dragonlands.'

'Yes?' said Yogi Baird expectantly.

'Go home. No matter what prophecy you've heard, the Dragon has done nothing wrong. He is fit and well and will doubtless last for years.' I suddenly felt very angry. 'What is the matter with you people? A noble beast may die, and all you are thinking about is lining your own pockets. You're like a bunch of vultures hopping around a wounded zebra, waiting for the moment to poke your heads into the ribcage and greedily pluck out a piece of—'

I was almost shouting in my anger but stopped when one of the TV lights popped.

'That's it!' said the engineer, looking up from his mixing panel. 'They've pulled the plug. We're off air.'

Yogi pulled his earpiece out and glared at me.

'I have *NEVER* been pulled on a live programme before, Miss Strange! Who do you think you're talking to? This is *my* show and I like to keep it light. You want to get on a soapbox? Go on *Tonight with Clifford Serious.*'

'But—'

He hadn't finished.

'I've been on TV for twenty years so I think my opinions count for something. Let me give you some advice: act a bit more responsibly in front of thirty million people. The bosses at Yummy-Flakes are not going to be pleased. If I knew you were a trouble-maker I would have interviewed Sir Matt Grifflon instead. At least he has a song he's promoting—!'

'Yogi, darling!' yelled his producer, holding the tele-phone. 'I've got the Zebra Society on the phone; they think we're negatively portraying zebras as passive victims. Will you have a word? They're a bit upset.'

Baird glared at me.

'And I've got the Vulture Foundation on line two. They think your programme is spreading unfair stereo-types about a noble bird.'

'See what you've done? A few badly placed words in this business and it's curtains. Ratings are every-thing – how could you be so selfish?'

He turned, glared at me and took the phone from his producer.

'No, sir,' I heard him say. 'I simply *adore* zebras . . .'

Foundling Trouble

I walked back to Zambini Towers. There seemed to be a buzz in the city. The influx of people eager to stake a claim had been huge, and all the shopkeepers had been doing a roaring trade, keeping those in constant vigil up by the Dragonlands well supplied with food, bedding and drink. Stocks of string had long ago run out, and a consignment of ten thousand claim forms had sold out in thirteen minutes.

Lady Mawgon was sitting in the lobby and looked as though she had been waiting to see me.

'Miss Strange,' she said, rising to meet me, 'don't think that becoming a Dragonslayer has in any way altered the low opinion that I hold of you and Master Prawns. Despite that frightful hag Zenobia refusing to supply us with any alternative foundlings, I have negotiated with the King of Pembroke to send us replacements. They arrive on Monday, so I will expect you to be packed and back at the Blessed Ladies of the Lobster by Monday lunchtime.'

She glared at me with a triumphant grin.

'With the greatest of respect, my Lady,' I replied,

'I believe only Mr Zambini can sign our release papers.'

'On the contrary,' sneered Lady Mawgon, who had obviously been doing her homework, 'the Minister for Foundling Affairs is King Snodd's useless brother, and he owes me a favour. He will sign your papers.' She smiled unpleasantly, but I wasn't out of ideas quite yet.

'I am acquainted with the King,' I told her, 'and he has charged me with an important task within the Dragonlands.'

This was true, of course – he had. But I wasn't going to tell Lady Mawgon I'd refused the King's request to claim the Dragonlands in his name.

'Your influence ends at noon on Sunday,' said Lady Mawgon, 'the predicted time of the Dragondeath. After that, no one will much care what happens to you. The useless brother signs your 'return to orphanage' papers on Sunday evening.'

I stared at her hotly. There didn't seem to be much I could say.

'That wiped off your silly smirk, didn't it? And don't try to steal any cutlery – I'll be searching you both as you leave.'

'Jennifer?'

It was Tiger with a message.

'Yes?'

'There's been a news flash. The Duke of Brecon

has raised an army to advance upon the Dragonlands as soon as the Dragon is dead. They aim to claim most of the land for themselves. Every able-bodied man or woman in the Kingdom of Brecon is to be mobilised.'

A cold hand fell on my heart. I hadn't thought that it would come to this so quickly. The Kingdom of Hereford and the Duchy of Brecon had been itching for a scrap for years, and the size of their armies made it potentially the biggest land battle fought in the Kingdoms since the Fourth Troll War. Worse, I knew for a fact that King Snodd was dying to try out his super-dreadnought landships, vast tracked vehicles of riveted steel seven storeys high that crushed and destroyed all in their path.

'We haven't had a good war for years,' said Lady Mawgon, 'and never one on live TV. Colourful costumes, the clank of machinery, rousing songs. It will be most enjoyable.'

'If your idea of enjoyment is watching people killed in an unspeakably unpleasant way,' replied Tiger sarcastically, 'then I guess so.'

'Your impertinence knows no bounds,' remarked Lady Mawgon scornfully, 'but since you will not be here for long, I shall ignore it. There won't be any death – it'll be a walkover. Brecon won't be able to muster anything more than five thousand troops. Hereford has a lot of seriously good military hardware, at least eighty thousand men – and that doesn't include the Berserkers.'

'King Snodd would use Berserkers?' I asked.

'He would,' replied Lady Mawgon. 'Nothing like the sight of a Berserker in a crazed frenzy to get the enemy to beg for peace.'

I was shocked. Berserkers were highly unstable individuals possessed of such grossly volatile temperaments that it allowed them to fight with extraordinary powers in every civilised nation they were defined under the Geneva Convention as 'illegal weapons of war that could cause unnecessary suffering and injury'.

'Would you excuse me, Lady Mawgon? I have to make a telephone call.'

She inclined her head to dismiss us, and we hurried off towards the offices.

'Here,' I said, handing Tiger a signed photo of Yogi Baird, 'I was going to tear this up into small pieces but thought you might like to instead.'

'That's very thoughtful of you,' said Tiger, 'thank you. Did Lady Mawgon tell you about us being replaced?'

'That's not until Monday,' I said. 'Lots can happen.'

'I don't want to go back to the Sisterhood.'

'It won't come to that, I promise.'

I wished I could believe it. The rights that foundlings possessed could be written on an ant in quite large letters. I was in no doubt that Mawgon could do precisely as she said, and there was nothing we could do to stop her.

'Think that's small enough?' asked Tiger, showing me the torn-up picture of Yogi Baird.

'That bit there,' I said, pointing out a piece that still might be smaller. I dialled the number Lord Tenbury had given me and was soon through to the switchboard at Snodd Hill Castle.

'I'd like to speak to the King, please.'

'I'm sorry,' said a snotty telephonist with a plummy voice, 'the King doesn't take person-to-person calls.'

'Tell him it's Jennifer Strange.'

There was protracted silence and a few minutes later the King came on the line.

'I don't make a habit of using the phone, Miss Strange,' he announced loftily, 'but since it is you I am willing to make an exception. You wish to tell me you will lay claim to the lands for me?'

'You cannot go to war over the Dragonlands,' I said, all royal protocol now vanished. There was silence for a few moments.

'Cannot?' questioned the King. 'Cannot? It is *your* behaviour that tempers me to this extremity, my dear. If you had made claim to the lands as we requested, then none of this would be necessary. Brecon amasses his troops at the border, so we must meet force with force.'

'But the Dragon is not going to die. He has done nothing wrong!'

'The court soothsayer Sage O'Neons is rarely

mistaken, my dear. Are you willing to lay claim to the Dragonlands for the Crown?'

'Will it stop the battle?'

'Sadly, no. It will merely give us the benefit of international law being on our side.'

'Then I gain nothing; I refuse.'

Royal politics was not something I was good at. But the King had other ideas.

'There is something you *can* do to avert serious loss of life even now.'

'What?'

'You can kill the Dragon earlier than is expected. Our spies tell us Brecon is unprepared; we can sweep across the lands before he even realises it. Dead Dragon now, dead Dragon later, what's the difference? How about Saturday at teatime? Do we have a deal?'

'No.'

'I will make you a rich woman, Miss Strange. Richer than you can imagine. I will raise your title to Baroness Strange of Hay and make you junior minister for traffic. I will pledge fifty thousand moolah to the Troll Wars Widow Fund. What do you say?'

'My answer is the same.'

'Very well. I was talking just recently to my useless brother. He tells me that you have . . . foundling problems over at Kazam. Do what I ask and I shall release you and your assistant from your indentured servitude. You will both be free citizens, my dear.'

I fell silent. I had only two years to run, but Tiger had six. I looked across at him, but he was busy doing the filing.

'I'm waiting for your answer, Miss Strange,' said the King. 'I am a generous man, but also an impatient one. Cash, freedom, and a title. What will it be?'

'No,' I said at last.

'*What?*'

'The life of a Dragon is not for sale at any price – not even for freedom. It is due to *your* intransigence that Troll Wars widows are reduced to begging at all. I reject your offer and will never compromise my position as Dragonslayer to assist your military conquests. Not now, not ever.'

There was renewed silence for a moment.

'You disappoint me, my dear. I hope you will not regret your decision.'

The line went dead. I looked up. Tiger was staring at me.

'Did you just turn down an offer from him to lift your servitude?'

'No,' I said, feeling a bit stupid, 'I turned it down for both of us.'

'Hmm,' he said after a moment's thought. 'I hope this Dragon friend of yours is worth it.'

'I don't know,' I said. 'The Mighty Shandar's recorded message told me not to trust men *or* Dragons. I know I can't trust Snodd and the Earl of

Tenbury. Brian Spalding is dead and Zambini indisposed. The only thing to trust is my own gut feeling, and that tells me Maltcassion is the one to follow. If I'm wrong, I apologise now.'

'No apology necessary,' replied Tiger cheerfully. 'Sister Assumpta bet me a moolah I wouldn't last the week, but aside from that, I'll only be back where I started.'

He was taking it quite well, all things considered.

'I need to somehow level the playing fields,' I said, mostly to myself. 'War can always be averted – you just have to find out how.'

'You know what you should do?'

'Strike Lady Mawgon on the back of the head with a cabbage?'

'A fine idea – but I was thinking you should speak to the Duke of Brecon and tell him his army is seriously outnumbered and outgunned.'

'Tricky,' I said, 'not to mention treasonous. I preferred the cabbage idea. But you're right,' I added, 'the problem is, how? All the phone lines between the two states were cut years ago and the border is closed.'

'Jenny,' said Tiger, 'what does a Dragonslayer care about borders?'

Conversation with Moobin

I waited until the evening and then drove up to the Dragonlands in my Volkswagen with Wizard Moobin and Brother Stamford, who were eager to see for themselves the spectacle of almost a million people waiting for Maltcassion to die.

'Any developments?' I asked as we drove across the River Wye.

Moobin showed me the Shandarmeter. The needle was almost off the scale.

'More magic?'

'And how. Every hour that passes the meter jumps another five hundred Shandars.'

'Where is it coming from?'

'It seems,' said the wizard, 'to be centred on the Dragonlands.'

I had a thought.

'How much power do you need to start a Big Magic?'

'I don't know.'

'Make a guess.'

'At *least* ten GigaShandars.'

'And at this rate, when would you expect the combined wizidrical energy to exceed that?'

'Yes,' he said, getting my drift, 'Sunday around noon.'

'The time of the predicted Dragondeath. Don't tell me it's all a coincidence.'

'I think not,' replied Moobin. 'But all that energy has to come from *somewhere*. There aren't ten GigaShandars of power on the planet. The most generous estimate of the world's power is barely five, and that includes the power locked up in those marker stones. Even with every magician on the planet we'd still be at least three GigaShandars short. I think the rate of increase will level out and leave us short by a long way. And even if we do get ten Gigs of power around the Dragonlands, no one's sure how we might be able to channel it.'

'We've still got a couple of days.'

'Would you look at that . . .' murmured Brother Stamford, who was staring out of the window. We all followed his gaze to where rows of colossal tracked machines of riveted iron and steel stood silent against the night sky, their substantial bulk brought into sharp relief by the large floodlights that illuminated the edge of the Dragonlands.

'Landships,' said Moobin in a quiet voice.

It showed that King Snodd meant business. Each landship was capable of carrying two hundred soldiers and enough firepower to attack even the most robustly held defences. But despite appearances, they weren't invincible. Many lives had been lost in these towers of iron during the disastrous campaign that became known as the Fourth Troll Wars.

We said nothing more as we approached the Dragonlands, and I threaded the car amongst car parks, military outposts, hamburger vans and television vans. But most of all, we noticed the people. More people than I had ever seen in one place before, and ever would again. They were all ready and waiting in case the Dragon died early and the force-field fell. They were holding stakes, mallets and lengths of string. All that was required was to enclose a section of land and peg a claim form to the grass with your name and signature. It was part of the Dragonpact.

I drove as close as I dared, not wanting to attract attention. The area was being patrolled by members of the elite Imperial Guard. I turned to Moobin and Brother Stamford.

'You had both better get out. I'm going into the Dragonlands.'

They needed no further bidding and clambered out, wishing me good luck in whatever I was about to do. I thanked them, and accelerated towards an unguarded piece of land between the marker stones. Suicide by force-field was not uncommon, and I suppose this was what most people must have thought I was up to as I passed, amid frenzied shouts, between the marker stones and into the Dragonlands. They would have realised then who I was as I drove on, but I was soon lost to view, bumping across the turf in the darkness. I drove over a rise and was soon within the relative quiet of the Dragonlands.

It was dark but a full moon had risen. I didn't suppose I would have much trouble finding my way to the other side of the Dragonlands, to where the land bordered that of the sworn enemy of the King of Hereford: the Duke of Brecon.

The Duke of Brecon

The Duchy of Brecon was a place I had never visited. Stories of the iniquity of the Duke of Brecon were common in the Kingdom and I was taking no chances as regards the Duke's possible treachery. As soon as I thought I had driven far enough I descended the hill and came within sight of more floodlights, crowds and military – but these were Brecon's troops, who were very surprised to see me but soon guessed who I was; most people watched the same news channels, and the Yogi Baird show was syndicated everywhere.

'I wish to meet with the Duke of Brecon,' I said to an officer who came running up once I had parked my Volkswagen.

'I shall take you to him, gracious Dragonslayer,' said the officer, bowing low.

'No,' I replied, staying safely behind the buzzing marker stones, 'I would be grateful if the Duke would come to see me.'

The officer told me that the Duke didn't make house calls, but when he saw I was adamant, ran off. I sat down on the grass and waited while the soldiers asked me what it was like to live in the Kingdom of Hereford, where they had heard the roads were paved with gold, cars were given away free with breakfast cereals and a man could make a million pounds in a year selling string. I tried to put them right and it wasn't long before they all drew apart as a tall man dressed in a heavy greatcoat walked up the hill towards us. He had with him three aides-de-camp, all dressed in the costume of the Breconian Royal Guard. All of the foot soldiers were cleared back so we could talk in private, and for a moment we both stood there, facing each other across the humming boundary. One of the aides-de-camp took it upon himself to make a formal announcement.

'May I present his Worshipfulness, his Worthiness, his Beauteous—'

'That's enough!' The Duke of Brecon smiled in a kindly fashion. 'Miss Strange, I am at your service; my name is Brecon. Please join me.'

He clicked his fingers and two chairs and a table were carried up and placed upon the grass. The table was set with a candelabra and a bowl of fruit.

'Please!' he said, indicating the chair.

I was suspicious and stayed behind the boundary marker where he could not reach me. He nodded his head and strode over to where I was standing, tossed some dust into the barrier to see where it was and held out his hand just inches from the force-field.

'Then allow me to shake the hand of the last Drag-onslayer?'

I put out my hand almost instinctively, through the force-field, and grasped his. It was a mistake. He held my hand tightly and pulled me through to his side of the boundary, and I cursed myself for falling for such a stupid trick. I had expected to be set upon but instead the Duke released me.

'You are free to return, Miss Strange. I only did that to show that you could trust me.'

Not one of his people moved as Brecon sat at the table.

'Come,' he said, 'sit with me, and we will talk like civilised human beings.'

From television reports and the papers I had always supposed him an ogre of a man, but he seemed quite the opposite. To be truthful, those news stations *were* Hereford- and state-controlled so I reasoned there was a natural bias involved. I sat down opposite him.

'I take many risks in coming to see you, my Lord,' I began. 'I want to avoid war at all costs.'

The Duke tapped his fingers on the table.

'Your King thinks ill of me for wanting to expand my territory into the Dragonlands when Maltcassion passes on. He does not appreciate that my Kingdom is one tenth the size of his and considerably poorer. But Snodd's designs are not wholly centred on the Dragonlands. He has been looking for a good reason to invade my country for years; if a battle starts on the Dragonlands it will end in only one way for me: the invasion of our territory and an end to the Duchy of Brecon. Wales is suffering disunity at present, and would be a walkover for King Snodd. I would expect this to be the first step in a potential invasion. Snowdonia might put up a fight, but Hereford has many friends in the east who might willingly form an alliance – the tourism dollars of the mountainous nation alone are potentially worth billions.'

'Invade Wales?' I repeated incredulously. I knew the King was warlike, but this seemed a little far, even for him. 'He would never do that!'

'Alas, I think he might. You are too young to remember the previous king's annexation of the Monmouth Principality on the grounds of historical ownership, but I am not. Snodd is looking to increase and consolidate his lands, and I will not let him do it.'

'I think you're wrong.'

'He has thirty-two landships,' remarked Brecon, 'when it would take only one to crush my small duchy. Think about it, Miss Strange.'

Brecon's words had the ring of truth about them. It had always been thought that the King of Hereford simply liked having parades, but perhaps there was a more insidious reason for his love of military hardware.

'How will you react?' I asked. 'If the force-field comes down?'

Brecon stared at me for a moment.

'Come Maltcassion's demise we do not aim to move into the Dragonlands at all.'

'Then what are the soldiers for?'

'Defence,' replied the Duke, 'pure and simple.'

'Why are you telling me all this?' I asked, not understanding why Brecon should be giving me delicate state secrets.

'I tell you because I know I can trust you. The Dragonslayer is historically a neutral party, belonging to no kingdom, making no decision for one dominion in favour of another. King Snodd appears a fool but is well advised – I suspect he has offered you inducements to help stake claims within the Dragonlands.'

I thought of the promises that King Snodd had made to me, the land, money, freedom and title in exchange for staking his claim.

'So you will make me a better offer?' I asked, thinking naively that Snodd and Brecon were different fleas on the same Quarkbeast.

'No,' asserted the Duke, 'I offer you nothing and will pay you nothing. Not one Breconian groat. I simply ask you to abide by the rules of your calling.'

I noticed that several excavators were starting to build large defensive ditches for the expected invasion on Sunday afternoon. It would be a waste of time. Landships would pass over them as if they were not there. Brecon had nothing compared to the military might of King Snodd.

'It will be bows and arrows against the lightning,' I told him.

'I know,' replied Brecon sadly, 'my artillery will barely dent the landships. But we will fight to maintain our freedom. I will be here, next to my men, defending my beloved country to the last shot in my revolver, and the final breath in my body.'

'I wish you luck, Sire.'

He thanked me but said nothing. He had a lot of work to do. I returned to the Dragonlands deep in thought. Right now, I couldn't see anything but bad news in every direction. But then it suddenly struck me that everyone kept forgetting about Maltcassion himself, even though he was at the heart of everything that was happening. And the fact remained that the pre-cogs had spoken of a Dragondeath at the hand of a Dragonslayer. Destiny had me killing Maltcassion at noon on Sunday. But the fact of the matter was, if Maltcassion didn't transgress the Dragonpact, I didn't have to.

I slipped back to Zambini Towers to tell Tiger what had happened. More sorcerers and magicians had arrived, and a party seemed to be going on. All the retired magicians of the lands were making their way to the small kingdom, following an instinct to lend whatever power they had to the Big Magic.

Dragon Attack

I was awakened by Gordon van Gordon, who was pulling on my sleeve and urging me to wakefulness. I had been dreaming of Dragons again, but not all the dreams were good ones. Maltcassion had been looking at me with a grim expression, explaining what it meant to him to be a Dragon, but I hadn't really been listening and missed something important, which annoyed me.

'What's that noise?' I asked.

'It's the red phone.'

'I don't have a red phone. And what are you doing in Zambini Towers?'

'We're not in Zambini Towers.'

He was right. I was in the Dragonstation. 'Oh,' I said, shaking the fog of sleep from my head and looking at the hotline phone that was ringing under its cake-cover, 'don't worry, it'll probably be someone wanting a pizza. Benny's number is quite similar.'

But it wasn't someone wanting a pizza, it was someone wanting a Dragonslayer.

Within ten minutes the armoured Rolls-Royce was heading south of the city. Gordon was driving as he needed more to do, I was fretting at what we would find, and the Quarkbeast was yawning and wondering why we had got up so early.

The low sun was just spreading its rays across the land as we drove towards Longtown, a village right on the edge of the Dragonlands. A 'Police line do not cross' tape was stretched across the road near the castle, and Gordon parked the Rolls-Royce next to a large contingent of police cars. I introduced myself to a policewoman, who guided me among the many emergency personnel and news crews. The road underfoot was awash with water and the number of fire appliances made me uneasy.

'We meet again, Miss Strange,' said Detective Norton, who was standing with Sergeant Villiers near an upturned eighteen-wheeled truck. 'I should arrest you right now for withholding evidence.'

'I didn't know I was the last Dragonslayer then.'

'That's *your* story.'

'Events have moved on,' I told them. They looked me up and down.

'Kind of young for a Dragonslayer?' said Norton finally.

I stared back at him.

'Perhaps you'd tell me what's going on?'

'We found the claw marks in the cab.'

He beckoned me to follow, and we walked towards

where a large ConStuff truck was lying upended in a field. It had been completely gutted by fire, and the water used to extinguish the flames had run down the field and flooded the road with mud. Norton pointed. On the bodywork, just below the roofline, were two large grooved holes, as though something very massive and very strong had simply squeezed it.

'Vandals?' I asked, somewhat dubiously.

Detective Norton stared at me as though I were an imbecile.

'Talons, Miss Strange, *talons*. This van was taken from Gloucester last night and turns up here. When the fire services arrived they were positive there were no wheel tracks; if you look here . . .'

He indicated an area of damage to the rear of the truck, which had been heavily stoved in – the back axle had almost been torn off.

'It looks as though the truck was dropped from a great height.'

'So what are you saying?' I asked him.

'You tell me, Miss Dragonslayer. Looks as though Maltcassion picked up this van, tried to fly with it back to the Dragonlands but dropped it on the way. To try and disguise the crime, he torched it.'

'A truck hardly counts as livestock, does it?'

'A technicality. The Dragonpact cites damage to *property* as a punishable offence. I think what we've got here is a rogue Dragon.'

'That's sort of far fetched,' I said, trying to play the incident down. It was a serious accusation. A rogue Dragon was a Dragon out of control; one that had transgressed the rules of the Dragonpact. Such a Dragon could legally be destroyed. That's the trouble with premonitions; they have an annoying habit of coming true.

'Did anyone see it?'

Norton looked at his feet.

'No.'

'Anyone hear anything, see it being flown out here?'

'No.'

'Then by the rules of the Dragonpact I'm going to have to see at least two other uncorroborated incidents of Dragonattack before I can even consider this a rogue Dragon.'

Norton rounded on me angrily.

'It's pretty clear cut—!'

'Then *you* punish him, Norton,' I responded. 'I'm going to need to see better evidence than this.'

I left Norton, lifted the 'do not cross' tape and was instantly assailed by a wall of journalists.

'Was this an attack by a Dragon?' asked a reporter from *The Whelk*.

'Unlikely.'

'How could you know it wasn't Maltcassion?'

'I didn't say it wasn't. I said it was *unlikely*.'

'So you're confused?'

'No.'

'Is it true,' asked another pressman, 'that you stated on the *Yogi Baird Show* you aim to study Maltcassion?'

'If I can.'

'Then you have a vested interest in keeping the Dragon alive?'

'What is this all about?'

'We're wondering whether you are qualified to make an objective decision on Dragondeath. Perhaps in light of your dubious conflict of interests you had best leave Dragonslaying to someone else. We understand Sir Matt Grifflon has just held a press conference in which he stated his eagerness to assume your duties; has he contacted you?'

I didn't answer and another reporter took a turn as I walked in the direction of the Rolls-Royce.

'Sophie Trotter of the UKBC,' announced the reporter. 'Miss Strange, does the prospect of having to carry out your duty fill you with trepidation?'

'It won't come to that.'

'But if Maltcassion reneges on the Dragonpact, you will act to destroy him?'

'If he does, I will carry out my duty.'

'Do you think King Snodd's declaration of "no confidence" in your abilities will make you reconsider your decision to resign?'

I stopped so fast the pack of journalists nearly walked into the back of me.

'King Snodd said that?'

'At Sir Matt Grifflon's press conference late last night. He called for your resignation and endorsed Sir Matt taking your place. Such an undertaking is allowed under the Dragonslayer's charter, we take it?'

'I can transfer my calling ... but only to a *knight*,' I murmured, realising that I was being steadily outmanoeuvred.

'So will you be resigning?'

'Listen,' I replied somewhat testily, 'I am the last Dragonslayer. I will uphold the rule of law as laid down by the Dragonpact of 1607 to the best of my abilities. I have no plans to do otherwise. Excuse me.'

I climbed aboard the armoured Rolls-Royce and Gordon drove us away from the mob and headed back to town.

'Are you all right?' he asked.

'Sure. I was hoping to be able to study Maltcassion at my leisure; that hope is rapidly fading.'

Gordon nodded in the direction of the truck.

'What was all that about?'

'Villiers thought it was a Dragonattack; talon marks on an eighteen-wheeler. Even if it was Maltcassion – which I doubt – it isn't enough to have him destroyed. If he does it several times, then I might have to do something. The good thing is that no one was killed. So long as no lives are lost, I can drag this beyond the prophecy deadline. Pre-cogs only see a version of the future. As soon as a deadline is missed, the prophecy becomes less and less likely.'

'So who did this if not Maltcassion?'

'Who knows? Both Hereford and Brecon could have done it. The Dragonlands are of great strategic importance to them both. I've got no way of knowing who is telling the truth. Brecon says he doesn't want the land at all and is fearful of being invaded, whereas King Snodd is convinced that Brecon wants to take over the whole area. I don't know who to believe, so I've cancelled them both out like opposite ends of an equation. I'll have to judge all this on merit as we go along.'

I lapsed into silence as we drove back to the Dragonstation. There were a lot of reporters there too, but I avoided them all as Gordon drove me straight into the garage. The news of my refusal to kill the Dragon without corroboration spread quickly and I had to leave the phone off the hook after some unpleasant calls. A jeering mob started to yell outside the Dragonstation that I was a coward or something, which went on for an hour until some animal-rights campaigners turned up on my behalf. There was a short battle and the police waded in with water cannon and tear gas. I don't think anyone was hurt but a brick came through the front window.

'Tea?' said Gordon with a masterful piece of good timing. 'I've made a cake, too.'

'Thank you.'

Mr Hawker

I was reading *The Dragonslayer's Manual* over breakfast and had just got to the bit about using a banana to sharpen Exhorbitus when there was a sharp rap at the door. I opened it to reveal a small man dressed in a worn suit. He was flanked by two huge men whose knuckles almost touched the ground.

'Yes?'

'Miss Strange, Dragonslayer?'

'Yes, yes?'

'My name is Mr Hawker. I represent the Hawker & Sidderley debt collection agency.'

The alarm bells started ringing. I had expected King Snodd to make life difficult, but this was not what I had anticipated. Hawker handed me a sheath of papers, all headed with the Kingdom's judicial seal and looking terribly formal. I was in no doubt that it was all official, very legal, and wholly dishonest.

'What does it mean?' I asked Hawker, who seemed to be enjoying himself.

'This property has been given rent free by the Kingdom for almost four hundred years,' he

explained. 'We have discovered that this was a cler-
ical error.'

'And you found out just this morning, I suppose?'

'Indeed. Back rent, back electricity bills, gas bills,
rates, you name it. Three hundred years' worth.'

'I've only been here two days.'

Hawker – and the King's advisers, presumably – had
already thought of that.

'As Dragonslayer you are legally responsible for
yourself and the previous members of your calling.
The Kingdom has been generous for many years, but
feels now that circumstances have changed.'

He looked at me with a smile.

'You owe us 97,482 moolah, and forty-three
pence.'

I patted my pockets, drew out some change and
handed it to the debt collector, who wasn't laughing.

'Now how much do I owe you?'

'I think you fail to appreciate the seriousness of the
situation, Miss Strange. I have a warrant for your arrest
if you do not pay the monies owed. Failure to pay
will result in you being jailed for debt.'

He obviously meant it. I could only assume that
the King thought a brief stay in jail would make me
more compliant. But I wasn't about to be arrested just
like that. I asked Mr Hawker to wait and called Gordon
to fetch the accounts. Brian Spalding had said we had
funds available in the bank.

'How long do I have to pay?'

The debt collector smiled and one of his heavies started cracking his knuckles.

'We're not totally devoid of a sense of fair play,' replied Hawker with a gloat. 'Ten minutes.'

'Well?' I said to Gordon, who had returned with the bank statements.

'Not too good, ma'am,' he said. 'It seems we have a fraction under two hundred moolah.'

'Oh dear,' said Hawker. 'Officers, arrest her.'

The policemen stepped forward but I raised a hand.

'Wait!'

They stopped.

'I thought you said I had ten minutes?'

Hawker gave a rare smile and checked his watch.

'Think you can raise a hundred thousand in, let's see . . . eight minutes?'

I thought quickly.

'Well,' I replied, 'actually, I rather think I can.'

Maltcassion again

An hour later I was heading off to the Dragonlands again, the Rolls-Royce bedecked with Fizzi-Pop stickers. Painted on the door was a big sign saying:

Dragonslayer

Personally sponsored by
Fizzi-Pop, Inc.
The Drink of Champions

Sometimes you have to do things you don't want to do for the greater good. After Mr Hawker's warning I had dashed out and collared the Fizzi-Pop representative who had been camping outside the Dragonstation. He and his opposite number at Yummy-Flakes breakfast cereals had quickly called their bosses and bid over the phone for my endorsement of their product. Yummy-Flakes had pulled out at M95,000 but Fizzi-Pop had gone all the way to my asking price of M100,000. It was a simple deal: I was to wear one of their hats and jackets whenever in public, and the

Slayermobile had to be similarly adorned. I had to appear in five commercials and do nothing to impinge on the good name of the product. The alternative was debtor's prison so I didn't have much choice. Hawker, as you might expect, was furious. He had called his lawyers and tried to find a way round the problem, but this was something they had not expected. It wasn't the end of it, I could see that, but at least it was the first round to me. And actually, I quite liked Fizzi Pop.

I saw as I approached that even more people had gathered at the Dragonlands. Just behind the marker stones there was now a 500-yard-deep swathe of tents, mobile eateries, toilets, marquees, first-aid posts and parked cars. The word was spreading, and citizens were arriving from the farthest kingdoms of the land. It was rumoured that claimants were arriving from the Continent and masquerading as unUK citizens in order to be able to stake a claim. A coachload of Danes had been detained at Oxford, a boot-load of rollmop herrings having given them away.

Sunday at noon was a little over twenty-four hours away, and if the premonition came true there would be an unseemly rush to claim everything there was as soon as the force-field was down. It was estimated that a total of approximately 6.2 million people would claim the 350 square miles in under four hours, and the vast majority would be disappointed. The injury rate was pegged at about two hundred thousand, and the fight over land would, it was thought, lead to an estimated three thousand deaths.

As I approached the Dragonlands along one of the access roads kept clear for deliveries of food and other essentials, ten thousand heads swivelled in my direction, and the buzz of conversation dropped to silence. The crowd parted to give me free access to the marker stones, but this was doubtless less from respect and more from the possibility of profit: I was key in the whole affair.

My progress unimpeded, I bumped on to the Dragonland and drove up the hill towards Maltcassion's lair. It was a beautiful day and peace and tranquillity still reigned within the lands. Birds were busy building nests and wild bees buzzed among the wild flowers, which grew in cheerful profusion on the unspoilt land. I found Maltcassion in the clearing in the forest that was his lair, the marker stone in the middle humming a bit louder than the last time. The old Dragon was busy scratching his back against an old oak that bent and creaked under his weight.

'Hello, Miss Strange!' he said in a cheerful tone. 'What brings you here?'

'To speak with you.'

'Well, cheer up, old girl, your face looks long enough to reach your feet!'

'You don't know what's going on out there!' I replied miserably, waving my hand in the direction of the outside world.

'Oh, but I do,' replied Maltcassion. 'You can see the visible spectrum of light, can't you? Violet to red, yes?'

I nodded and sat down on a stone.

'A pretty poor selection, I should think!' said the Dragon, stopping his scratching, much to the relief of the oak tree. 'I can see *much* further. At the slow end of the electromagnetic spectrum lie the languorous long radio waves that move like cold serpents. Next are the bright blasts of medium and short radio waves that occasionally burst from the sun. I can see the strange point-sources of AM radio stations, like raindrops striking a pond. I can see the strange thermal images of the low infrared and beyond this is the visible spectrum that we share; then we are off again, past blue and out beyond violet to the ultraviolet. We go past google rays and manta rays and then shorter still to the curious world of the X-ray, where everything bar the densest materials are transparent. I can see all this, a beautiful and radiant world quite outside your understanding. But it's not all just for fun. You see this?'

He showed me one of his ears. It folded into a flap behind his eye and was of a delicate mesh-like construction, a bit like the ribs on a leaf. He unfurled it for my benefit, rotated it and then slotted it away again.

'A Dragon's senses are far more keen than yours. In the radio part of the spectrum I can see your television and radio signals. But more than that, I can *read* them. I can pick up sixty-seven TV channels and forty-seven radio stations. I thought you were great on the Yogi Baird show.'

'How about cable?'

'Luckily, no.'

'Then you heard about the incident this morning? The truck the police thought was you?'

'I heard something about that, yes. Quite what I would be doing stealing eighteen-wheelers is anyone's guess; I don't even have a driver's licence. Have you had lunch?'

'*And you're not bothered!*' I jumped up, my voice rising. 'There are crowds of people outside waiting for you to die and take over this haven! Doesn't that worry you?'

Maltcassion stared at me and blinked the lids above his jewel-like eyes.

'It bothered me once. I am old now, and have been waiting for you for a number of years. But there is another place we can see. Not radio waves or gamma waves but another realm entirely – the cloudy subether of *potential outcome*.'

'The future?'

'Ah, yes!' said Maltcassion, raising a claw in the air. 'The future. The undiscovered country. We all journey there, sooner or later. Don't let anyone tell you the future is already written. The best any prophet can do is to give you the *most likely* version of future events. It is up to us to accept the future for what it is, or change it. It is easy to go with the flow; it takes a person of singular courage to go against it. It was long foreseen that the Dragonslayer who oversaw the last of our kind would be a young woman of singular mind, remarkable talents and generosity of spirit. She would set us free.'

'Are you sure you've got the *right* Jennifer Strange?' I asked.

The Dragon changed the subject abruptly.

'There is more, but it's all so vague. I could remember it once, but there are so many thoughts in here that it's difficult to work out.'

'You heard about King Snodd and the Duke of Brecon lining up for battle?'

'Yes; all is going to plan, Miss Strange.'

'All to plan? This is your doing?'

'Not everything. You will have to trust me on this.'

'But I don't understand.'

'You will, little human, you will. Leave me. I shall see you Sunday morning – and don't forget your sword.'

'I won't come!' I said as defiantly as you can in front of forty tons of Dragon.

'Yes you will,' answered Maltcassion soothingly. 'It

is out of your hands as much as it is out of mine. The Big Magic has been set in motion and nothing will stop it.'

'This is the Big Magic? You, me, the Dragonlands?'

He shrugged in a very human-like manner which seemed vaguely comical.

'I know not. I cannot see beyond noon on Sunday; there can be only one reason for that. Premonitions come true because people want them to. The observer will always change the outcome of an event; the millions of observers we have now will almost guarantee it. You and I are just small players in something bigger than either of us. Leave now. I will see you on Sunday.'

Reluctantly, and with more questions than answers, I departed.

By the time I had got back to Zambini Towers, there had already been fresh allegations about Maltcassion's supposed misdemeanours. I was called to them both, one after the other. To not cause undue panic or be trailed around by the press, I took my car rather than the Slayermobile.

Inspector Villiers was waiting for me on a side road that had as many police cars and forensic teams as the last supposed Dragonattack. This time, however, he was more confident: Villiers had what could only be described as a large smirk etched across his features.

'Try and tell me this wasn't a Dragon!' He leered.

He led me past the police cordon he had set up near the village of Goodrich and pointed at the ground. There was a black scorch mark on the road, the sort of mark an over-hot iron might make on a shirt. The scorch mark had left the clear imprint of a man, a spreadeagled pattern; I didn't like the look of it.

'Scorch mark, no body, classic sign of a Dragon. *And,*' he paused for dramatic effect, 'I have a witness!' He introduced me to a wizened old man who smelt of marzipan. He was eating the foul substance out of a paper bag and was unsteady in speech and limb.

'Tell the Dragonslayer what you saw, sir.'

The old man's eyes flicked up to mine. He explained in a stammered and broken voice about balls of fire and terrible noises in the night. He spoke of his friend being 'there one moment' and 'gone the next'. He showed me his scorched eyebrows.

'Enough for you?' asked Inspector Villiers in a humourless way.

'No,' I replied. 'Maltcassion is being framed. I was with the Dragon not two hours ago. This witness of yours wouldn't last ten minutes in a court of law. The same burden of proof is required for a Dragon as it is for any other living creature.'

'You're becoming something of a pest,' responded Inspector Villiers. 'I've been a policeman for over twenty years. Who do you think did this if it wasn't Maltcassion?'

'Someone keen on getting the Dragonlands for themselves. King Snodd perhaps, or Brecon. Both of them have an interest in the lands.'

'You're crazy!' he said, pointing a finger at me. 'And what's more, you're dangerous. Accusing the King of complicity in murder? Have you any idea what could happen to you if I decided to make that public?'

He glared at me and I glared back.

'C'mon,' he said finally, 'there's another incident that I want you to see.'

We drove in convoy the ten miles towards Peterstow, where a field of cows had been torn literally limb from limb. It was not a pretty sight, and the flies were already buzzing happily in the heat.

'Seventy-two heifers,' announced Villiers, 'all dead. Talons, Miss Strange. Your friend Maltcassion. You have a duty to protect your charges and carry on your work. Maltcassion has gone loco in his old age. You *must* defend the realm.'

'He didn't do it.'

Villiers rested his hand on my shoulder. His demeanour was less triumphant. Even he, I suspect, did not wholly believe what he was seeing. When you work for the King's Law Enforcement Agencies, you can usually learn to spot a stitch-up when you see it. And ignore it.

'It doesn't matter whether he did it or not, to be honest. All that matters is that there have been three separate incidents. You can check *The Dragonslayer's Manual* if you want.'

I didn't need to. He was right. To counter a Dragon's Deceit, to have three incidents with all the hallmarks of Dragonattack was enough. These were the rules laid down by the Mighty Shandar four centuries ago and ratified by the Council of Dragons. Perhaps it was my destiny to kill Dragons; I was, after all, a Dragonslayer.

Sir Matt Grifflon

The door to the Dragonstation was open when I got back. There was no sign of Gordon. Instead, sitting at the kitchen table and reading through *The Dragon-slayer's Manual* was a striking-looking man with a lantern jaw and long flowing blond hair. He looked up at me and smiled his best smile as I entered, and rose politely to his feet. I knew who he was well enough as his face was emblazoned almost everywhere around the Kingdom: Sir Matt Grifflon. I felt a bit stupid as although I had good reason to dislike and even fear him, my pulse was still racing excitedly in his presence. I had all his albums, several posters and also, to my infinite shame, was a member of his fan club. In panic, I did the first thing I could think of when meeting a celebrity face-to-face – I pretended I didn't know who he was.

'Who are you?' I asked.

He looked shocked.

'You're kidding, right?'

'No,' I replied, 'I've absolutely no idea. Let me guess: you're here to do the drains?'

'Let me remind you,' he muttered sharply, 'I was in King Snodd's chambers when you visited.'

'You're the footman? Sorry, didn't recognise you without the wig and pantaloons.'

He scowled.

'Let me give you a clue: ever heard the song: "A Horse, a Sword, and Me"?'

'You're a songwriter?'

'Okay, fun's over,' he said, suddenly sensing my deliberate impertinence, 'my name is . . . Sir Matt Grifflon.'

He said it in a dramatically deep voice that set the teacups rattling in the corner cupboard.

'His Gracious Majesty King Snodd IV,' he continued in a businesslike tone, 'has ordered me to personally oversee the Dragon-killing process in order that this whole sorry business can be brought to a successful conclusion as soon as possible. I have been given free rein over the manner in which this is done, and any order from me can be taken to have come from King Snodd himself.'

He was sickeningly full of self-confidence.

'I'm sorry,' I said, 'what did you say your name was again?'

He glared at me.

'I don't think you fully appreciate the seriousness of the situation. The rule of the Dragonpact is clear: three attacks and the Dragon must be destroyed. Proof is no longer a burden in this investigation, Miss Strange. If you do not have the stomach for the job then step aside.'

He was right, of course. As Villiers had pointed out, the rules were clear and I was bound by them.

'I will do my duty.'

'And kill the Dragon?'

'If that is what my duty entails.'

'Not good enough,' he said, his voice rising.

'No one can replace me unless I agree,' I replied hotly.

'Will you kill the Dragon? YES or NO?'

'*If* the Dragon is rogue, I will do my duty.'

'YES or NO!'

He was shouting at me now, and I was shouting back.

'NO!' I yelled as hard as I could. The knight fell silent.

'I thought as much,' said Grifflon in a normal tone of voice. 'King Snodd feels that you have been beguiled by the charm of the beast and I agree with him. Action must be taken to remove you from your post. You have failed in your fundamental duties as a Dragonslayer and as a loyal citizen of Hereford.'

'Listen, Grifflon,' I said, purposefully not calling him 'Sir' because I knew it would annoy him, 'why don't you do yourself a favour and head on home? The only way you get this job is over my dead body.'

Grifflon was staring at me in a dangerous sort of

way and I suddenly felt as though my last sentence was probably *not* the right thing to say.

'You force my hand in this, Miss Strange,' murmured Grifflon. 'By your stubborn refusal to kill the Dragon. According to Old Magic from the days of Mu'shad Waseed, the first person to lay their hands on Exhorbitus after the violent death of a Dragonslayer is, by Dragonpact decree, the next in line.'

Sadly, this was true. Sir Matt Grifflon was smiling rather nastily at me and had taken a step closer. There was no weapon to hand and to be honest I probably would not have known how to protect myself if there had been.

'Don't make this too hard on yourself,' he said, pulling a small dagger from his pocket. 'If you stand still I can make it painless.'

He was between me and the door, and I was just thinking of leaping out of the window when a single word came to my rescue and stopped Grifflon in his tracks. It was a simple word. Short, to the point and quite unmistakable in its meaning. The word was *Quark*, and the Quarkbeast said it.

'Quark,' said the Quarkbeast again, positioning himself defiantly between myself and Grifflon.

My outrageously handsome would-be assassin looked at the Quarkbeast nervously. It had its mouth open and was revolving its five canines in a menacing fashion.

'Call him off, Miss Strange.'

'And let you kill me? Just how stupid do you think I am?'

'Quark,' said the Quarkbeast, taking a step towards Grifflon, who backed away nervously.

'You can't hide behind a Quarkbeast for ever, Miss Strange.'

'It's Sunday tomorrow,' I told him. 'After the premonition of Maltcassion's death is proved wrong I won't need to hide behind anything.'

He glared at me and ran quickly out of the door. The Quarkbeast sat on the rug and looked up at me with his large mauve eyes.

'You did good,' I told him. 'Thank you.'

I looked out of the Dragonstation and into the street. The crowds, which up until that point had been thronging around outside the Dragonstation, had thinned out dramatically, doubtless to find a good place from which to stake a claim in the land rush tomorrow. On the street outside only a few diehard Dragonslayer fans, some journalists and Sir Matt's squires were in attendance, the latter doubtless to keep an eye on me in case I decided to make a run for it. I went back inside, locked the door and caught the mid-morning TV bulletin. King Snodd was giving a speech about how the Dragonlands were 'historically part of Hereford', and that the whole Kingdom had to act together to prevent the perfidious Duke of Brecon invading the country and threatening 'all that we know and love'. I switched off the TV and went through to the kitchen, where I found a note from Gordon van Gordon. It read:

Dear Miss Strange,

I am sorry but I have been called away to look after my mother, who has gout. I wish you the very best on this most difficult of days for you, and hope you will find the courage to act in the way that you think correct.

Yours, Gordon van Gordon

'Coward,' I muttered angrily, tearing up the note and throwing it aside. I sat down to ponder my next move, and hadn't come up with a plan half an hour later, when there was a loud hammering at the door. The Quarkbeast's hackles rose.

'Hello?' I yelled without opening the door.

'Police,' came the reply.

'What do you want?'

'The Quarkbeast has been declared a dangerous animal,' announced the impassive voice of the officer, 'harbouring one is considered unlawful.'

'Since when?'

'Since when the King decreed it, seven minutes ago.'

The rug was being pulled rapidly from under my feet.

'I need the Quarkbeast for protection,' I answered a bit feebly.

'King Snodd has thought of that,' bellowed the officer through the door. 'His Majesty has sent Sir Matt Grifflon to guarantee your safety.'

A shiver ran down my spine.

'Grifflon wants to kill me so he can take over as Dragonslayer.'

There was a pause.

'You have been beguiled by the Dragon, Miss Strange. Sir Matt tried to help you and you set the Quarkbeast on him. King Snodd has given his word that no harm will come to you. There is no higher guarantee in the Kingdom.'

He then added in a patronising manner:

'We don't want to hurt you or the Quarkbeast, Jennifer. All we want to do is *help* you.'

I peeped cautiously out of the window. The street had been blocked off and three police cars were parked outside. There were about a dozen officers, and two of them were dressed in heavy armour. They had between them a riveted titanium box in which to imprison the Quarkbeast. A half-inch of titanium was about the only metal he couldn't chew through.

Standing on one side but still looking very much in charge of the operation was Sir Matt Grifflon.

'Please, Jennifer,' said the officer, 'open the door.'

'Wait a minute,' I said, running to the rear window and looking out. There were police out there, too. I was trapped.

'Either you surrender the Quarkbeast or we come in and take it and arrest you for non-compliance with a royal decree,' said the officer as I returned to the front door. 'If the Quarkbeast so much as looks at us in a funny way, we will have no choice but to use lethal force. The choice is yours. I'll give you a minute to decide.'

I looked down at the Quarkbeast.

'It's fourteen against two, chum. What do you say?'

'Quark.'

'I thought you'd say that. But I'm not risking your life for mine. Let's find another way out.'

I ran to the Rolls-Royce and unclipped Exhorbitus. As the Quarkbeast watched me with growing interest, I attacked . . . the *wall*. The sword cut deep into the brickwork, slicing the masonry as though it were wet paper. Three quick slashes and we were through to the property next door.

'Sorry!' I said to the surprised-looking resident who had been watching *The Snodd v. Brecon War Show Live* when his wall came down and a Dragonslayer and her Quarkbeast jumped through.

We didn't stop there, either. Holding the sword in front of me, I ran across the room and went through the next wall and into a coin-operated launderette. Water sprayed everywhere as the sword sliced easily through the washing machines. We heard an explosion from the Dragonstation as the police blew the door down; but by that time we had cut our way out of the launderette and were into the house beyond *that*. Luckily this one was empty and the next wall brought us out into the daylight at the end of the terrace. Exhorbitus was too unwieldy to allow me to run far, and I wasn't going to use it on anyone anyway, so I hid it beneath some rubbish in an empty building site and ran into the network of small alleyways in the Old Town behind the cathedral. We heard yells behind us, and I stopped. We couldn't run for ever, my Volkswagen was in the other direction and the safety of Dragonlands almost twenty miles away. I turned to the Quarkbeast and told him to run off and hide. He looked all doleful and made signs that his place was by me so I had to be cross and explain that this wasn't the time for a final stand that would doubtless leave us both dead, and that given a choice they would follow me sooner than him. He understood my every word, and eventually lolloped off. I waited until Sir Matt and his officers could see me from the far end of the street, then darted off in the opposite direction. I ran through the narrow streets with Grifflon and the officers barely a hundred yards away. I turned left, then right, then found myself outside Zambini Towers. I was out of breath, luck and ideas, and before I knew what I was doing I had darted inside and thrown the bolt.

I had hoped that Wizard Moobin might have returned and would help me, but I knew as soon as I entered that the old building was empty. For the first time ever I noticed an eerie silence within the echoing corridors of the old hotel. There was no hum, no static, no strangeness – nothing. All the sorcerers – even the mad ones from the eleventh floor – were doubtless up at the Dragonlands, presumably to assist with the Big Magic in whatever form it might take. There was no one to help me, no one to turn to. I was entirely on my own.

I dashed through the open doors of the Palm Court, looking for a place to hide, but my heart fell as I entered. Sitting next to the fountain was Lady Mawgon. She was sitting bolt upright with her hands on her lap. She was dressed even more funereally than usual in her blacker-than-usual crinolines, gloves and a veil. It would have been a child's spell to make me decide to run left when I entered the lobby.

'Good afternoon, Lady Mawgon.'

'I've been waiting for you, Jennifer.'

'Listen,' I said, 'I know we've not been getting on very well at present, but there's a Big Magic going on tomorrow at noon, and I've got to be there.'

I didn't get to say anything more as there was a sharp report from the front door as the lock was shot off, and a cry from Sir Matt. There were footfalls on the steps of at least six officers and I heard shouts and cries in the lobby. I hurriedly hid behind the central fountain. I'd be unseen from the door, but even a cursory search of the Palm Court would uncover me.

'Sir Matt?' called out Lady Mawgon. 'Would you come into the Palm Court please?'

Sir Matt stepped in and nodded respectfully to Lady Mawgon.

'My Lady,' he said, 'will you give her to me?'

There was one of those long pauses that seem to go on for ever. I closed my eyes.

'I have not seen the wretched child all afternoon,' she announced. 'After you find her, you may send her to me.'

'Don't think me untrusting,' said Sir Matt, and he beckoned his officers to search the Palm Court. He stepped forward and Lady Mawgon placed her hand lightly on my shoulder. Sir Matt could not have missed me, but he did – and I breathed a sigh of relief. Lady Mawgon had *occluded* me from his sight. It's not the same as invisibility, which has eluded even the finest magicians for centuries, but a spell whereby I would not easily be noticed – exploiting the same phenomenon that stops you seeing your car keys when they are sitting on the desk in front of you. To make it work, I stood perfectly still and made no noise.

'Nothing in here, sir,' said an officer, and trotted out to search the rest of the building.

'She won't get far,' replied Grifflon. 'The whole of the Old Town is sealed off.'

He turned back to Lady Mawgon and lowered his voice.

'If I find out you've hidden her, I will return – and my revenge will be frightful.'

She gave him one of her most imperious looks, and Sir Matt called off the search since the wizards, ever worried about thieves, had left frighteners in their rooms, and even the burliest officers were quaking with fear at what they had seen. Within five minutes they had gone, and Lady Mawgon took her hand off my shoulder.

'There is a Big Magic to be completed,' she said in a quiet voice and without looking me in the eye, 'and it behoves me to set our differences aside. Get a good night's sleep. I will watch over you.'

I wanted to give her a hug, but decided against it.

'Thank you, Lady Mawgon, I—'

'It is my duty,' she said, 'nothing more.'

I said nothing, and went to find Tiger.

Escape from Zambini Towers

Lady Mawgon was true to her word. She sat up all night in the lobby, and whenever any of Grifflon's men came in to look for me, she gave them such a devastatingly withering look that they scurried out again, tail between legs. Tiger and I talked deep into the night down in the kitchens. At 1 a.m. a thump in the laundry room made us nervous until we found that it was the Quarkbeast, who had managed to sneak back into Zambini Towers by way of the laundry chute without being noticed.

The early morning radio bulletins estimated that the crowds up at the Dragonlands had topped eight million people, and anticipation was high. Neither King Snodd nor Sir Matt Grifflon had made any further proclamations, so I could only assume that they were still looking for me. Unstable Mabel made us pancakes for breakfast, and then a special batch for the Quarkbeast, who liked them with curry powder instead of flour.

'Every exit is covered by at least three Imperial Guards,' said Tiger, who had been around to check. This was not good news.

'I need to retrieve Exhorbitus from some waste-ground and then get to the Dragonstation,' I replied. 'No one is permitted to hinder a Dragonslayer while on official duties, and to be honest, once I'm in the armoured Rolls-Royce, nothing but an artillery shell could stop me – and even King Snodd would think twice before trying to kill me in broad daylight and in front of the TV cameras.'

'It's five hundred yards to the Dragonstation,' said Tiger. 'They're not after me. Perhaps I could fetch the Slayermobile for you?'

'Can you drive?'

'How hard can it be?'

Just then, Lady Mawgon walked into the kitchen and handed me a copy of *The Daily Mollusc*. The front page had banner headlines explaining how everything was fine after all and it was no longer necessary for me to slay Maltcassion. It added that the Duke of Brecon and King Snodd had kissed and made up, the Quarkbeast was no longer an illegal animal, the sale of marzipan had been banned and all foundlings everywhere were to be reunited with their parents.

'This is all far too good to be true,' I muttered, and as soon as I had, the enchantment crumbled. I was no longer reading a newspaper but simply staring at a colourless grey pebble.

'What you have in your hand is a Pollyanna stone',

explained Mawgon. 'Whoever holds the pebble will see what they expect or hope to see. It might be of use if you are stopped on the way.'

She turned away, thought for a moment, then turned back.

'If you tell *anyone* I've been nice to you,' she said, narrowing her eyes, 'I will make it my solemn duty to render both your lives as unbearable as possible. And don't think I'm not going to have you both replaced on Monday, for I will.'

And without another word, she left the room.

'The sorcerers are an odd bunch, aren't they?' said Tiger with a smile.

'They grow on you,' I replied, 'even Lady Mawgon-Gorgon there.'

'I heard that!' came a voice from outside.

We finished breakfast and talked about a plan to get me to the Dragonstation. There were several possible ideas mooted, but none passed the stringent 'remotely plausible' test. We were still scratching our heads when we heard a noise outside, and found that the Quarkbeast had dragged a pram from one of the building's many boxrooms, and was looking at us excitedly and wagging its tail.

'Brilliant!' said Tiger. 'The Quarkbeast's a genius! Listen carefully: we'll need some baby clothes, a piece of card, a felt-tip pen, some old clothes and a wig.'

★

Twenty minutes later, and after Tiger had wished me all the very best of luck, I let myself out of the garage doors at the back of Zambini Towers and walked towards where the guards were standing on the corner. I was dressed in one of the Sisters Karamazov's old outfits and a red wig I had borrowed from Mr Zambini's dressing-up box, and was pushing the Quarkbeast in the pram. The Quarkbeast was wrapped up in a baby shawl and wearing a pretty pink bonnet. A placard tied to the front of the pram announced that I was collecting for the Troll Wars Orphans Fund. I wasn't convinced this would work but Tiger was smart and it was the only idea we had had.

'Everyone has lost someone in the Troll Wars,' he had explained, 'so no one will stop you.'

He was right. Since Troll Wars widows begging for coins were not at all uncommon, I was ignored by the members of the Imperial Guard who were searching every car on the roads. There were posters of me up on the walls, telling the general public how I was a dangerous lunatic and a traitor and had to be stopped as a matter of national security. As I crossed the road a police car passed with a large loudspeaker on the roof, offering an earldom and a guest spot on the *You Bet Your Life!* quiz show to whoever turned me in. I quickened my pace and made it to the waste ground where I had hidden Exhorbitus. I wrapped the sword in a blanket, hid it under the pram and turned into the road in which the Dragonstation was located.

There was a 'Police line do not cross' tape barring my way, and outside the Dragonstation were two Imperial Guard armoured cars, and upwards of a dozen soldiers, all armed. I took a deep breath and walked towards them. It was all going well; if I could make it to the Rolls-Royce all would be—

'Quark.'

'Shhh.'

'Good morning, ma'am. Going somewhere?'

Two of the Imperial Guards had walked across to see who I was and what I was doing there. It was galling. I was almost within spitting distance of the Dragonstation.

'Spare a groat for a poor Troll War widow?'

'This road's closed,' announced the first soldier sharply. He didn't look as though he had a very charitable nature. 'What are you doing here?'

'Taking my poor, sweet, orphaned, fatherless and ill child to his check-up. He has bad calluses on his legs, a bald patch and his poor orphaned heart, well, it's—'

'I get the point. Identification papers?'

I handed him the Pollyanna pebble. If he thought I was a war widow then all would be well. If he was expecting the worst or was even vaguely suspicious, all would be lost. I was lucky. The guardsman looked at the pebble as though it really *were* identification papers, turned it over and said:

'Name?'

'Mrs Jennifer Jones.'

'Identification number?'

'86231524.'

He nodded and passed the pebble back to me.

'Okay, move along.'

I thanked him and started to walk off.

'Wait!' said the second soldier, and I held my breath.

He dug into his pocket and pulled out . . . a *coin*.

'Here's a groat for you. I fought in the Troll Wars and I lost some good friends. May I see the baby?'

Before I could say or do anything he looked into the pram at the Quarkbeast. I held my breath. The Quarkbeast stared up at him.

'What's his name?'

'Quark?' said the Quarkbeast, blinking nervously.

'Sweet kid. Okay, Mrs Jones, move along.'

I walked on, my heart beating heavily and a cold sweat on my forehead.

'Well,' I heard the second soldier whisper to his colleague, 'I've seen some ugly babies in my time but that little Quark Jones was uglier than all of them put together.'

The two officers turned away, and as soon as I was opposite the broken-in front door of the Dragonstation I jumped inside and ran to the Rolls-Royce. The

Slayermobile whispered into life, I engaged first gear and floored the accelerator. With a splintering of wood I drove through the locked garage doors, and pushed the Imperial Guard's armoured car out of the way. I pulled the wheel over and accelerated up the street, the *spang* of rifle fire bouncing off the heavy iron plating. At the end of the street was a barricade of cars, manned by a group of policemen whose puny weapons could not hope to damage the heavily armoured Slayermobile. They jumped out of the way as the vehicle tore through their cars, the sharp spikes ripping the bodywork as though it were tissue paper.

Once I was out of the tight police cordon that had ringed the Old Town, I found quite a different scene awaiting me. The public, who had been told that a Dragonslayer – although not necessarily me – would be heading up to the Dragonlands that morning, had lined the route in eager expectation. An excited yell went up as the Slayermobile appeared and several hundred flags were waved in unison. Somewhere a brass band started up and garlands of flowers were thrown in the path of the Rolls-Royce. Sir Matt Grifflon had laid all this on for himself. He had thought, in his arrogance, that I would be caught and dispatched before morning.

I slowed down as the danger subsided. There was little that Grifflon or even King Snodd would dare try with all these potential witnesses about. As I drove past, the crowds broke ranks and followed the Slayermobile in one long procession. We were joined by the Guild of Master Builders, two marching bands and a contingent from the Troll Wars Veterans' Association. TV cameras at every corner beamed my journey live to half a billion viewers worldwide. From China to Patagonia and from Hawaii to Vietnam, my progress was being eagerly watched.

Back to the Dragonlands

My journey unimpeded, I arrived at the Dragonlands an hour later and drove slowly through the parting crowd, felt the slight *fizz* as I passed through the marker stones, and then stopped the car. Safe at last, I climbed out of the Slayermobile as the news crews came as close as they dared to the boundary markers.

First on the scene was a MolluscNews film crew. The reporter, jostled from behind, made a short introduction to what would turn out to be the biggest news scoop of her career.

'I am speaking live from the Kingdom of Snodd where we are about to witness the last round of a titanic struggle that began four hundred years ago with the Dragonpact, and finishes at twelve o'clock noon here high on a hill just outside the Kingdom of Hereford. A struggle that will finally see the Ununited Kingdoms rid of Dragons once and for all.'

She pointed the microphone at me.

'A few words? We're live.'

'My name is Jennifer Strange,' I began, 'I am the last Dragonslayer. I have grave doubts over the claims of the supposed crimes but by the laws of the Drag-onpact I am not permitted to refuse. I hope that one day you will all forgive me, although I know I shall never be able to afford myself the same privilege.'

The pressmen clamoured for more but I ignored them. I caught a glimpse of Sir Matt Grifflon staring at me with daggers in his eyes. He was standing next to a couple of Berserkers who were hitting each other with bricks in readiness for the battle. I gave them all a wan smile and drove away from the baying crowd. Once out of their sight I stopped the Rolls-Royce and climbed out. It was barely eleven o'clock; I had time to catch my breath.

'You're back,' said a voice.

I knew who it was. I didn't even bother turning around.

'Hello, Shandar,' I replied.

He was sitting on a rock.

'You must *not* kill the Dragon,' he said quite simply. 'I *order* you not to kill the Dragon. You will regret it. The Dragonpact will be destroyed. The Dragons will be free to once again roam the land, killing and plundering, and the Ununited Kingdoms will collapse into a new dark age more evil and sinister than you can imagine. Humans, made slaves, will be ruled over by the Dragons, whose hearts are as black as the deepest cavern, their one wish the destruction of the human race.'

'Is this another recording?'

'I have placed this recording here as a warning against anyone trying to kill the last Dragon. Believe nothing that they say to you. They can lie in thought, deed and gesture. I repeat: return now and leave the Dragon alone.'

I was confused.

'But by the terms of your decree, the Dragon is rogue and must be destroyed!'

The image twitched and went back to the beginning again.

'You must not kill the Dragon,' he said quite simply. 'I order you not to kill the Dragon . . .'

I watched the speech again but the magic was old and weak and before I had heard the message three times Shandar was merely a voice on the wind. Naturally, I agreed with him, but was suspicious of his strong wish for me *not* to kill the last Dragon, when he had been paid twenty dray-weights of gold to do precisely that. Had I been beguiled by the Dragon? Did he have another agenda? Was I smart enough to see through the possible lies? Thoroughly confused, I set off into the Dragonlands.

I drove up a hill, followed the ridge for a little way and then descended into a beech forest. I had to steer the large Rolls-Royce very carefully among the tree stumps and fallen branches. Twice I had to back up and try a new way through, but soon the forest thinned out and I found myself looking out on to a large, flat meadow next to a stream. I drove across the short grass as grazing sheep moved lazily out of my way, and then crested a low rise and stopped, not believing what I could see.

I turned off the engine and stepped out on to the springy turf. Across the low valley was a sea of white tape that criss-crossed the untouched land, tied at intervals to pegs hammered into the ground. Someone was in the Dragonlands. Someone was already staking claims.

I heard a cheery whistling on the breeze and walked to the brow of a low hill, where I saw a small man wearing a brown suit and an unmistakable derby hat. It was Gordon van Gordon. I stared for a moment, not quite sure what I was seeing. He had *lied* to me. He wasn't valiant or trustworthy – and it didn't look as though he was looking after his mother, either. I cursed myself for my stupidity, for I had made all this possible by his appointment – only a Dragonslayer or their apprentice may enter the Dragonlands. He was cheerfully banging claim stakes into the ground, and hadn't noticed I was watching him.

'I trusted you, Gordon.'

He jumped as I spoke and looked up at me, but he didn't seem too worried.

'Trust is a trait you should be proud of, Jennifer – and I'm very glad you're so pleasant. If you'd been obnoxious this would have been ten times as hard.'

'Let me see.'

He gave me one of the stakes. There was an aluminium disc attached, and it was stamped with the name of the company Mr Trimble had been negotiating for earlier: The Consolidated Useful Stuff Land Development Corporation. Gordon had successfully claimed the land. The area enclosed within the named stakes legally belonged to ConStuff – or it would do, as soon as the Dragon was dead and the marker stones lost their power. And Gordon had claimed a *lot*. As far as I could see there were marker tapes tied to stakes.

I shook my head sadly.

'Why did you do it, Gordon?'

'Business, Miss Strange – nothing personal. You have many fine qualities that I admire. But you are out of time. You should have been born a century ago when values such as yours meant something.'

Gordon smiled. But it was a smile I hadn't seen before. It was as though I was meeting a different person. The Gordon I knew, the friendly and helpful Dragonslayer's apprentice, had never been real at all.

'You had me fooled.'

'Don't beat yourself up over it,' he said kindly, 'we've been running Last Dragonslayer Drill for a number of years now.'

I frowned.

'This was all *planned*?'

He knocked a peg in, wrapped a tape around it and walked off in the direction of a stream. I followed, more out of a sense of shocked disbelief than anything else.

'We knew that Brian Spalding was expecting someone to replace him. He resisted all our attempts to get him to appoint an apprentice so we watched him, waiting for the time the new Dragonslayer would come and take his place. It just so happened that you chanced along on my shift.'

'How long were you waiting?'

'Sixty-eight years. A team of six people, working round the clock. My father gave his working life to ConStuff. He watched Brian Spalding for over thirty years.'

'Thirty years? Just for some real estate?'

'You don't get it, do you?' he said, as though I were some sort of idiot. 'Snodd and the Duke of Brecon are powerful, Miss Strange. They have the power, as you have seen, to change the law at a whim and outlaw their citizens at their command. But even they are merely transient when it comes to the might of commerce. Governments may come and go, wars will reshape the Ununited Kingdoms many times. But companies will stay, and flourish. Show me any major event on this planet and I will show you the economic reason behind it. Commerce is all powerful, Miss Strange. Commerce rules our lives. ConStuff have put a lot of time and money into Project Dragon, and their investment is about to bear fruit.'

'Money,' I murmured.

'Yes,' he agreed, 'money. And lots of it.' He spread his arms wide and looked around to make the point. 'Do you have any idea just how much this parcel of land is worth?'

'Of course,' I replied, 'I have a very good idea of the value of the Dragonlands. But you and I are talking about different currencies. You're talking about gold and silver, cash and securities. I'm talking about the sheer beauty of the land, the value of unpolluted parkland made wild and staying wild for ever.'

'Dream on, Strange,' he sneered, 'in every direction are millions of greedy speculators eager to lay claim to a few square yards. While you have been gallivanting around pondering the imponderables, I have potentially laid claim to sixty per cent of the lands. We already have plans drawn up. We will build an access road through that oak forest and just over there' – he indicated a small copse of silver birches – 'will be a retail park for over seventy different shops, with parking for a thousand cars. Over there,' he pointed to another hill in the other direction, 'will be a luxury housing development. Just beyond that hill there will be a power station and a marzipan refinery. This is progress, Miss Strange. A billion moolahs' worth of progress. We were lucky you turned out to have such high ideals – if you had fallen for King Snodd's schemes to claim the Dragonlands on his behalf you might have been something of a nuisance to us. As it is, everything has turned out admirably.'

'Then I pity you,' I replied, 'pity you because you will never know or see a decent act. You have given nothing, you will receive nothing.'

'I have a bank balance that proves you wrong, Jennifer. My share alone in this project amounts to over thirty million. I watched Brian Spalding doggedly for over twenty-three years. Don't tell me I don't deserve it!'

'You don't deserve it.'

We stared at each other for a few moments.

'So all those Dragonattacks. They were arranged by ConStuff?'

'Certainly. As soon as the prophecy began we could see how we could use it to our advantage. Even King Snodd and the Duke of Brecon wouldn't have dared fake a Dragonattack. We just helped things along. Massaged fate, if you like. Look at it our way – we have actually *helped* solve the Dragon Problem. I think the Mighty Shandar would be grateful.'

'And the prophecy that began all this? You as well?'

'If only!' said Gordon, laughing. 'If *that* was in our power we could have engineered all this sixty-eight years ago. Nope, that wasn't us.'

We continued to stare at each other for a moment longer. ConStuff and Gordon were playing with things quite outside their understanding. 'Money is a form of alchemy,' Mother Zenobia had often told me, 'it turns kind, normal people into greed-mongers, intent only on acquisitiveness.'

'You have no idea what's going on, have you?' I told him, my voice rising. 'I know that,' I added, 'because *I* have no idea what's going on, and I'm the Dragonslayer. Everyone wants the Dragon dead except me and Shandar. Even the Dragon wants the Dragon dead. If I were you I'd get out of the Dragonlands while you still can.'

'You're blabbering, Jennifer. I'll be staking claims until the first Berserker comes over that hill.'

I couldn't think of much to do, so as a pointless gesture I pulled up a marker stake and threw it in the river. Gordon wasn't impressed. He pulled a service revolver out of his waistband and pointed it at me.

'Be a good little girl and leave me alone. Do something useful like kill the Dragon so we can finish this all up and get to the bit where I am handed wads of—'

There was a growling and a snapping noise and I looked up. The Quarkbeast had left the safety of the Rolls-Royce and was running down the hill as fast as his short legs could carry him. He'd been keeping his anger in as I had ordered, but out in the Dragonlands his instincts were taking over. He was going to protect me whether I liked it or not. I wasn't mad keen on Gordon but no one deserves to be savaged by a Quarkbeast.

'Call him off, Miss Strange. I'll shoot him, I swear I will!'

'Stop!' I shouted to the Quarkbeast. 'Danger!'

But he kept on coming, his jaws rattling dangerously, the sharp obsidian teeth glinting unkindly in the sunlight. There was a sharp report and the Quarkbeast fell, rolled over twice in the heather and lay still. I looked across at Gordon, who now turned the smoking revolver back to me.

'Don't even think about it!' he said angrily. 'I never liked the little tyke anyway. Run along and do your duty or by King Snodd and St Grunk, I'll shoot you where you stand and get Sir Matt Grifflon in here to do your work for you – I could even claim the reward on your life!'

I tried to find something to say but nothing came out.

'Well!' sneered Gordon. 'Quite the Dragonslayer, aren't you? I was wondering how you could possibly have handled this any worse. All you had to do was kill a Dragon, and instead we've got a major war about to break out. Destiny is unkind sometimes, isn't it? How many deaths will you have on your conscience? Ten thousand? Twenty thousand? How much are your fancy scruples worth now?'

'Stop!' I shouted angrily, but he wouldn't.

'Stop?' he repeated as he smiled a triumphant smile. 'Or what? What will you do?'

I suddenly knew *exactly* what I'd do.

'Or I'll fire you, Gordon.'

'Well you can't,' he sneered. 'I resign.'

'You resign?'

'Yes, I—'

'You mean you're *not* my apprentice?'

He clapped his hand over his mouth as he realised what he had just said, and his face drained of colour.

'NO!' he yelled, throwing the gun away and changing his tone to a mournful plea. 'I don't resign! I'm sorry, *please* take me on again, I don't want to end like—'

There was a bright flash and a smell of burnt paper as Gordon was reduced to little more than the sort of powder you might find in a cup-a-soup sachet. Only his clothes, derby hat and a steaming revolver remained to show that he had ever been. None but a Dragonslayer or their apprentice could enter the Dragonlands. His arrogance had got the better of him; his thirty million meant nothing.

I walked over to where the Quarkbeast was lying still in the heather. I dropped to my knees and rested my hand gently on his forehead. His large eyes were closed; he might have been asleep. There is a legend about Quarkbeasts that tells they are sent by the spirits of dead relatives to watch over you in times of uncertainty. My father had sent the Quarkbeast, I was sure of it. The small animal, although repulsive to many and possessed of disgusting personal habits and, yes, a bit smelly, had done his duty without regard for his own safety. I moved his body to a hillock above a bend in the river and placed a pile of stones over his small form. I topped this with a larger rock upon which I scratched the word *Quark* and the date. In the warm summer sunshine I stood for a moment in silent contemplation. He was a good, loyal friend, and he gave his life to save me.

Noon

I returned to the Slayermobile and drove to Maltcassion's lair, the clearing in the forest. I parked up and stepped out. The large marker stone was humming louder than usual. The Dragon was sitting up on his hind legs. He was far taller than I had supposed – at least the height of one of King Snodd's landships. He sniffed the air and listened carefully with his finely tuned ears.

'I am sorry for your small friend,' he said, looking down at me. 'He had a good soul, despite his appalling table manners.'

I thanked him, and he told me he knew I would come, despite my own misgivings.

'The Mighty Shandar just spoke to me,' I said. 'He demanded that you were to be spared. How do you account for that?'

Maltcassion growled angrily.

'Don't you dare speak of that scoundrel in my presence!'

I was shocked.

'Scoundrel? You mean Shandar?'

Maltcassion roared and a sheet of flame burst from

his throat and shot across the clearing in front of me, where it ignited a mature Douglas fir. The tree went up like a Roman candle. I took a few hasty steps back from the heat.

'I told you not to mention his name!'

'I don't understand,' I yelled above the crackling of the burning tree. He beckoned me to move away and I joined him.

'Why do you think you are the first Dragonslayer to ever come up to the Dragonlands?'

'I don't know.'

'Then let me ask you something else. Why do you suppose you are here at all?'

I thought the question a bit obvious but answered nonetheless.

'To slay any Dragons guilty of violating the Dragonpact?'

'But in four centuries none of us has *ever* violated the pact. Have you any idea why?'

'Because you respect the Dragonpact?'

'No. I'll tell you. Shandar suggested the use of a force-field surrounding the marker stones to keep humans out. Such an act of magic is vast; he requested that we help him and we readily agreed, binding the magic of the marker stones so tightly it could never be undone except by the death of the Dragon it was there to protect.'

'And?'

'He tricked us. The weave of the magic was tighter than we imagined. The marker stones don't just keep humans out, *but us in*. These Dragonlands are not a safe haven but a prison!'

I digested this new information.

'Then the Dragonpact wasn't a pact at all!'

'Exactly. Shandar earned his twenty dray-weights of gold, believe me. The first Dragon who tried to get out of his lands was vaporised instantly. We sent around a message warning of the danger, and here we have sat, dwindling in numbers, communicating rarely and watching our magic slowly siphoned out of us by the energy of the very force-field that was meant to protect us!'

'So why have Dragonslayers at all?'

'Window dressing,' replied the Dragon. 'The Dragonslayers, far from being a most noble profession, are really nothing more than a contractual obligation. In Shandar's plan you would never have come up here at all.'

'Then . . . I don't have to kill you.'

The Dragon raised a claw in the air and wagged it at me.

'Well, that's the *wrong* answer, I'm afraid,' he said reproachfully. 'We've planned this for a long time. You were chosen by us to do this deed; at midday you *have* to kill me!'

I could feel large salty tears well up in my eyes. It all seemed so unfair.

'But I've never killed anything in my life!'

'Big Magic is by definition highly specific. Someone like you *must* do it.'

'What's special about me? Why can't Sir Matt Grif-flon do it?'

'You are more special than you realise, Jennifer.'

I stared up at the old Dragon, hearing what I had suspected for a while, and had been confirmed to me by Mother Zenobia and recent events. Something astonishing was going to happen, and I was going to be part of it. My life had been leading up to this moment. I had a purpose.

'I'm ready,' I said in a quiet voice, 'tell me what is expected of me.'

The Dragon fixed me with his jewel-like eyes.

'You already know what is expected of you, Jennifer. I wish I had the answers but I don't. I am only the last in a long line of greater minds. All I know is that you have to discharge your duty using your own free will and judgement. This is your moment. You will do the right thing.'

I picked up Exhorbitus as a clock started to strike twelve somewhere in the distance, and Maltcassion lifted his chin to reveal the soft flesh beneath his throat. I started to cry, large drops that ran down my face and on to the soft earth. Sometimes one's destiny takes you to dark places that you'd rather not be, but destiny, as they say, is destiny.

I held the sword aloft as a light wind whipped the leaves and twigs into motion. I placed the tip against his skin and paused.

'Goodbye, Jennifer, *Gwanjii*. I forgive you,' he said.

I closed my eyes and thrust the sword upwards as hard as I could. The effect was immediate, and dramatic. Maltcassion shuddered and slumped to the ground with a mighty crash. A large cloud of dust was thrown up by his falling bulk and knocked me backwards into the dirt. I was momentarily winded and struggled to my feet, expecting some sort of magic to start happening. I stole a glance at Maltcassion then hurriedly looked away. The jewel in his forehead had stopped glowing and an unnerving silence invaded the forest.

Abruptly, the marker stone in the centre of his lair stopped humming. What if I had been wrong? Big Magic, Wizard Moobin had told me, has rarely more than a 20 per cent success rate. I had trusted Maltcassion and done what he had asked but there was no magic. No high winds, no noises, no mysterious flashes of light, no 'bzzz' sounds – *nothing*. If this was Big Magic, it was a grave disappointment. I suddenly felt very small and solitary. One person alone in 320 square miles of disputed territory, sandwiched right between two huge armies with artillery and landships, and with only forty tons of dead Dragon for company. I apologised to the large beast but he could not hear me. It was over. The ancient order of the Dragons was dead.

Anger

I stood up and looked around at the forest, wondering what to do. Far in the distance there was the crack of an artillery piece. A few seconds later and a faint whistle preceded a shell that exploded somewhere in the Dragonlands. That was the sign. The war had begun. Everything that had happened over the past few days now seemed unimportant. I had failed Wizard Moobin and the Big Magic, I had failed Maltcassion and the centuries-dead Dragon Council. Maltcassion had suggested I was chosen for this task because of some kind of purity or moral rectitude that he thought I possessed. I was obviously not good enough. I had felt no remorse when Gordon of Stroud was vaporised and I felt nothing but disgust for ConStuff, King Snodd and the hordes of claimants that waited eagerly outside the Dragonlands. I had once tugged at the convent cat's tail, too. Perhaps there had been a mistake; perhaps there was *another* Jennifer Strange somewhere. One with true purity and goodness. A Jennifer with nothing but forgiveness who had never tugged at a cat's tail and led a blameless and charitable life. Perhaps she would have triumphed.

There was another distant *crack* and a second artillery shell came whistling over and exploded, opening up a hole in the fertile earth of the Dragonlands. I looked again at the old Dragon. He looked more like a huge pile of rubble than he ever had before. Perhaps in years to come someone would remember what had happened here and open a small museum that explained what the Dragonlands had been like, the treachery of the Mighty Shandar and the final effort of the Dragons to survive. On the other hand, perhaps they wouldn't bother. They'd probably build a museum to Yogi Baird – and it would as likely as not be sponsored by Yummy-Flakes breakfast cereals.

I sat on the trunk of a fallen tree and listened as another shell was lobbed into the lands. Only a few more minutes and the battle would begin. King Snodd's massive landships would lumber across the hills, churning up the ground with their heavy tracks, laying waste to all before them as they pushed their way towards the Duchy of Brecon and beyond in their campaign to conquer Wales. I ducked instinctively as a shell landed in the forest about a hundred yards away and felled an old Douglas fir, which crashed into the undergrowth with a tearing of foliage. But their aim was wild and erratic. The Hereford gunners were firing blind into the Dragonlands.

I noticed that my pulse had started to race, and I felt hot and angry. I pulled at the collar of my shirt as a bad feeling started to rise within me like a fever. I clenched my fists as a red veil of rage descended upon me. I tried to swallow the anger down but it was too strong. I simmered for a few seconds, then I boiled. All rational thought vanished. I was out of control. The image of the Quarkbeast and the leering face of Gordon assaulted my mind.

I thought of the crowds around the Dragonlands, waiting for the moment of the Dragon's death with greedy expectation. Suddenly, I wanted to run to the marker stones and attack and kill and maim as many of the greedy, bloodsucking, Dragon-hating people as I could.

I leapt for Exhorbitus and grasped the hilt. My hand latched on to it with a tightness that made me cry out in pain. I felt strong enough to take on a land-ship, tear at its iron hull with my bare hands and face the guns with an iron resolve. I let fly at a boulder with the sword, hoping to release the rage that rose within me; the boulder fell neatly in two but I felt more angry, not less. A noise like a hurricane had started in my head and every muscle in my body tightened like a spring.

Then the pain started. It was like a burning sensation that attacked every nerve ending in my body. Instinctively I knew of only one form of relief; I opened my mouth and screamed. It was quite a scream. They heard it at the marker stones. They heard it in Hereford. Animals turned and fled and milk curdled in the churns. Babies cried in their cots and horses bolted. But it wasn't just a scream. It was more. It was a pointer, a marker, a conduit for other energy to follow, like the small spark that precedes a lightning bolt.

I pointed the blade of Exhorbitus at Maltcassion and from the blued steel there flowed a sinuous white source of energy that moved into the old Dragon's body and made the lifeless husk squirm and dance. I carried on screaming, the noise dominating everything around me. The dust started to lift from the ground and the water began to steam. The trees shed their leaves and birds dropped unconscious from the sky. I saw more shells falling to earth in a slow and lazy arc, but I could not hear them. One of them exploded near by and I felt a piece of shrapnel pluck at my sleeve.

A tree fell in the clearing but I didn't flinch. All that mattered to me was the power of the scream, the uncontrolled rage that wrung the energy from the air. The sky darkened and a bolt of lightning descended to the marker stone, splitting it in two. But it couldn't last. A darkness opened up in front of me as I screamed the last of the air from my lungs. I knew then that my scream was everything. It was all consuming. It was the scream of Dragons long dead, it was the collective emotion of millions of people. It was other things but most of all it was a scream of renewal. It was the Big Magic.

The New Order

'Is it dead?' said a voice.

'Not it, *she*,' said a second.

'I can never tell the difference. Is *she* dead, then?'

'I hope not.'

I opened my eyes and found myself staring into the kindly face of not one but *two* Dragons. They were not that much different to Maltcassion except considerably smaller and a great deal younger. My temper had left me; all I was left with was an aching body and throbbing temples.

'Have either of you a paracetamol?' I croaked, my throat feeling as though I had slept with a toad in my mouth.

The Dragon who had spoken first gave a sort of harrumphing cough that I took to be a snigger.

'We are glad you still have your sense of humour.'

I sat up.

'My sense of humour I kept,' I replied, clutching my head and groaning. 'What I lost was Maltcassion, the Quarkbeast, the Dragonlands and most of free Wales.'

'You could do with a drink,' said the second Dragon. He nodded and a glass of water appeared beside me.

'How did you do that?' I asked suddenly.

'*Magic,*' replied the Dragon.

I smiled and sipped at it gratefully.

'Hmm,' said the first of the Dragons as he unfurled his wings and looked at them thoughtfully, the same way a baby might examine its own foot and wonder what it was for.

'Two of you?' I asked. 'Two from one? Is that how it works?'

'Usually,' replied the second Dragon. It sneezed violently and a small jet of flame leapt across the clearing and ignited a shrub.

'Whoops,' he said. 'I'm going to have to get *that* under control.'

The two Dragons sniffed around, eager to investigate their new world. Of Maltcassion there was no sign, just a forehead-jewel on top of a pile of grey ash that was being blown by a light wind into the Dragonlands.

'Shh!' I said. 'Listen!'

They both cocked an ear into the breeze and frowned.

'We don't hear anything.'

'That's exactly it!' I replied. 'The guns. They've *stopped.*'

'Of course,' countered the Dragon. 'The Old Magic

is unwoven. New Magic has taken its place. The force-field is back up but we may pass freely in both directions. The Dragonlands are still Dragonlands. But I have no manners. Allow me to introduce myself. My name is Feldspar Axiom Firebreath IV, and this is Colin.'

Colin the Dragon bowed solemnly and said:

'We would like to thank you, Miss Strange, for without your fortitude and adherence to duty, dear Maltcassion really *would* have been the last Dragon.'

I thought for a moment, trying to make sense of the strange course of events. I had lost my temper in a big way; I was confused.

'I wasn't chosen for my purity, was I?'

'I'm afraid not,' replied Feldspar. 'But don't be disappointed. It's as well that true virtue is rare, for it would have to be balanced by the purest evil. The Dragon Council chose well. I would never have guessed in a million years that you were a Berserker.'

I looked at them both in turn.

'A Berserker? Me?'

'Of course. Didn't you know?'

Now I came to think of it, I had always been in control of my temper – perhaps as a result of long-forgotten tantrums as a child. Perhaps Mother Zenobia knew more about me than she had ever revealed. Now I knew, of course, I would have to be careful – I was a member of a rare class of fearless warriors – a person who could draw energy from those about them during uncontrollable bouts of rage and channel it with terrifying violence against a foe. Even rarer, I was a Berserker who could *contain their temper.* If I let it be known I would almost certainly be the subject of relentless study. I shuddered at the prospect.

'You won't tell anyone?'

'You would be surprised how many concealed Berserkers walk among the citizenry. You have a gift. Learn to use it wisely.'

'So you planned all this?'

'It was a grand plan, Jennifer, a plan forty decades in the making. When Shandar imprisoned us we knew that as individuals we could do nothing to unweave the strong magic. Dragons have always been renewed by death. Kill one and two rise in its place. Mu'shad Waseed didn't know that but Shandar did. That's why he didn't want you to kill Maltcassion. A Dragon that dies of old age leaves no offspring.'

'So any time in the past four hundred years a Dragonslayer could have killed a Dragon and added one more to the population?'

'It wouldn't have done much good. Two Dragons imprisoned instead of one? No; we needed to do more. We needed a spell to overcome all that Shandar had done and a little bit more besides. A spell of almost incalculable size and complexity. A spell that could release us and also recharge the power of wizardry, lest Shandar return to make good his promise to destroy the Dragons. He is an evil man, but an honourable one, and twenty dray-weights of gold is a sizeable chunk of change – and I'm not sure he's the sort of Wizard who likes giving refunds.'

'Big Magic.'

'*Precisely*. But Big Magic is unpredictable stuff, and we were still without the vast quantity of raw wizidrical energy to make it work. Shandar cast the spell, so we would need *more* than the power of Shandar to undo it. Such a power is spread too thinly upon this planet to be useful – we needed to find a way to collect it.'

'Like the grains of gold on the beach,' I murmured, remembering Mother Zenobia's words.

'Just so. Valuable but essentially worthless since you can't extract it. The power that comes closest to the energy that makes up what we call magic is human emotion. The power in one person is negligible, but a large group of people can generate an almost limitless amount of energy.'

'Emotion? You mean like love?'

'Powerful, I agree,' conceded Feldspar, 'but impossible to generate artificially. *Avarice*, on the other hand, is far more simple to create. All we needed to do was gather together a lot of humans and the tantalising possibility of something for nothing.'

'The claims,' I whispered. 'The Dragonlands.'

'Precisely. At eleven fifty-nine and fifty-five seconds

284

there were eight million people staring anxiously at their watches, their hearts beating faster, the sweat raised on their brows in expectation of claiming enough land to retire. Greed is all powerful, greed conquers all. Greed channelled the Big Magic; greed set us free.'

'But why leave so much to chance?'

'Big Magic works in mysterious ways, Jennifer. If you push destiny it has a nasty habit of pushing back. All things must come together, in confluence. There had to be you, death by Exhorbitus and all that raw emotion. Once Maltcassion was sure you were ready, he used the last of the Dragon's magic to send out the premonition of his own death and a broad feeling of greed that caught on like a virus. He knew a bit about ConStuff and a lot about human nature. Once the crowds were gathered the death of a Dragon would kickstart the spell, with you as the Berserker to draw the power from those around you and Exhorbitus to channel the power. I think you'll agree that it all turned out rather well.'

I digested what he had said. Maltcassion had sown, farmed and then harvested the emotional energy from eight million people. The Dragons had defeated the most powerful wizard the world had ever known, and taken over four hundred years to do it. Maltcassion had given his life to make it happen. I sighed.

'We sense your sorrow, Jennifer. If it's any consolation

there is much in us that was Maltcassion. He hasn't gone for good, just, well, *fragmented* slightly.'

'So what happens now?'

'Well,' said Colin, 'the Dragonslayer's work is done. We will live here and grow strong. We want only peace with humans and have much to teach you. You will come and see us, and you will be our ambassador. We thank you again for all you have done.'

I picked up Exhorbitus from where it had fallen. It was a fine weapon, worthy of a Berserker if he or she were ever to have need of it. When I had grown older and was stronger, perhaps I might even learn to wield it with skill. I bowed to both Dragons using the traditional method of departure and they returned the compliment. I walked a few paces then turned back. There was still one question I wanted to ask.

'Maltcassion used a word just before he died. He called me a *Gwanjii*.'

'Ah,' replied Feldspar solemnly, 'that is an old Dragon word. A word that one Dragon might use to another perhaps twice in his lifetime.'

'What does it mean?'

'It means *friend*.'

The End of the Story

I drove back to the marker stones to find that the avaricious spell had been broken. Everyone was packing up to leave, wondering why they had sat on a hillside for five days drinking stewed tea and eating stale cake. The landships and artillery stood silent, the soldiers waiting for orders to advance that never came. The Berserkers had stopped hitting each other with bricks and were calming themselves by doing tricks with yo-yos.

Wizard Moobin met me as I stepped across the boundary. He was grinning wildly and shook my hand vigorously.

'You did it!' he shouted as he hugged me.

'At a price, Moobin, at a price.'

He guessed my meaning and wrapped a blanket about my shoulders. I was shaking badly and had a fever. My throat was badly inflamed; I was to sleep for almost three days.

Within a week only a sea of wastepaper and acres of mud around the Dragonlands gave you any idea that eight million people had eagerly awaited an event that never took place. King Snodd and Brecon did not go to war, or at least, not then. Magic had returned to the planet with added vigour. Every one of the sorcerers at Zambini Towers found their powers had increased; it would make it much much easier to hire out their talents.

I gave the entire Dragonslayer merchandising rights to the Troll Wars Widows Association, which made very good use of it. We often see the Dragons flying across the town as they explore the land, and I noted that the Consolidated Useful Stuff Land Development Corporation was made bankrupt a month later.

After some legal wranglings and a week in prison I was granted a reluctant pardon by the King and returned to run the Kazam Magic Agency, where both Tiger Prawns and I remain – after several adventures – to this day. I keep the sword Exhorbitus in a cupboard in case I have any need for it in the future, and I am careful never to lose my temper. I give as much time and energy to the Berserkers' Benevolent Fund as I can but never tell anyone why. It's safer that way. I was delighted to speak at Mother Zenobia's 182nd birthday two months later, although we told her it was only her 160th in case she got depressed. Transient Moose is still hanging around Zambini Towers, the Mysterious X became *more* mysterious and Lady Mawgon remains our most aggressive critic. The Great Zambini has still not reappeared and, luckily, neither has the Mighty Shandar – but we hold frequent strategy meetings on what to do if he does.

As for the Quarkbeast, without whom there would be no Jennifer Strange and thus no Big Magic or Dragons, we thought it would be fitting to raise a large statue in his honour outside Zambini Towers. Several people screamed and fainted at the unveiling and it often frightens animals and small children.

I think it's what he would have wanted.

Jasper Fforde is the critically acclaimed author of *Shades of Grey*, the Nursery Crime books: *The Big Over Easy* and *The Fourth Bear* and the Thursday Next novels: *The Eyre Affair*, *Lost in a Good Book*, *The Well of Lost Plots*, *Something Rotten*, *First Among Sequels* and *One of Our Thursdays is Missing*. The next instalment in the Last Dragonslayer series, *The Song of the Quarkbeast*, comes out in 2011.

After giving up a varied career in the film world, Jasper now lives and writes in Wales, and has a passion for aviation.

You can visit www.jasperfforde.com to find out more.

Loved *The Last Dragonslayer*?
Read on for a taste of the next fantastic
book in the series . . .

The Song of the Quarkbeast

Jasper Fforde

As the background Wizidrical Power slowly builds after
the Big Magic, King Snodd IV of Hereford realises the
man who controls magic controls almost anything.

But one person stands between him and his plans for
power and riches: Jennifer Strange, sixteen-year-old
acting manager of Kazam.

It may involve a trip on a magic carpet at the speed
of sound to the Troll Wall, it may involve a second
Quarkbeast sniffing around town. It might also involve
the mysterious Transient Moose, and a powerless
sorceress named Once Magnificent Boo. But one thing
is certain: Jennifer Strange and her faithful assistant Tiger
Prawns will not relinquish the noble powers of magic
to big business and commerce without a fight.

Available from November 2011

HODDER &
STOUGHTON

'For every Quarkbeast there is an equal and opposite Quarkbeast'

Miss Boolean Smith, Sorcerer (Rtd)

Where we are right now

I work in the Magic industry. I think you'll agree it's pretty glamorous: a life full of spells, potions and whispered enchantments; of levitation, vanishings and alchemy. Of titanic fights to the death with the powers of darkness; of conjuring up blizzards, and quelling storms at sea; of casting lightning bolts from mountains; and bringing statues to life in order to vanquish troublesome foes.

If only.

No, magic these days was simply *useful*. Useful in the same way that cars and dishwashers and can-openers are useful. The days of wild, crowd-pleasing stuff like commanding the oceans, levitating elephants and turning fish into taxi drivers were long gone, and despite the advent of a Big Magic[1] two months before, the return of unlimited magical powers had not yet happened. After a brief surge that generated weird cloud shapes and rain that tasted of elderflower cordial, the wizidrical power had dropped to nothing before

---

[1] It's a sort of rekindling of magic that happened two months before the time of this story, and in which Jennifer played a large part.

rising again almost painfully slowly. No one would be doing any ocean commanding for a while, elephants would remain unlevitated and a herring wouldn't be losing anyone wanting to get to the airport. We had no foes to vanquish except the taxman, and the only time we got to fight the powers of darkness was during one of the Kingdom's frequent power cuts.

So while we at Kazam waited for magic to re-establish itself, it was very much business as usual: hiring out sorcerers to conduct low-level, mundane and very practical magic. You know the sort of thing: plumbing and rewiring, wallpapering and loft conversions. We also lifted cars for the city's clamping unit, conducted flying carpet pizza deliveries and could predict weather with 23% more accuracy than SNODD-TV's favourite weather girl, Daisy Fairchild.

But I don't do any of that. I *can't* do any of that. I organise those who can. I'm in 'Mystical Arts Management' or an agent, more simply put. The person who does the deals, takes the bookings and then gets all the flak when things go wrong – and little of the credit when it goes right. And the place I do all this is a company called Kazam, the biggest House of Enchantment in the world. To be honest that's not saying much – there are only two: Kazam and Industrial Magic, over in Stroud. Between us we have the only eight licensed sorcerers on the planet. And if you think that's a responsible job for a sixteen-year-old, you're right – I'm really only *acting* manager until the Great Zambini gets back.

If he does.

So as I said, it was very much business as usual at Kazam, and this morning we were going to try to find something that was lost. Not just 'mislaid-it-whoops' lost which is easy, but 'never-to-be-found' lost which is a good deal harder. We didn't much like finding lost stuff as in general lost stuff doesn't like to be found, but when work was slack, we'd do pretty much anything within the law. And that's why Perkins, Tiger and I were sitting in my parked Volkswagen one damp autumn morning in a roadside rest area not six miles from our home town of Hereford.

'Do you think a wizard even knows what a clock is *for*?' I asked, somewhat exasperated, as I had promised our client that we'd start at 9:30 a.m. *sharp*, and it was twenty past already. I'd told them to get here at 9:00 for a briefing, but I might as well have been talking to the flowers.

'If you have all the time in the world,' replied Tiger, referring to a sorcerer's often greatly increased longevity, 'then I suppose a few minutes either way doesn't matter so much.'

Horton or 'Tiger' Prawns was my assistant and had been with us only for the past two months. He was tall for his twelve years and had close-curled sandy-coloured hair and freckles that danced around a snub nose. Like most foundlings of that age, he wore his oversized hand-me-downs with a certain pride. He was here to learn the peculiar problems associated with a finding – and with good reason. He was to take over from me in two years' time. Once I was eighteen, I was out.

Perkins nodded an agreement.

'Some wizards do seem to live a long time,' he observed. This was undoubtedly true, but they were always cagey about how they did it, and changed the subject to mice or onions or something when asked.

The Youthful Perkins was our best and only trainee all wrapped up in one. He had been at Kazam just over a year and was the only person in the company roughly my own age. He was good-looking, too, and aside from suffering bouts of overconfidence that sometimes got him into trouble when he spelled quicker than he thought, he would be good for the company and good for magic in general. I liked him, too, but since his particular field of interest was *remote suggestion* – the skill of projecting thoughts into people's heads at a distance – I didn't know whether I actually liked him or he was *suggesting* I like him, which was creepy and unethical all at the same time. In fact, the whole remote suggestion or 'seeding' idea was banned once it was discovered to be the key ingredient behind advertising and promoting talentless boy bands, something that had until then been something of a mystery.

I looked at my watch again. The sorcerers[2] we were waiting for were the Amazing Dennis 'Full' Price and Lady Mawgon. Despite their magical ability, Mystical Arts Practitioners – to give them their official title – could barely get their clothes on in the right order, and often needed to be reminded to have a bath and attend regular mealtimes. Wizards are like that – erratic, petulant, forgetful, passionate, and *hugely* frustrating. But the one thing they weren't was boring, and after a difficult start when I first came to work here, I now regarded them all with a great deal of fondness – even the *really* insane ones.

'I should really be back at the Towers revising,' grumbled the Youthful Perkins, who had his Magic Licence hearing that afternoon and was understandably a bit jumpy.

'Full Price suggested you come along to observe,' I explained, 'Finding lost stuff is all about teamwork.'

'I thought sorcerers didn't like teamwork?' asked Tiger who, after ice-cream and waffles, enjoyed questions more than anything else.

'The old days of lone wizards mixing weird potions in the top of the north tower are over,' I said, 'they've got to learn to work together, and it's not just me who says it – the Great Zambini was very keen on

2 After a well-argued plea for gender equality at the World Magic Expo of 1921, 'sorcerers' refer to male or female practitioners. The feminine 'sorceress' is no longer used, except by some of the old duffers who think that a female sorcerer's place is in the home, conjuring up food and cleaning the house by thought power alone.

rewriting the rulebook.' I looked at my watch. 'I hope they actually *do* turn up,' I added, for as Kazam's acting manager in the Great Zambini's absence, I was the one who did the grovelling apologies to any disgruntled clients – something I did more than I would have liked.

'Even so,' said Perkins, 'I've passed my Finding Module IV, and always found the slipper, even when it was hidden under Mysterious X's bed.'

This was true, and while finding something random like a slipper was good practice if you wanted to learn to find stuff, there was more to it than that. In the Mystical Arts, there always is. The only thing you really get to figure out after a lifetime of study is that there's more stuff to figure out. Frustrating and enlightening, all in one.

'The slipper had no issues with being found,' I said in an attempt to explain the unexplainable, 'if something doesn't want to be found, then it's harder. The Mighty Shandar could hide things in plain sight by simply *occluding* them from view. He demonstrated the technique most famously with an unseen elephant in the room during the 1826 World Magic Expo.'

'Is that where the 'elephant in the room' expression comes from?'

'Yes; his name was Daniel.'

'You should be taking the Magic Test on my behalf,' remarked Perkins gloomily, 'you know a lot more than

I do; there are whole tracts of the *Codex Magicalis*[3] I haven't even read.'

'I've been here three years longer than you,' I pointed out, 'so I'm bound to know more. But having me take your test would be like asking a person with no hands to sit your piano exam.'

No one knew why some people could do magic and others couldn't. I'm not good on the theory behind magic, other than knowing it's a fusion between science and faith, but the practical way of looking at it is this: magic swirls about us like an invisible fog of energy which can be tapped by those gifted enough using a variety of techniques that centre around layered spelling, mumbled incantations and a channelled burst of concentrated thought from the index fingers. The technical name for this energy was the 'variable electro-gravitational mutable subatomic force' which doesn't mean anything at all — confused scientists just gave it an important-sounding name so as not to lose face. The more usual term was: 'wizidrical energy', or more simply: 'the crackle'.

'Hey,' said Perkins in a breezy manner, 'I've got two tickets to see Jimmy "Daredevil" Nuttjob have himself fired from a cannon through a brick wall.'

Jimmy Nuttjob was the Kingdom's most celebrated travelling daredevil, and tickets to see his madcap stunts

---

3 The so-called 'Book of Magic', which while full of useful stuff, also has a lot in it that is nonsense. The skill is finding out which is which.

were much in demand. He had eaten a car tyre to live orchestral accompaniment the year before; it had been a great show until he nearly choked on the valve.

'Who are you taking?' I asked, glancing at Tiger. The 'will Perkins gather up the courage to ask me out?' issue had been going on for a while.

Perkins cleared his throat as he built up the courage.

'You, if you want to come.'

I said nothing and stared at the road for a moment, then said: 'Who, me?'

'Yes, of course you,' said Perkins.

'You might have been talking to Tiger.'

'Why would I ask Tiger to watch a lunatic fire themselves through a brick wall?'

'Why *wouldn't* you ask me?' asked Tiger in a mock-aggrieved tone, 'watching some idiot damage themselves might be just my thing.'

'That's entirely possible,' agreed Perkins, 'but while there's a prettier alternative, you'll always remain ninth or tenth on my list.'

We all fell silent.

'Pretty?' I said, swivelling in the driver's seat to face him, 'you want to ask me out because I'm pretty?'

'Is there a problem with asking you out because you're pretty?'

'I think you blew it,' said Tiger with a grin, 'you should be asking her out because she's smart, witty, mature beyond her years and because every moment in her company makes you want to be a better person – pretty of face should be at the *bottom* of the list.'

'Oh, blast,' said Perkins despondently, 'It should, shouldn't it?'

'At last!' I muttered as we heard the distinctive *dugadugadugaduga* of Lady Mawgon's motorcycle, and we climbed out of the car as she came to a stop. I caught her eye almost immediately, but wished I hadn't as she was wearing her 'I'm about to harangue Jennifer' sort of look. Of course, being harangued by Lady Mawgon was nothing new; in fact, I was often harangued by her at lunch, dinner, and teatime – and at random times in between. She was our most powerful sorcerer, and also the crabbiest. She was so crabby, in fact, that even really crabby people put their crabbiness aside for a few minutes to write her gushing yet mildly sarcastic fan letters.

'Lady Mawgon,' I said in a bright voice, bowing low as protocol dictated, 'I trust the day finds you well?'

'An idiotic expression made acceptable only because it is adrift in a sea of equally idiotic expressions,' she muttered grumpily, stepping from the motorcycle that she rode side-saddle, naturally, 'is that little twerp attempting to hide behind what you jokingly refer to as a car?'

'Good morning,' said Tiger in his best 'gosh, didn't

see you there I wasn't really hiding' voice, 'you are looking *most* well this morning.'

Tiger was lying. Lady Mawgon looked terrible, with lank hair, a complexion like dented bells and a sour, pinched face. Her lips had never seen a smile, and rarely passed an intentional friendly word. She was dressed in a long black bell-shaped crinoline dress that was buttoned up to her throat in one direction, and swept the floor in the other. When she moved it was as if on roller skates; she didn't so much walk but *glide* across the ground in a very disturbing manner. Tiger had bet me half a moolah that she actually did wear roller skates. Trouble was, neither of us could think of a good, safe or respectful method of finding out.

She greeted Perkins more politely as he was, like her, of the wizidrical calling, and talked briefly about his magic test and how important it was he passed. She didn't waste a salutation on either of us as Tiger and I were foundlings and thus of little social rank or regard. Despite our low status, our presence aggravated Lady Mawgon badly as Tiger and I were crucial to the smooth running of the company. It was how Kazam's founder the Great Zambini liked it. He always felt that foundlings were better equipped to deal with the somewhat bizarre world of Mystical Arts Management. He thought that 'pampered civilians' would panic at the weirdness or think they knew better, or try to improve things, or get greedy and try to cash in.

'While you're here,' announced Lady Mawgon, breaking into my thoughts, 'I need to run a test spell later this morning.'

'How many Shandars, Ma'am?'

The 'Shandar' was the unit of wizidrical power, named after the Mighty Shandar himself, a mage so powerful his footsteps spontaneously caught fire when he walked. The practical use of flaming footprints was questionable and most likely just for dramatic effect – the Mighty Shandar was not only the most powerful wizard who had ever lived, but also something of a showman.

'About ten Meg[4],' said Lady Mawgon sullenly, annoyed at the ignominy of having to run her test spells past me first.

'That's a considerable amount of crackle,' I said as I wondered what she was up to, and hoped she wouldn't attempt to bring her pet cat Mr Pusskins back to some sort of semi-life, an act not only *seriously* creepy, but highly frowned upon, 'may I inquire as to what you are planning to do?'

'I'm going to try and hack into the Dibble Storage Coils. It may help us with the bridge job.'

I breathed a sigh of relief. This changed matters considerably, and she was right. We had agreed to rebuild Hereford's medieval bridge on Friday, and we needed all the help we could get, which was why

---

4 One thousand Shandars = one MegaShandar, more usually referred to as a 'Meg' after 'Old Meg McMeddoes', an early proponent of Magical Field Theory.

Perkins was taking his magic test today rather than next week. He'd still be a novice, but six sorcerers would be better than five – magic always worked better with the wizards in use divisible by three.[5]

'Of course,' I said, consulting my pocket-book to check we had no clashes. Two sorcerers spelling at the same time could deplete the crackle, and there is nothing worse than running out of steam when only two-thirds of the way through the spell – a bit like having a power-cut just when you get to the good bit in a book.

'At eleven the Price Brothers are moving Snamoo[6], so anytime after eleven-fifteen would be good – but I'll double check with Industrial Magic just in case.'

'Eleven-fifteen it is,' replied Lady Mawgon stonily, 'You may observe, if you so choose.'

'I'll be there,' I replied, then added cautiously: 'Lady Mawgon, please don't think me insensitive, but any attempt to reanimate Mr Pusskins on the back of the Dibble Coil Hacking enchantment might be looked on unfavourably by the other wizards.'

Her eyes narrowed and she gave me one of those stares that seem to hit the back of my skull like a dozen hot needles.

---

5 No one knows why. The 'Rule of Three' crops up often and is often referred to as 'Mandrake's 3rd Dictum' after the sorcerer who first wrote about it.

6 Snamoo is the Snodd Seaworld's performing walrus. He can play *Eine Kleine Nacht-musik* on a xylophone, amongst other tricks. He only liked being moved by the Prices, and it's tricky to argue with 1.4 tons of recalcitrant sea-mammal.

'None of you have any idea what Mr Pusskins meant to me. Now, what are we doing here?'

'Waiting for the Amazing Dennis Price.'

'How I deplore poor timekeeping,' she said, despite being almost half an hour late herself, 'Got any money? I'm starving.'

Perkins gave her a one moolah coin.

'Most kind. Walk with me, Perkins.'

And she glided silently off towards a roadside snack bar that was close by.

'Do you want anything?' asked Perkins as he made to follow Lady Mawgon.

'Eating out gives foundlings ideas above their station,' came Lady Mawgon's decisive voice, quickly followed by an admonishment to the owner of the snack bar: 'How much for a bacon roll? Scandalous!'

'A running sore has more charm,' said Tiger, leaning against the car, 'and since when was a roadside snack bar eating out? That's like saying listening to the radio out-of-doors is like going to a live show.'

'She is an astonishing sorceress of considerable power and commitment, so don't be impertinent. Or at least,' I added, 'not within earshot.'

'Speaking of live shows,' said Tiger in a lowered voice, 'will you go to Jimmy "Daredevil" Nuttjob's stunt show with Perkins?'

'Probably not,' I said with a sigh, 'it's not a good idea to date someone you work with. If he and I are meant to be, it'll certainly wait the two years until I leave.'

'Good,' said Tiger.

'Why is that good?'

'Because he may give away your ticket, and I'd like to watch someone with more bravery than sense being fired from a cannon into a brick wall.'

'Is there a support act?'

'A brass band, cheerleaders, and someone who can juggle with bobcats.'

'The big cat or the earthmover?'

'I'm not sure.'

We turned to see a taxi approaching. It was the Amazing Dennis 'Full' Price, and after I had paid for the taxi, he climbed out and looked around.

'Sorry I'm late,' he said, demonstrating the difference between him and Lady Mawgon almost immediately, 'I got delayed talking to Wizard Moobin. He wants you to witness an experiment he's got cooking.'

'A dangerous one?' I asked with some concern. Wizard Moobin had destroyed more laboratories than I'd had cold and inedible dinners.

'Does he know any other?' he replied. 'Where's Mawgon?'

I nodded in the direction of the roadside snack bar.

'Not with her own money, I'll be bound,' he said, and after giving us a wink strode off to talk to her.

'Full' Price was another of our licensed operatives.

He and his brother David – known as 'Half' – were famous as the most *unidentical* identical twins on record. David was tall and thin and lofty and oft to sway in a high wind, while Dennis was short and squat like a giant pink pumpkin, only with arms and legs. They hailed from the ramshackle collection of warlord-controlled regions in mid-Wales that was loosely referred to as 'the Cambrian Empire'. Details were sparse, but it seemed the Prices had refused to work with the Cambrian Potentate who was the well-named 'Tharv the Insane', and then made their way to the Kingdom of Hereford to escape. They joined up with the Great Zambini soon after, and had been at Kazam for over twenty years.

As Tiger and I stood there smelling the faint aroma of frying bacon on the breeze, a Rolls-Royce whispered to a halt next to us.

In Pursuit of Lost Stuff

The Rolls-Royce was one of the top-of-the-range six-wheeled Phantom Twelves. It was as big as a yacht, twice as luxurious and had paintwork so perfect it looked like a pool of black paint sitting in the air. The chauffeur opened the rear passenger door and a well-dressed girl climbed out. She was not much older than me, but from a world far removed from the upbringing of a foundling – a world of privilege, cash and a sense of entitlement. I should have hated her, but I didn't – I envied her.

'Miss Strange?' she said striding confidently forward, hand outstretched, 'Miss Shard is glad to make your acquaintance.'

'Who's she talking about?' asked Tiger under his breath, looking around.

'Herself, I think,' I said, smiling broadly to welcome her, 'Good morning Miss Shard, thank you for coming. I'm Jennifer Strange.'

This was our client. She didn't look old enough to have lost something badly enough to call us, but you never knew.

'One must call me Ann,' she said kindly, 'your recent exploits of a magical variety filled one with a sense of thrilling trepidation.'

'I'm sorry?'

'It was a singular display of inspired audaciousness,' she replied.

'Is that good?' I asked, still unsure of her meaning.

'Most certainly,' she replied, 'we followed your adventures with great interest.'

'We?'

'Myself and my client. A gentleman of some knowledge, position and bearing.'

She was undoubtedly referring to someone of nobility. By long tradition royals in the Ununited Kingdoms employed others to do everything for them; only the very poorest did anything for themselves. It was said that when King Wozzle of Snowdonia tired of eating he employed someone to do it for him. He was quickly succeeded by his brother.

'I can't understand a word she's saying,' whispered Tiger.

'Tiger,' I said, keen to get rid of him before she took offence, 'why not fetch Dennis and Lady Mawgon, hmm?'

'Were they of a disingenuous countenance?' Miss Shard asked, smiling politely.

'Were who of *what*?'

'The Dragons[7],' she said, 'were they . . . unpleasant?'

'Not really,' I replied in a guarded fashion. Almost everyone wanted to know about the Dragons, and I revealed little. They valued discretion more than anything. I said nothing more, and she got the message.

'I defer to your circumspection on this issue,' she replied, with a slight bow.

'O-kay,' I said, not really getting that either, 'this is the team.'

Tiger had returned with Full Price and Lady Mawgon with Perkins bringing up the rear in his 'observing' capacity. I introduced them all and Miss Shard said something about how it was 'entirely convivial' and 'felicitous' to meet them on 'this auspicious occasion', and in return they shook hands but remained wary. It pays to distance oneself from clients, especially ones who used too many long words.

'What do you want us to find?' asked Lady Mawgon, who was always keen to get straight to the point.

'It's a ring that belonged to the mother of my client,' she said, 'he would be here personally to present his request, but finds himself unavailable due to a prolonged sabbatical.'

'Has he seen a doctor about it?' asked Tiger.

'About what?'

---

7 She was referring to Jennifer's connection with Dragons. Of the only two Dragons on the planet, she knew them both well enough for them to return her calls. Dragons usually don't.

'His prolonged sabbatical. It sounds very painful.'

She stared at him for a moment.

'It means he's on holiday.'

'Oh.'

'I apologise for the ignorance of the staff,' said Lady Mawgon, glaring at Tiger, 'but Kazam sadly requires foundling labour to function. Staff can be so difficult these days, wanting frivolous little luxuries like food, shoes, wages . . . and human dignity.'

'Please don't worry,' said Miss Shard politely, 'foundlings can be refreshingly direct sometimes.'

'About the ring?' I asked, feeling uncomfortable with all this talk of foundlings.

'Nothing remarkable,' replied Miss Shard, 'gold, plain, large like a thumb-ring. My client is keen to present it to his mother as a seventieth birthday gift.'

'I'm sure she'll be pleased,' remarked Full Price, 'do you have anything that might have been in contact with this ring?'

'Such as your client's mother?' added Tiger.

'There's this,' said Miss Shard, producing a ring from her pocket, 'This was on her middle finger, and would have clicked against the lost ring. You can observe the marks, look.'

Lady Mawgon took the ring and stared at it intently for a moment before she clenched it in her fist, murmured something and then opened her hand. The ring hovered an inch above her open palm, revolving slowly. She passed it to Full Price who held it up to the light and then popped it in his mouth, clicked it against his fillings for a moment, then swallowed it.

'Meant to do that,' he said in the tone of someone who didn't.

'Really?' asked Miss Shard dubiously, doubtless wondering how she was going to get it back and in what condition.

'Don't worry,' said Full Price cheerfully, 'amazing how powerful cleaning agents are these days.'

'Why did you ask us to meet you here?' asked Lady Mawgon, thankfully changing the subject.

It was a good question. We were on an unremarkable lay-by and rest area on the Ross–Hereford road near a village called Harewood End.

'This is where she lost it,' replied Miss Shard, 'she had it when she got out of a car here, and when she left she didn't have it any more.'

Lady Mawgon looked at me, then at our client, then at Dennis. She smelled the air, mumbled something and looked thoughtful for a moment.

'It's still around here somewhere,' she said, 'but this ring does not want to be found. You agree, Mr Price?'

'I do,' he said, rubbing his fingers together as he felt the texture in the air.

'How can you know this?' asked Miss Shard.

'It's been lost for thirty-two years, ten months and

nine days,' murmured Lady Mawgon thoughtfully, 'am I correct?'

Miss Shard stared at her for a moment. It appeared this was indeed true, and it was impressive. Mawgon had picked up the lingering memory that human emotion can instil on even the most inert of objects.

'Something that wants to be lost is lost for a good reason,' added Full Price, 'why doesn't your client give his mother some chocolates instead?'

'Or flowers,' said Lady Mawgon, 'we can't help you. Good day.'

She turned to move away.

'We'll pay you a thousand moolah[8].'

Lady Mawgon stopped. A thousand moolah was serious cash.

'A thousand?'

'My client is inclined toward generosity regarding his mother.'

Lady Mawgon looked at Full Price, then at me.

'Five thousand,' she said.

'Five thousand?' echoed our client, 'To find a ring?'

'A ring that doesn't want to be found,' replied Lady Mawgon, 'is a ring that *shouldn't* be found. The price reflects the risks.'

Miss Shard looked at us all in turn.

---

8 The moolah is the unit of currency in the Kingdom of Snodd. One hundred Herefordian washers = 1 moolah, which is roughly equivalent to the spondoolip, at 2007 exchange rates.

'I accept,' she said at last, 'and I will wait here for the results. But no find, no fee. Not even a call-out charge.'

'We usually charge for an attempt—' I began, but Mawgon cut me short.

'—we're agreed,' she said, and made a grimace that I suspect might have been her version of a smile.

Miss Shard shook hands with us again and climbed back into her Rolls-Royce, and a few seconds later the limousine moved off to park opposite the snack bar. The allure of a bacon sandwich was no barrier to class.

'With the greatest of respect,' I said turning to Lady Mawgon, 'if it gets around that we've been fleecing clients, Kazam's reputation will plummet. And what's more, I think it's unprofessional.'

'How can civilians hate us any more?' she said disdainfully and with some truth, as despite our best efforts, the general public still regarded the magic trade with suspicion, 'more importantly, I've seen the accounts. How long do you think we can give our skills away for free? Besides, she's in a Phantom Eight. Loaded with moolah.'

'It's a Phantom Twelve,' murmured Tiger, who being a boy, knew precisely the difference.

'Shall we get a move on?' said Full Price, 'I've got to move a walrus in an hour, and if I'm late David will start without me.'

'The sooner the better,' said Lady Mawgon,

dismissing Tiger and I with a sweep of her hand so she and Full could have a meeting. I leaned against the car with Tiger, took several deep breaths and watched them talk.

'Mawgon's a pest,' said Tiger, 'five grand is a total rip-off.'

'Borderline larceny, I'd say. I agree she's a pest, but quite brilliant.'

Maybe that was what it took to be an excellent sorcerer – being troublesome. Mind you, neither of the Prices were annoying, nor Wizard Moobin – just strangely unpredictable.

'I lost my luggage once,' said Tiger thoughtfully, eager to contribute something relevant to the 'losing stuff' conversation, 'On an orphanage trip to the steel mills of Port Talbot.'

'What was it like?' I asked, glad of the distraction and never having been to the industrial heartland of the Ununited Kingdoms myself.

'Red with castors and an internal pocket for toiletries.'

'I meant Port Talbot.'

'Oh. Hot and very noisy.'

'The steam hammers?'

'The steam hammers were fine. It's the *singing*.'

We watched as Perkins circled Mawgon and Price, attempting to hear what was going on.

'Is Perkins going to get his licence, do you think?'

'He'd better. We need him for the bridge job. Fumble that and we'll all look a bit stupid.'

'And on live TV, too.'

'Don't remind me.'

Our concerns about Perkins only become apparent when you consider that the person we had to get the licence from was the one person more bone-headed and corrupt than our glorious ruler King Snodd – his useless brother, who was the Minister for Infernal Affairs, the less-than-polite term used to describe the office that dealt with all things magical.

'You swallowed it?' we heard Lady Mawgon demand angrily, 'Why in Snorff's name would you do something like that?'

She must have meant the ring, and since there wasn't any real answer to this, Full Price just shrugged in a lame manner. I walked up, ready to mediate if required. Mawgon put out her hand.

'Hand it over, Dennis.'

'Can't we wait until it passes out of its own accord?' he replied somewhat sheepishly.

'We don't have the luxury of time,' replied Lady Mawgon testily, 'nor the stomach for such a thing. Migrate it.'

Full Price looked annoyed, but knew better than to argue. He closed his eyes and took a deep breath, then made a series of odd facial expressions and huffy-exertion noises before rolling up his sleeve. We saw the shape of the ring *beneath* the skin as it moved down his forearm, and as it migrated he sweated and grunted with the effort. I had seen this done several times before, the most recent to expel a bullet lodged perilously close to a patient's spine, the result of a shooting accident.

'Ah!' said Full Price, as the ring-shaped lump moved across the top of his hand, 'Ow, ow, *OW!*'

The ring travelled down the tighter skin of his finger, rotated around his fingertip and after a lot of swearing, he succeeded in expelling it from under his nail-bed.

'That is so gross,' said Tiger.

'I agree,' replied Perkins, 'but it's sort of impossible not to look, don't you think?'

'There,' said Full Price, wiping off the ring and handing it to Mawgon, 'happy now?'

But Lady Mawgon was already thinking of other things. She took the ring, murmured something around it and handed it back to Dennis who held it tightly in his fist.

'I don't like the feel of this,' he said, 'something bad happened.'

'I agree,' replied Mawgon, taking out a small crystal bottle with a silver stopper. We had stepped back to allow them to work, and Perkins, now fully mystified by what was going on, had joined us.

'They'll try to animate the memory,' I said.

'Gold has a memory?'

'Everything has a memory. Gold's memory is quite tedious – got mined, got crushed, went to the smelters, banged with a hammer – big yawn. No, we're looking for a stronger memory that has been induced on to the gold – the recollections of the person wearing it.'

'You can transfer your memories to inanimate objects?'

'Certainly. And the stronger you feel for something, the longer it will stick around. Some people think that objects like jewellery and paintings and vintage cars actually have a *soul*, but as far as we know they don't – just the memories of the people who had been around them. The more something is loved, enjoyed and valued, the stronger the memory, and the more we can read into it.'

'And the crystal bottle?'

'Watch and learn.'

Lady Mawgon placed a single drop on the ring that Full Price was holding, and in an instant a small dog was sitting on the floor wagging its tail happily. It sparkled slightly, indicating that it was not real, and seemed to be made of solid gold.

'Good boy,' said Lady Mawgon, 'Find it.'

The small memory-dog[9] gave a low bark, then scuttled off happily, sniffing the ground this way and that as it tried to remember where the ring might have

---

9 The technical term is a *Canis Mnemonicus*, or 'Mnemonic Hound'. The ability of dogs to find things has a long tradition, and was exploited quite early on by sorcerers.

gone. Lady Mawgon and Full Price followed the hound away from the road, opened a gate to let it in and then chased the small dog across a field, much to the amusement of several cows. Mawgon and Full Price stopped occasionally as the memory-dog paused to think for a while or scratch its ear with a hind leg, then carried on as it chased off in another direction. It would often double back on itself as it tried to catch the memory-scent, all the while with Lady Mawgon's index finger steadily pointed at it. Once, it thought its tail was the quarry and snapped at it, then realised and moved on.

'I wonder what did happen to it?' said Tiger as we followed the sorcerers and the dog across the field, over a stile and a smaller road, then into a small wood.

'Happened to what?'

'My luggage,' replied Tiger, who wasn't yet done on his missing luggage problem, 'luckily, it didn't have anything in it. I don't have any possessions. In fact, the luggage was my only possession. It was the one I was found in.'

Owning very little or even being found in a red suitcase with castors and a separate internal pocket for toiletries was not unusual when you consider Tiger's foundling heritage. He had been abandoned on the steps of the Sisterhood of the Blessed Ladies of the Lobster the same as me, then sold into servitude with Kazam Mystical Arts until he was eighteen. I still had two years to run before I could apply for citizenship; Tiger had six. We didn't complain because this was how things were. There were a lot of orphans due to the hideously wasteful and annoyingly frequent Troll Wars, and hotels, fast-food joints and laundries needed the cheap labour that foundlings could provide. Of the twenty-three Kingdoms, Duchies, Socialist collectives, Public Limited Companies and ramshackle Potentates that made up the Ununited Kingdoms, only three of them had outlawed the trade in foundlings. Unluckily for us, the Kingdom of Snodd was not one of them.

'When we have some surplus crackle we'll retrieve your luggage,' I said, knowing how valuable any connection to parents was to a foundling. I had been left on the front seat of the Volkswagen Beetle that I drove today, and little would part me from my car.

'It's okay,' he said, demonstrating the selflessness and humility by which most foundlings carried themselves, 'It can wait.'

We followed Mawgon, Full Price and the memory-dog out of the small wood and through a gate into an abandoned farm. Brambles, creepers and hazel saplings had grown over much of the red-brick buildings, and rusty machinery stood in abandoned stables with dilapidated roofs. No one had been here for a while. The memory-dog ran across the yard and stopped at an abandoned water-well where it wagged its tail excitedly. As soon as Lady Mawgon caught up with it she made a flourish and the dog started to chase its tail until it was nothing more than a golden blur, then back into the ring which continued spinning on a flag-stone with a curious humming noise.

Lady Mawgon picked up the ring and gave it back to me. It was still warm and smelled of puppies. Full Price pulled an old door off the wellhead, and we all gazed down the brick-lined well. Far below in the inky blackness I could see a small circle of sky with the shape of our heads as our reflections stared back up at us staring down.

'It's in there,' she said.

'And there it should stay,' replied Full Price, who still wasn't happy, 'I can feel something wrong.'

'How wrong?' I asked.

'Seventh circle of wrong. I can sense the lingering aftertaste of an old spell, too.'

There was silence for a moment as everyone took this in, and a coldness seemed to emanate up from the well.

'I can sense something, too,' said Perkins, 'like that feeling you get when someone you don't like is looking over your shoulder.'

'It doesn't want to be found,' said Full Price.

'No,' said Perkins, '*someone* doesn't want it to be found.'

They all looked one another. Missing objects are one thing, but purposefully hidden objects quite another.

'I can think of five thousand good reasons to find it,' said Lady Mawgon, 'so find it we shall.'

She put her hand above the well in order to draw the ring from the mud below, but instead of the ring rising, her hand was tugged sharply downwards.

'It's been anchored and resists my command,' she said with a voice tinged more with intrigue than concern, 'Mr Price?'

Full joined her and they both attempted to lift the ring from the well. But no sooner had they started the lift than a low rumble seemed to come from the earth beneath our feet and the bricks that made up the low wall started to shift. Tiger and I took a step back but the others simply watched as an old and long-forgotten enchantment moved the bricks into a new configuration, sealing the wellhead tight. Within a few seconds there was only a solid brick cap.

'Fascinating,' said Lady Mawgon, for this was in effect a battle of wits between sorcerers – just separated by thirty years. Whatever enchantment had been left to keep the ring hidden, it was still powerful.

'I vote we walk away now,' said Full Price.

'It's a challenge,' retorted Lady Mawgon excitedly, 'and I like a challenge.'

She was more animated than I had seen her for a

while, and within a few minutes had formulated a plan.

'Right then,' she said, 'listen closely. Mr Price is going to reopen the wellhead using a standard Magnaflux Reversal. How long, Mr Price?'

Full Price sucked air in through his teeth thoughtfully.

'About thirty seconds – maximum forty.'

'Should be enough. But since the ring is *resisting* a lift we will have to send someone down to get it. I will levitate them head downwards to the bottom of the well, where they will retrieve the ring. You, Mr Perkins, will channel the crackle to Mr Price and myself. Can you do that?'

'To the best of my ability, Ma'am,' replied Perkins happily. Lady Mawgon had never asked him to assist her before.

'He doesn't have a licence,' I said, 'you know what the penalty could be.'

'Who's going to snitch on him?' she retorted, 'You?'

'I can't allow it,' I said.

'It's Perkin's call,' said Mawgon, looking at me angrily, 'Mr Perkins?'

Perkins looked at me and then Lady Mawgon.

'I'll do it.'

I didn't say anything more as we all knew the consequences of operating without a licence were extremely unpleasant. The relationship between the populace and

Mystical Art Practitioners had always been one of suspicion, a relationship not helped by a regrettable episode in the nineteenth century when a wayward sorcerer who called himself 'Blix the Barbarous' thought he could use his powers to achieve world domination. He was eventually defeated, but the damage to magic's reputation had been deep and far-reaching. Bureaucracy now dominated the industry with a sea of paperwork and licensing requirements. Reinventing sorcery as a useful and safe commodity akin to electricity had taken two centuries and wasn't done yet. Once lost, trust is a difficult thing to regain. But I said nothing more. I was there to remind them of the rules, not to police them.

'Good,' said Lady Mawgon, 'let's begin.'

'Wait a minute,' said Tiger, who had just figured out that the 'going down a well headfirst' plan doubtless included him as he was lightest, 'it's going to be as dark as the belly of a whale down there.'

I passed him a glass globe from my bag, just one of the many useful objects that I liked to have with me on assignment.

'It runs off sarcasm,' I said, handing it to him.

'Great,' he replied, and the globe lit up brightly.[10]

'You'll also need this,' I told him as I tied a toddler's

---

10 The correct term for this is 'sarcoluminescence' and efficiently converts emotion to power, one of the central pillars of magic. It is one of the first spells to be taught to trainees.

shoe around his neck. When done, I spoke into the matching shoe I held in my hand.

'Can you hear me?'

'Yes,' he replied, 'I can hear you. Do I have to go down a well upside down while being sarcastic with a shoe tied around my neck?'

'You could use a conch[11] to talk,' said Perkins helpfully, before he added less than helpfully: 'only we haven't got any.'

'And you'd look pretty daft with a conch tied to your head,' added Full Price.

'Like I am so not worried about looking a twit,' said Tiger, and the globe went up to full brightness again.

'You're going to have to find the ring within thirty seconds,' announced Lady Mawgon, 'and since it might be tricky to find in the rank, fetid, disease-ridden muddy water, you'll need my help.'

'You're coming down too?'

'Good Lord no. What do you think I am? An idiot?'

'I'm not sure it would be healthy to answer that question,' replied Tiger carefully.

'Answer it how you want – I'd ignore it anyway. Here.'

She handed him a neat leather glove and told him to put it on while she placed its pair on herself. Like

---

11 Conch: The shell of a sea snail that lends itself well to medium-range communication. Giant clams have been used (and still are) for transcontinental message transmission. Toddler's shoes have a range of about sixty yards, but are a lot lighter to carry than conches, and not as delicate.

toddler's shoes and conches, gloves have left-and-right symmetry and can thus be *amicably* linked to one another to work together while separated by physical distance. Lady Mawgon clenched and unclenched her fist as Tiger's hand did the same. She revolved her arm around in the air and the paired glove copied her actions perfectly while Tiger stared at his arm and hand. He was, to all intents and purposes, now partly Lady Mawgon. Better still, the gloves were feedback enabled. Lady Mawgon would be able to feel what Tiger was feeling.

'How's that?' asked Lady Mawgon.

'Peculiar,' he replied, 'what if I can't find the blasted ring in thirty seconds?'

'Then the well will close with you inside and it's entirely possible you'll spend the rest of your life at the bottom of a deep well with only bacterium and leaches for company, then utter darkness when your sarcasm runs out.'

'I'm not so sure I want to do this any more.'

'Don't be such a cry-baby,' chided Lady Mawgon, 'If our roles were reversed and you were the skilled practitioner and I was the worthless foundling with the silly name, I'd be down that hole like an actor after a free lunch.'

Tiger looked across at me and raised an eyebrow.

'You don't have to do this if you don't want to,' I told him.

'Lady Mawgon is relating a worst-case scenario,' said

Full Price in a soothing voice, 'we'll call the fire brigade if we can't reopen the well. The longest you'll be trapped is an hour.'

'Then how could I possibly refuse?' replied Tiger grumpily, 'Let's get on with it.'

Lady Mawgon and Full Price took up their stances, index fingers at the ready. At the count of three Full Price pointed at the wellhead and the bricks opened again, revealing the deep hole in the ground. At the same time, Lady Mawgon pointed at Tiger and my young assistant was lifted from the ground, turned upside down and plunged headfirst down the well. We peered over to look in. It was all dark until Tiger said 'What super fun this is,' and the globe lit up to reveal a brick-lined well all the way down. After a few moments Tiger's voice came through the shoe that he was at the bottom and that it was wet and muddy and very smelly and all he could see was an old bicycle and a shopping trolley.

'They get everywhere,' I said, 'let Lady Mawgon have a feel around.'

Mawgon already was. With one hand keeping Tiger floating a few inches above the water level, the other was grasping, feeling and churning above her head, while her other glove on Tiger's hand sixty foot below did the same thing. Tiger kept us informed of what was going on while interspersing his speech with some top-quality sarcasm.

'Fifteen seconds,' I said, staring at my watch.

'I can feel something odd,' said Perkins, who was standing to one side, doing little except direct the ambient crackle more efficiently into Mawgon and Price, in the same way as a guttering directs rain into a storm-drain.

'Me too,' said Full Price, eyes fixed intently on the well-head and his index fingers beginning to vibrate with the effort, 'Look at that.'

I looked down the well. Before, only the top course of bricks had closed over to prevent us getting in, but now *other* bricks were starting to pop out from the well sides all the way down. The well was starting to constrict.

'We need Tiger out,' I said to Lady Mawgon, who was still feeling about above her head, eyes closed as she searched the muddy bottom of the well.

'Nearly,' she muttered.

'Twenty-five seconds.'

'What's going on?' came Tiger's voice over the toddler's shoe.

'You'll be out soon, Tiger, I promise.'

The bricks were starting to move inwards with increased speed, and brick dust, soil and earwigs were tumbling down the well. Full Price was sweating with the effort and shaking badly.

'I . . . can't . . . hold . . . it!' he managed to mutter between clenched teeth.

'The walls,' came Tiger's tremulous voice, 'they're moving in!'

'Lady Mawgon,' I said as calmly as I could, 'It's only a ring. We can leave it be.'

'Almost there,' she said, feeling around with her gloved hand in increased desperation.

'Thirty seconds,' I said as I stared at my watch, 'that's it. Abort.'

She continued on, undeterred.

'Mawgon!' yelled Full Price, who was now shaking so hard his index fingers were a blur, 'get the lad out NOW!'

But Mawgon was unmoved by our entreaties. She was so intent on finding her quarry that nothing mattered – least of all a foundling being crushed to death by an ancient spell sixty feet below ground. The well had shrunk to half its size by now, and Full Price was crying out in pain as he tried to keep the spell at bay. Perkins was shaking with the effort, too, and Lady Mawgon was still wildly looking around with Tiger's arm below when several things happened at once. Lady Mawgon cried out, Perkins fell over and the well shut with a teeth-jarring thump that we felt through the ground. I looked at my watch. Price had kept it open exactly forty-three seconds. Of Tiger there was no sign; the well was now a solid plug of brick, and down below, somewhere, Tiger was part of it.

There was silence. I couldn't think of anything to

say. Full Price and Perkins were both on their hands and knees in the dirt coughing after their exertions, but Lady Mawgon was just standing there, her gloved hand half open as if clasped around something. She might have found something, but it didn't matter. The price had been too great.

I felt my head grow hot as anger welled up inside of me. I may have boiled over then as I have a terrible temper once riled, but a small voice brought me back from the edge.

'Hey Jenny,' went the voice, 'I can see Zambini Towers from here.'

It was Tiger's voice. I frowned, and then looked up. So high above us that he was nothing but a dot, was a small figure free-falling back towards earth. Lady Mawgon had brought Tiger so rapidly out of the closing well that we hadn't seen him pass, and he had carried on and up, and was now on his way back down. I looked across at Lady Mawgon who winked at me, and opened her gloved hand wide. She swiftly moved a hay-rick twenty feet to the right where Tiger landed with a thump a few seconds later, and at the same time she caught a muddy object in her gloved hand which she then passed to me.

'There,' she said with a triumphant grin, 'Mawgon delivers.'

Jasper Fforde

Shades of Grey

Hundreds of years in the future, the world is an alarmingly different place. Life is lived according to The Rulebook and social hierarchy is determined by your perception of colour.

Eddie Russett is an above average Red who dreams of moving up the ladder. Until he is sent to the Outer Fringes where he meets Jane – a lowly Grey with an uncontrollable temper and a desire to see him killed.

For Eddie, it's love at first sight. But his infatuation will lead him to discover that all is not what it seems in a world where everything that looks black and white is really shades of grey . . .

Out now

HODDER

Jasper Fforde

One of Our Thursdays is Missing

It is a time of unrest in the BookWorld. Only the diplomatic
skills of ace literary detective Thursday Next can avert a
devastating genre war. But a week before the peace talks, Thursday
vanishes. Has she simply returned home to the RealWorld or is
this something more sinister?

All is not yet lost. Living at the quiet end of speculative fiction is
the written Thursday Next, eager to prove herself worthy of her
illustrious namesake.

The fictional Thursday is soon hot on the trail of her factual
alter-ego, and quickly stumbles upon a plot so fiendish that it
threatens the very BookWorld itself.

Out now

HODDER &
STOUGHTON

Jasper Fforde

The Big Over Easy

It's Easter in Reading – a bad time for eggs – and no one can remember the last sunny day. Humpty Dumpty, well-known nursery favourite, large egg, ex-convict and former millionaire philanthropist is found shattered beneath a wall in a shabby area of town.

Following the pathologist's careful reconstruction of Humpty's shell, Detective Inspector Jack Spratt and his Sergeant Mary Mary are soon grappling with a sinister plot involving cross-border money laundering, the illegal Béarnaise sauce market, corporate politics and the cut and thrust world of international chiropody.

As Jack and Mary stumble around the streets of Reading in Jack's lime green Austin Allegro, the clues pile up, but Jack has his own problems to deal with.

And on top of everything else, the Jellyman is coming to town . . .

Out now

HODDER

To find out more about

The Last Dragonslayer

keep up to date with Jasper Fforde, or for
fun, forums, merchandise, blogs, photos,
games, the Fforde Ffiesta, book upgrades, newsletters,
questionariums, competitions, Thursday Next X-Treme,
films, special features, free stuff, appearances, signings, tour
details, reader parodies, fan clubs, songbooks, dodo
emporiums, the Toast Marketing Board
and much, much, more, go to

www.jasperfforde.com